RALPH COMPTON: BULLET CREEK

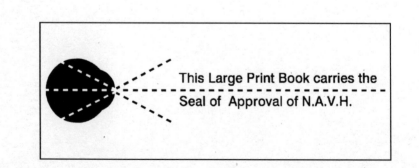

This Large Print Book carries the
Seal of Approval of N.A.V.H.

A RALPH COMPTON NOVEL

RALPH COMPTON: BULLET CREEK

PETER BRANDVOLD

THORNDIKE PRESS
A part of Gale, Cengage Learning

Farmington Hills, Mich • San Francisco • New York • Waterville, Maine
Meriden, Conn • Mason, Ohio • Chicago

GALE
CENGAGE Learning·

LIBRARY OF CONGRESS CATALOGING-IN-PUBLICATION DATA

Names: Brandvold, Peter, author. | Compton, Ralph.
Title: Ralph Compton : Bullet Creek : a Ralph Compton novel / by Peter
  Brandvold.
Other titles: Bullet Creek
Description: Large print edition. | Waterville, Maine : Thorndike Press, 2016. |
  Series: Thorndike Press large print western
Identifiers: LCCN 2016019229 | ISBN 9781410488299 (hardcover) | ISBN 1410488292
  (hardcover)
Subjects: LCSH: Large type books. | GSAFD: Western stories.
Classification: LCC PS3552.R3236 R345 2016 | DDC 813/.54—dc23
LC record available at https://lccn.loc.gov/2016019229

Published in 2016 by arrangement with New American Library, an
imprint of Penguin Publishing Group, a division of Penguin Random
House LLC

Printed in Mexico
1 2 3 4 5 6 7 20 19 18 17 16

THE IMMORTAL COWBOY

This is respectfully dedicated to the "American Cowboy." His was the saga sparked by the turmoil that followed the Civil War, and the passing of more than a century has by no means diminished the flame.

True, the old days and the old ways are but treasured memories, and the old trails have grown dim with the ravages of time, but the spirit of the cowboy lives on.

In my travels — to Texas, Oklahoma, Kansas, Nebraska, Colorado, Wyoming, New Mexico, and Arizona — I always find something that reminds me of the Old West. While I am walking these plains and mountains for the first time, there is this feeling that a part of me is eternal, that I have known these old trails before. I believe it is the undying spirit of the frontier calling, allowing me, through the mind's eye, to step back into time. What is the appeal of the Old West of the American frontier?

It has been epitomized by some as the dark and bloody period in American history. Its heroes — Crockett, Bowie, Hickok, Earp — have been reviled and criticized. Yet the Old West lives on, larger than life.

It has become a symbol of freedom, where there was always another mountain to climb and another river to cross; when a dispute between two men was settled not with expensive lawyers, but with fists, knives, or guns. Barbaric? Maybe. But some things never change. When the cowboy rode into the pages of American history, he left behind a legacy that lives within the hearts of us all.

— Ralph Compton

CHAPTER 1

"They smell the springs," yelled Tom Navarro. "Turn 'em east!"

The Bar-V foreman, his craggy, sun-seared face shaded by his wide-brimmed hat, hunkered low in his saddle and turned his galloping claybank hard right. The horse ate up the ground, weaving around saguaros and clay-colored boulders, leaping sage and barrel cacti, until it had raced out ahead of the two west-galloping leaders — a big dun with a cream-speckled rump and a bay with an evangelical fire in its eyes.

"Hee-ya now," Navarro called, throwing up his right arm and reining the claybank gently east. "You *git* now! *Mooove* your ornery asses!"

Both leaders jerked their heads stubbornly and slowly turned south, Tom hazing them along with his coiled lariat, yelling epithets and yammering coyotelike, until the entire remuda of twelve half-wild, mountain-bred mustangs was once again trotting and loping east.

The kid, Lee Luther, appeared out of the dust sifting over the catclaw and greasewood on Tom's right, and put his buckskin into step beside Navarro's claybank. The lad looked sheepish under his battered Stetson, his faded red kerchief bibbing over his hickory shirt, his chaps flapping on his knees. "Sorry, Mr. Navarro. I forgot about the springs!"

"You gettin' tired, Lee Luther?"

"No, sir, I ain't!"

"Oh, then you must've been sayin' your prayers back there in that canyon, when I looked over and you had your chin on your chest."

The kid, sixteen years old and fresh and new to the Bar-V role, looked outraged. "Wha . . . ? I never . . ." He paused, then looked away as he and Navarro trotted abreast, heading east along the stage road between Tucson and Benson. "I reckon I mighta nodded off there for a minute. Sorry, Mr. Navarro."

Tom didn't say anything as he rode along behind the remuda's bouncing butts and dusty manes flashing in the midafternoon sun. Having grown up in the saddle himself, he knew how Lee Luther felt. A green drover never liked to be out alone with the ramrod. There was damn little fun in it, and too much pressure. Lee Luther would have preferred making this trip with Sparky or Bill Tobias or Ray Fisher or even Bear Winston, the big Welshman who'd never been known to smile.

"I reckon I had you up a little late last night, foggin' Tomahawk Wash for strays." With that, Navarro reined out around the remuda's left flank to gather up a meandering paint and to begin turning the group slightly south.

"I'll do better next time," he heard the kid call over the clomps of galloping hooves.

"I know you will," Navarro said, amazed at himself. Christ, was he getting soft . . . or just old?

Ten minutes later, the Butterfield station rose from the liquid mirages and the chaparral, the long, low cabin puffing smoke from its field rock chimney and the corrals swaying up against the split cordwood behind the barn. Navarro saw that Mordecai Hawkins had the main corral gate open. He waved to the old man, who returned the gesture.

Deftly maneuvering their well-trained cutting ponies, Tom and Lee Luther rode back and forth along the remuda's left and right flanks, hazing the herd with their lariats and barking orders, breathing into the neckerchiefs and squinting their eyes against the dust.

They strung the horses out single file, three or four wide, and guided the leader through the gate. Not a minute later the entire remuda was inside the corral's peeled log fence, blowing and shaking their heads.

The dry dust and manure sifted. A big cream in the adjoining corral lifted its long snout and gave an obstinate whinny, setting off several answering nickers and deep-throated chuffs in the new remuda. The big bay pranced around the corral with an insolent, exasperated air, as though looking for a fight.

Mordecai Hawkins, an old hide hunter who'd started hostling for the Butterfield company a half dozen years ago, choked on the dust as he closed and latched the gate. The portly oldster — a good ten or fifteen years older than Tom's fifty — wore torn duck pants, suspenders, and mule-ear boots. His hide hat sat crooked on his salt-and-pepper head, slanting a shadow across his bearded face. "Nice-lookin' stock, Tom. Damn nice-lookin'. But can they pull a stagecoach?"

"That's your job, Mordecai," Navarro

said. "When you don't have nothin' else to do around here, you can break 'em to the hitch."

Hawkins offered a snide grin. "When I don't have nothin' else to do . . ."

"This is Lee Luther," Navarro said, leaning forward on his saddle horn and nodding toward the boy riding up on his right. "Lee Luther, Mordecai Hawkins. Mr. Hawkins is the hostler here."

"And chief Indian fighter and horseshoer," Hawkins said. "When I ain't repairin' windmill blades or —"

"Don't listen to that old reprobate," a woman's voice said. "I have to roust him out of bed with a shotgun most mornings and fire over his head every so often to keep him from nodding off."

Navarro turned to see a svelte, brown-eyed woman with cherry red hair walking toward them from the cabin. Her hair was pulled back in a French braid, and her dress, a shade darker than her hair, clung to her long, high-waisted body in all the right places. The low neckline, revealing a modest peak of freckled cleavage, was trimmed with white lace. The cameo pin on her right lapel winked in the desert sun.

"That only happened a couple times," Hawkins grumbled.

11

As the woman approached, she gazed up at Navarro, an affable light in her expressive eyes. "Hello, Tom."

Navarro pinched his hat brim. "Louise, nice to see you again."

"It's been a couple months." She held his gaze and smiled, her teeth flashing in her wide mouth as expressive as her eyes. She had lips neither too full nor too thin, but just right.

Navarro stared back at her for a long, awkward moment, then caught himself and jerked his thumb at the boy on the buckskin. "Louise, this is Lee Luther."

She reached up with her hand. "Hello, Mr. Luther."

"Pleased to meet you, Mrs. Talon. I heard a lot about you on the way down here."

She arched her brows at Navarro but spoke to the boy. "What did you hear?"

Under her gaze, Tom's face heated, and he turned his eyes to the corral, where several horses were drawing from stock tanks.

Lee Luther said, "Just about how you and Mr. Navarro met in Mexico last year, when you was trailin' them slavers that took your hired girl. Boy, he sure was right, though." Lee Luther shook his head, his eyes riveted on Louise. "You sure are pretty, Mrs. Talon."

"Why, thank you, Mr. Luther!" Louise slid her gaze back to Tom. "Or should I thank Mr. Navarro."

"I never thought it was true at all about pretty women," the boy continued.

"What?" Louise asked.

"That they was mulish and hard to get along with, and that *redheaded* ones were twice as hard. Why, I knew —" The boy stopped himself, his mouth frozen open. By turns, his smooth face blanched and flushed.

Mordecai Hawkins threw his head back, laughing.

Her smile fading quickly, Louise crossed her arms on her chest. "Who on earth would say such a thing?"

Navarro shot Lee Luther a pointed look, then swung his right leg over the claybank's rump. "Must've been a crazy uncle or some such, eh, boy?"

The boy shifted uncomfortably in his saddle. "Um . . . yeah, that must've been who it was."

Navarro said to Louise, "I know the stage line only agreed to pay us for the horses, but how 'bout throwin' in a late lunch? My stomach's been kissin' my backbone for the last two hours."

"It's already on the table," Louise said, "if

you don't mind breaking bread with a mulish redhead."

"I've managed before, haven't I?" Staring over his heavy Porter saddle at her, his craggy face so dark he could have been mistaken for an Indian if not for the close-cropped silver hair, he broke into a grin.

Movement at the cabin caught his attention, and he slid his gaze around Louise. Two men had just stepped out of the low shake-shingled hovel and were peering his way. One was tall and thin, with ash-colored curly hair tufting around his water-stained range hat. The other was the first man's height but heavier, his round, hairless face shaded by an elaborately stitched sombrero. Both men wore revolvers in cartridge belts thonged low on their thighs, gunman style.

The men held Navarro's gaze. After a time, the man in the sombrero pulled his gloves out from behind his cartridge belt. He lightly slapped the other man with the gloves, and they both turned slowly to the hitch rack, where a silver-gray and a line-back dun stood with dropped heads. The men climbed into the hurricane decks, thanked Louise for the meal she'd served them, then, pinching their hat brims, galloped northeastward from the barn and corrals and onto the main stage road, heading east. The thuds of their horses' hooves faded behind them.

Navarro shifted his gaze back to Louise, who'd turned to watch the strangers depart the station. "Friends of yours?"

"Just passin' through on their way from Tucson," Louise said. "They ride for Grant Sully."

To Navarro's left, Mordecai Hawkins said, "I don't know that I like the way they looked you over, Tom. You butt heads with them boys, did you?"

"Not yet," Navarro said. "Come on, boy." Ignoring Louise's wary glance, he turned and led his claybank toward the gaping barn doors.

When Navarro and the boy had unsaddled their horses and stalled them in the barn's fragrant shadows, with oats and cool spring water, they retired to the cabin. Louise stood inside, wiping her hands on a towel while her hired girl, Billie, cut into a loaf of steaming bread. When Louise saw Navarro, she smiled. "Ready to eat?"

Navarro stared at her. Her husky voice made everything she said sound sultry. As she held his gaze, her smile turned into a grin, and he felt his own lips pull upward. Damn, but she was a fine woman. He liked her crooked smile and the smoky way she looked at him, one eye slightly squinted as though she were always laughing.

"Are you goin' in, sir?" Lee said, tentative, from behind him.

Louise chuckled. Navarro shook his head and stepped aside so Lee could get past him.

Looking first at Louise, then at Navarro, Lee shrugged. "Well, she asked if we're ready to eat. I know I am."

Navarro dropped a hand on the boy's shoulder and returned his gaze to Louise. She enjoyed another moment, then turned her attention to Lee. "You men have a seat and dig in. I'll get the coffeepot."

Over a dinner of venison stew, thick slices of freshly baked bread, and strong black coffee, Navarro, Louise, and Hawkins discussed the horses and other details of the stage business. Lee Luther chatted shyly across the table with the pixie-faced Billie, who wouldn't look at the boy when she spoke and only picked at her food.

Afterward, they gathered in the shade on the east side of the cabin, where a barrel, some mismatched chairs, and a bench had been placed. They sat down to a dessert of dried apricot pie with big dollops of buttery cream. When Billie had replenished their coffee cups and taken away their dessert plates, Navarro leaned over to Louise and whispered, "Care for an introduction to your new hitch stock?"

She looked over the rim of her coffee cup. "Certainly."

Arm in arm, holding their coffee in their free hands, they strolled across the yard to the corral, where the new horses were still milling, sweat-silvered and nervous in their new surroundings. The other horses regarded them with wary curiosity, a tall bay wandering up close to the fence dividing them, lifting his head and snorting.

"They're beautiful," Louise said.

A black-and-white calico pranced back and forth along the far rail, expanding and contracting its nostrils as it blew, the west-angling sun gilding the adobe-colored dust in its coat. "Watch that calico. He tends to shoulder nip when you're not looking. That dapple gray? He's a fighter. Might want to separate him from other troublemakers. He'll make a good lead, though."

Leaning his elbow on the top corral slat, Tom turned to Louise, quickly running his eyes down the length of her body. He looked away, embarrassed. "That's a nice-lookin' dress."

A flush rose in her high-boned, finely wrought cheeks. Her eyes shined humorously. "Why, thank you." She paused. "I wore it because I knew you were coming."

They both turned and stared at the horses. Finally, she chuckled softly, and they were able to look at each other again. Tom removed his hat and brushed a big brown hand through his close-cropped gray hair with a sigh. "You know, I been thinking."

"Oh?"

He looked over her shoulder into the distance. "I might pull up stakes here. Maybe head north, start my own horse ranch. I've got some money saved, and ole Vannorsdell agreed to sell me some mares and a couple stallions. Good ranch stock."

The crinkles around her eyes went smooth. She blinked. "North, eh?"

The look on her face wrenched his heart. "I'm gonna be needin' help," he added quickly. "I know enough cowboys I can hit up to sign on, but I'll be needin' someone to keep a house. Cook, clean, tend a garden —"

The laugh returned to her eyes. "Did you have somebody in mind?"

He smiled and cocked his head. "I guess I was wondering if you might be interested. I mean, you know horses and all, and you've got a good head for business."

She arched a brow at him. "So you'd be

hiring me on to clean your house, tend your horses, and keep your books?"

"No!" Tom looked exasperated. "No," he said softly. "That's not what I'm saying."

She smiled. "What then?"

Keeping his eyes glued to the corral, he said, "I was askin' if you'd consider hirin' on as my wife." He could feel her gaze on him. When she didn't say anything, he said, "Of course, it'd be a hard decision to quit Butterfield, I know" — he paused — "and I know how much it means to you, runnin' this place, and I suppose you don't really want —"

She put a hand on his arm to stop his rambling. He turned to look at her, the tenderness in his eyes a sharp contrast to the hard angles and lines of his face.

"You'd want to marry a mulish redhead?" she said softly.

His eyes caressed her face. A corner of his mouth crooked up. "I reckon I couldn't live with no hothouse flower."

"Would Billie be invited?"

He nodded. "Mordecai, too, if he wants to give up hostlin' for the stage line."

Her eyes were pensive as she wrapped her hands over the corral and hooked one foot over the bottom rail. "Since my husband died two years ago, I've become right

19

independent. It's a good feelin', Tom."

"I didn't say —"

She held up a hand to shush him. "I told myself I wouldn't ever marry again. I've had a lot of men coming around wanting to court me, and I've never been the least bit tempted. But when I met you down in Mexico, I felt different. I liked how you saw me as just a nuisance."

He smiled. "You liked that, huh?"

"You know what I mean. You had a purpose. I could see you were a good man."

"So . . . does that mean yes?"

She pursed her lips. "When you figure out what you're gonna do, when you have a place in mind, you ask me again and I'll give you my answer."

"Fair enough."

She put a hand on his cheek, and he turned toward her. Rising up on her toes, she tilted her head back, lifting her mouth to his. He brushed his lips against hers, then stopped to look at her. She was a strong woman, but she felt delicate in his big arms. The feelings she aroused in him were so strong that he wondered if he shouldn't break away right now and take a cold dip in the creek.

"I'm going to get those plans into place quick," he warned.

20

She smiled, understanding, and pressed her warm lips and body to his. He kissed her, holding her tightly, and when she let him go, her eyes stared passionately into his until they heard Mordecai's booming laughter behind them, on the other side of the cabin, returning them both to the moment.

They turned to see Lee Luther angling toward the barn, his cheeks flushed a bright red beneath his tan. Billie appeared around the cabin's northeast corner, striding stiffly toward the front door. Behind her, Mordecai guffawed. Mordecai came toward Louise and Navarro, stretching out his spats with his thumbs. His boots kicked up little tongues of finely churned dust and manure.

Seeing the expressions on Tom's and Louise's faces, the old wrangler shrugged innocently. "The boy was tryin' to ask Billie out to the Rosehill barn dance next Saturday. I could tell it was gonna take him that long to get the words around his tongue, so I helped him out. Next thing you know, they're both scatterin' like donkeys with their tails on fire!"

Navarro turned to Louise. "I reckon it's time we headed back to the ranch."

She chuckled. "Don't be a stranger."

"Lee Luther and Billie might need chaperons next Saturday."

She smiled and swiped dust from his arm. "Tom Navarro, are you tryin' to spark me?"

"You called it."

"You'll be sorry. I dance like a mule."

He put a hand to her cheek. "I'd love to dance with a redheaded mule."

Chapter 2

At the same time that Tom Navarro and Lee Luther were starting back, the Bar-V's owner and operator, Paul Vannorsdell, left the ranch headquarters on an energetic Appaloosa.

He followed a horse trail that had existed long before Vannorsdell had single-handedly scratched his ten-thousand-acre spread out of the sage and catclaw nearly twenty-five years ago. The stocky, swarthy rancher, aged sixty-three, rode east of Apache Peak, over the Whipsaw Mountains, and into Bullet Creek Valley on the other side.

The old cattleman was glad he'd been able to leave the Bar-V before Navarro had gotten back from delivering the horses to the Butterfield station. Navarro, the mother hen, would have insisted another man tag along with the rancher, as this was Apache country, and owlhoots were known to fog the dry washes and creek bottoms.

Vannorsdell knew the dangers better than anyone, but he enjoyed a solo ride once a while. Basically a solitary man, like Navarro himself, the old rancher liked to look over the terrain without having to gab or share his thoughts with another, maybe dismount and climb a low scarp, and peering off a mesquite-stippled canyon, remember the old days, when he and this country were wild and free and he didn't have twenty-three wranglers and a cook to administrate.

He was following another trace around a mountain's steep shoulder, passing a tangle of wind-felled, long-leafed trees on his left, when he decided it was time to give the Appy a blow. He reined the horse to a halt under a gnarled ponderosa pushing up from a black lava scarp, fished his makings sack from his blue plaid shirt, and rolled a brown paper cigarette.

He was twisting the ends when the angry buzz of a bullet passed about eight inches above the Appy's ears and just over the rancher's right shoulder. At the same time the bullet spanked a tall scarp on the downslope to his right, the rifle's crack reached Vannorsdell's ears, echoing shrilly around the canyon.

Starting at the noise, the Appaloosa jerked to one side, bucked, and reared. It was really more of a crow hop, and Vannorsdell would have been fine had he not instinctively reached for the old Walker Colt jutting up from the holster on his right hip. The rancher lost his grip on the reins, as well as his balance.

As the horse twisted sharply left, Vannorsdell's freshly polished black half-boots popped free of the stirrups, and the rancher flew off the Appy's right hip. As the horse bolted down the trail, nickering and kicking, Vannorsdell hit the ground on his right hip and arm.

Feeling a sharp pain up close to his elbow, he rolled downslope, rocks and cactus scraping and gouging before, after about six slow rolls, a tangle of boulders and juniper shrubs broke the heavy man's descent.

On his belly, hands splayed on either side of his head, Vannorsdell grunted and gritted his teeth. He'd lost his leather hat in the fall, and his thin gray hair swirled about his head. Sand and debris stuck to his red cheeks.

"Son of a bitch!"

He looked around for his revolver, saw it propped against a rock twelve feet away, and pushed himself onto his hands. Nothing seemed broken, but blood dribbled down his arm, beneath his torn sleeve. He crawled up the slope, grabbed the gun, thumbed the hammer back, and continued crawling, loosing sand and scree in his wake.

Ahead and above rose the slow clomps of walking horses, iron shoes ringing off stones.

The rancher stopped and stretched a look over the brow of the slope. Two riders in bright serapes and huge straw sombreros rode slowly down the slope toward the trail. Both men carried Winchester carbines over their saddle bows.

"Mr. Vannorsdell!" one of the riders called, his voice pitched high with mocking humor. "Are you all right, senor? *Sacramento!* I didn't mean to shoot. I thought you were a deer!" The speaker and the other man chuckled.

Cursing and breathing hard, Vannorsdell heaved himself to his feet. Holding the pistol down at his side, he regarded the two with fury flashing in his gray-green eyes. "Thought I was a deer, did you, Alejandro?"

The lead rider — tall and slender, with a weak chin, heavy eyelids, drooping mustache, and thin brown eyebrows beneath the brim of his red-and-gold sombrero — jerked his gaze to the rancher and reined his Arabian to an abrupt halt. Continuing with feigned concern, he said, "Ah, there you are, senor. I was worried I'd killed you. I recognized you just in time to pull the shot!"

The other man, a small hombre with a patch over one eye and a long face hideously pitted with smallpox scars, showed his teeth through a broad grin. Chisos Gomez — one of the several pistoleros who'd suddenly appeared on the de Cava roll. "There he is, uh? He's okay."

Vannorsdell spit out several bits of sand. He'd known Alejandro de Cava all the young man's twenty-two years. Alejandro had always had a wild streak, which, coupled with a rough sense of humor, often gotten him in trouble.

Canting a squint-eyed look at the two Mexicans, Vannorsdell said, "What you both need is to be taken over a knee and have a belt laid across your behinds."

"Your knee, Senor Vannorsdell?" Gomez said, challenge brewing in his good eye.

Vannorsdell nodded. "If I was twenty years younger, I'd pull you two young scrubs off those horses and kick the holy hell out of you both."

Gomez started swinging his rifle toward the rancher. Alejandro slapped his arm. "Don't be a *pendejo.*" When the rifle lay across the one-eyed man's saddle bows, Alejandro smiled down at Vannorsdell and asked conversationally, "You go to see *mi padre?*"

"It's Sunday, isn't it?" the rancher grunted. He picked up his hat, brushed it off, donned it, and stuck two fingers in his mouth. He loosed an expert whistle, which echoed several times before dying.

Alejandro snugged the butt of his carbine against his right hip socket and canted his head at Vannorsdell, smiling knowingly, without humor. "You convince *mi* venerable old *padre* to sell to you, no? Make you big, rich *gringo.* Double the land you have now."

"It's no secret I'd like to buy Rancho de Cava if Don Francisco decides to sell. Lord knows you and you brothers can't run it."

Hoofbeats sounded to Vannorsdell's right. He turned to see the Appaloosa trotting toward him along the hill's shoulder, stirrups batting the tall horse's sides. Seeing the strangers standing with its owner, the horse stopped and eyed the two warily, twitching its ears and lifting an angry whinny.

The rancher turned back to to Alejandro. "It's in everyone's best interest — including your family's — to sell Rancho de Cava to me, but I don't intend to pressure your father into a sale. We're just gettin' together tonight like we do every Sunday, to discuss the old days, when him and me were the only two men within a hundred square miles of Bullet Creek, fightin' the Injuns together and sharin' our stud bulls. Now, if you boys'll excuse me . . ."

Vannorsdell holstered his Colt, walked stiffly up to his horse, toed a stirrup with a grunt, and pulled himself into the hurricane deck. With a parting glance at the two vaqueros watching him from where he'd left them, sitting their tall Arabians with disdainful sets to their shoulders, he reined the Appy around and set off once again in the direction he'd been heading before becoming the butt of Alejandro's practical joke.

As he rode, he couldn't help wondering how the joke might turn out the next time around. Maybe Navarro had been right.

Maybe, knowing how Don Francisco's sons felt about him these days, Vannorsdell should've taken an escort.

The grass became more and more plentiful as Vannorsdell, a half hour after leaving Alejandro and Gomez, descended the broad valley of Bullet Creek. When he was within a mile of the ranch headquarters, three vaqueros appeared on his flank, keeping their distance but making their presence known. They disappeared as he gained the creek, a trickle between broad, sandy banks, and followed the willow-lined cut into the cottonwood-shaded compound.

He rode past the peeled-log corrals and squat adobe hovels of the blacksmith shops and wagon sheds, and the two long bunkhouses, scattering chickens and attracting three dogs from the bunkhouse shade. The curs barked in circles around the Appaloosa, until the cook called to them from the cook shack door, admonishing them in Spanish.

The day was winding down, and the vaqueros sat smoking in the deep shade of the buildings. Some played cards, while two others butchered a goat hanging head down from a viga pole, blood from its slit neck trickling into a dented coffee tin. The segundo, Guadalupe Sanchez, met Vannorsdell at the wrought-iron gate surrounding the sprawling main house with its red tile roof glowing like pennies in the gathering dusk.

"*Con mucho gusto!* How good it is to see you again, senor!" greeted the medium-tall Mexican, whose abnormally dark features betrayed his Mexican Indian, or Quill, blood. He wore the traditional bell-bottomed trousers, fancily stitched and adorned with hammered silver conchos, and a fresh blue neckerchief. His gray mustache, recently waxed and combed, stood out against his deeply etched near-black face. Spying the rancher's torn sleeve, he frowned. "What happened, senor?"

"A little trouble on the trail," the rancher said, dismounting with a grunt, then removing his pistol belt from his waist and coiling it over his saddle horn. From seemingly nowhere, a young Mexican in rope sandals ran up, nodded, and took the Appy's reins, leading the horse off to a stable for fresh oats and water.

"Banditos?" the segundo inquired.

"No," Vannorsdell said, still seething. "Alejandro and Chisos Gomez. Decided to have a little fun at this Yankee's expense."

"Ah," the segundo said with a grim, knowing nod. "I see."

"No real harm done," Vannorsdell said as he stepped through the gate, which Sanchez held open for him.

He followed the segundo across the patio, past the transplanted orange and pecan trees, into a breezeway, and through a heavy oak door, the men's boots clacking on the cracked stone tiles as they wended their way between cool brown adobe walls.

The casa was a sprawling old adobe, built by Don Francisco's grandfather, with two stories, and inner courtyards to take advantage of every stray breeze. Vannorsdell had known the place when around every corner was a servant wielding a broom, feather duster, or mop. Masons armed with trowels were forever maintaining the adobe.

Now, however, a sepulchral silence lay amid the heavy doors and fissured walls. Dust had settled in corners and on the rich Brussels carpets, and the mahogany and *toya* wood furniture, dull and splintery, had gone too long without oil. Too many drought-ridden years, as well as poor speculation and failing health on the part of the Rancho de Cava's current *hacendado,* were chipping away at the old estate's very foundation.

"Ah, my good friend, Paul," the venerable old Mexican intoned when Vannorsdell and Sanchez entered a small patio and terrace surrounded by a low rock wall. "How good it is to see you again, my friend!"

"Francisco, how the hell have you been?" Vannorsdell said.

Don Francisco sat against the southern wall, at a wrought-iron table, in a wedge of golden sunshine. Across from him sat a lovely senorita, small and long-limbed, with high cheekbones and flashing black eyes and hair. A jeweled comb sat back in her hair. A lacy white mantilla hung from the comb, framing her face and setting off those lustrous eyes and full red lips like diamonds in a cameo pin.

On the table between the girl and the old Mexican rancher was a checkerboard and checkers.

Vannorsdell saw the girl only after he'd given his customary greeting and caught himself with a start. "Oh . . . pardon my English, Doña Isabelle." He gave the girl, the daughter of the housemaid, a nod. "It's so dark in your corner, I didn't see you there."

The girl's smile was set like a well-trimmed lamp. Regally, she rose, standing no higher than Vannorsdell's elbow. She bowed to Don Francisco and said in Spanish, "I shall leave you gentleman. I will come back with refreshments?"

"The usual," the don said, grinning up at her like a love-stricken schoolboy, showing decayed yellow teeth below his trimmed black mustache. The gold light glistened in his oiled black hair, which, in spite of his infirmities and seventy-odd years, bore not a single strand of gray. He cupped a hand to his mouth and said in a conniving whisper, "And a couple of those rum-soaked cigars from my office. Do not tell Lupita."

"Don Francisco, you mustn't!"

The old man held two fingers to his lips, his shoulders rising and falling with laughter.

"As you wish." Isabelle turned, nodded politely to Vannorsdell, and strode into the house, her beaded leather sandals ticking quietly along the tiles.

His hat in his hands, Vannorsdell glanced at the girl, then turned to Don Francisco with a conspiratorial grin. "She's becoming better company for you all the time. How old is she now — eleven, twelve?"

"Fourteen," the old don said, smiling after the girl, the orange-and-almond scent of her perfume lingering behind her. "She is a joy — one of the few I have left."

Vannorsdell collapsed into the chair the girl had vacated and set his hat on the stone wall to his left. "How are you, Francisco?"

The smile faded from the don's deeply seamed face, the bruise-colored pouches below his rheumy eyes sagging nearly to his mouth. He raised and lowered his hands to the quilt covering his legs. "Essentially my back has been broken these past twelve years, the doctors in Nogales have told me — from the fall I took when we were chasing those Coyoteros, remember? And my heart — it gurgles and leaps so that I can't catch my wind." He sat up straight and smiled broadly. "Other than that, I am spry as a young colt in green timothy."

The don's eyes fell on Vannorsdell's torn, bloody shirtsleeve. He nodded to it. *"Dano?"*

Guadalupe Sanchez had been standing quietly to the left of the arched doorway. Now the segundo cleared his throat and said quietly, "Alejandro and Gomez."

"Tell me," the don said, beetling his trimmed black brows at Vannorsdell.

"It's nothing. They were just trying to discourage me from making another offer on Rancho de Cava."

"Ahhh," the don said knowingly, his face flushing with sudden anger. "I will have them flogged. Sanchez!"

Vannorsdell jerked his eyes at the segundo, who stood in the shadows of the arched doorway, regarding his boss warily. The man's countenance bespoke little confidence in his own power at Rancho de Cava. Little confidence, it seemed, in his boss's authority, as well. Don Francisco and his first lieutenant may have ruled the rancho with an iron fist in their day, but the old wolves were losing their luster, and the jackals were starting to strut with their tails up.

Vannorsdell had seen it coming, with a raw feeling of dread in his loins. Once solely

in the hands of Don Francisco's wild sons
and their gun-savvy charros, who had more
interest in outlawry than stock raising and
range tending, Rancho de Cava would
become a devil's lair, a parasitic neighbor.

"Not on my account," Vannorsdell said,
raising a placating hand. A whipping would
only inflame the men's rage. It might even
jeopardize the old man and Sanchez. "Like
I said, *de nada.* Let's let it go. *Estoy de
ecuardo.*"

De Cava glanced at him. The old man
sighed, the haggard lines in his face deep-
ing. His expression at once sad, frustrated,
and chagrined, he shuttled his gaze to
Sanchez. "*No se que hacer.* You may go,
Guadalupe. Tell Henriqua we will eat in one
hour, Don Vannorsdell and I."

The segundo's boots still sounded on the
tiles when young Isabelle appeared with a
tray of drinks and two cigars, the stogies'
ends already clipped. The girl set two cut-
glass goblets before each man, removed the
decanter's glass stopper, and poured Spanish brandy into each glass. Setting the
decanter on the table between the two men,
she lit their cigars.

All the while, the old don grinned up at
the girl with open admiration. She seemed
unaware of the attention, her eyes never

meeting his.

"If my own daughter only treated me so!" he intoned as the girl walked away, black tresses of coal black hair bouncing beneath the mantilla, her breezy aroma lingering even amid the pungent scent of the rum-soaked cigars.

"Where is Lupita these days?" Vannorsdell said, exhaling a long plume of smoke and leaning back in his chair. "I haven't seen her in months."

Instantly, Vannorsdell was sorry he'd mentioned the name of the don's only daughter. De Cava grimaced as he puffed his cigar, then cast a brief glance up and over his right shoulder, indicating a second-story window.

"Not far," the don grumbled through a thick web of smoke. "Believe me, Lupita is never very far. . . ."

CHAPTER 3

"Tell me, kid, what made you leave home so young?" Navarro asked Lee Luther as they followed the Windom Creek trail toward Coyotero Ridge.

Doves flitted about the chaparral. It was moving on toward five in the afternoon, and Tom's and the kid's shadows grew long beside them.

"My pa was old — older than you, even — and when the sawbones in Tombstone told him he had to quit drinkin' and smokin', he came home and hung himself in the barn."

Lee Luther reined his horse around a sharp rock in the trail. "Ma, she went back to Pittsburgh, but I didn't want nothin' to do with a city: people walkin' around in suits all day, goin' to work in fancy offices. . . ."

"What happened to your family's spread?"

"Ma sold it to my uncle. Couldn't stand

the old bastard. I wandered up to the Bar-V after three other spreads turned me away. Thanks again for givin' me a job, Mr. Navarro — without no reference letter or nothin'."

"Anyone who stays on Sunset as long as you did earns a bunk at the Bar-V." Sunset was the one Bar-V horse that had been roped wild, snubbed, branded, and saddled, but never broken.

They rode along a wash for a time, the rocky terrain rising gently toward the ridge.

"Mr. Navarro, you mind if I ask *you* a question?"

"I reckon."

"How'd you get the name 'Taos Tommy,' like some o' the other boys calls you?"

Navarro hit the kid with an angry look, the foreman's sharp blue eyes flashing and his silver-gray brows bunching. "They don't call me that to my face!"

A rifle cracked. Navarro drew back on the buckskin's reins and peered straight ahead, against the sun reflecting off the rocks. His right hand slapped leather. "What the hell was that?"

"Gunshot," Lee Luther said.

Navarro glanced at him, the nub of his sun-scalded right cheek rising up into his right eye socket. "I *know* it was a gunshot."

"You asked me, sir."

"Junior, don't make me regret lettin' you ride Sunset." Navarro booted the claybank into a gallop. "Come on!"

Another shot rang out as Navarro neared the top of a low knoll. He turned the claybank sideways and raised his hand. Lee Luther reined his own buckskin to a skidding halt.

"What is it?" the kid said.

Navarro shushed him with a look and dismounted. Tossing his reins to Lee Luther, Navarro doffed his hat and walked to the top of the knoll, crouching beside a tall saguaro off the trail's left shoulder.

In a rocky hollow on the other side of the knoll, an old Texas seed-bed wagon, its box covered with a ratty tarp, was stopped in the middle of the trail, facing away from Navarro. Two mules fidgeted in the traces, one lowering its head and angrily braying.

Two men sat in the box, staring stiffly down at a man holding a rifle on them. One of the men in the wagon clutched his right arm. The man with the rifle turned his head back and forth between the two men in the wagon and another man standing off the trail, partially concealed by small boulders, saguaros, and barrel cactus. This hombre was yelling furiously and kicking at some-

40

thing or someone on the ground before him.

Navarro squinted at the slumped figure. A spray of hair flew up from behind a rock — long, dull blond hair.

"Goddamn it," Navarro grumbled, wheeling and heading back down the grade to where Lee Luther stood in the trail with the horses.

Tom shucked his Winchester from his saddle boot and glanced at Lee Luther. "Time to meet the neighbors, kid."

"What?"

"Come on. Leave the horses and grab your carbine." The horses would stay ground-hitched where their reins fell.

Navarro tramped off the left side of the trail, along the knoll's base. Lee Luther jogged up behind him, puffing nervously.

"What's over there?"

"Those two hombres from the Butterfield station are havin' a little fun with a family of three on the other side of this hill."

"Oh, boy. What're we gonna do?"

"Whatever we can." When they came to a gully snaking around the east side of the hill, Navarro stopped. The kid, close on his heels, nearly ran into him. "How good are you with that thing?" Tom asked, nodding at the kid's Spencer carbine.

Flushed with fear and excitement, the kid

looked at the gun and hesitated. "Ummm . . ."

"Never mind. Just stay behind me and watch for my signals."

Navarro dropped into the gully and followed it, walking and jogging, the kid huffing and puffing behind him, kicking rocks and grunting, nearly falling several times. At one point, Navarro stopped and indicated a snake coiled up under a catclaw shrub on the gully's east bank. Swinging wide around the tongue-flicking diamondback, Navarro set off again. The kid eyed the snake warily and traced the same path.

Laughter rose in the distance. Navarro stopped, got his bearings. He and the kid were east of the wagon. The laughter had risen just north.

Navarro cast a glance at Lee Luther. The kid had dropped to one knee for a breather. Indicating south with his eyes, Navarro climbed out of the gully and traced a winding path through the chaparral-shrouded rocks and boulders. The kid jogged along behind him, crouched over with the old Spencer in his gloved hands.

A gleeful whoop sounded. Navarro motioned for the kid to stop. He sidled up to a boulder slightly taller than himself and glanced around one side.

Twenty feet away, just beyond two entangled saguaros, one of the men shoved a tall blond woman dressed in dusty clothing against a rocky dike. The woman pushed him back, and he cuffed her hard with the butt of his six-shooter. The movement knocked his big sombrero down his back, where it hung from a horsehair cord. His head was as bald as a minie ball.

The woman grunted and fell back against the rock. Her knees buckled, but she didn't fall.

The man laughed again. "Now that we got a little privacy . . ." He holstered his .45, slipped a long-bladed skinning knife from a sheath behind his neck, and with one deft slicing motion, cut away the buttons of the woman's dark blue shirt. The tails still stuck in the woman's pants, the shirt opened, revealing a grimy gray undershirt.

"You son of a bitch!" she cried hoarsely. Raising her bruised face, she spit.

The man brought his right hand up to smack her, and she dropped to her knees, cowering and cursing. He kicked her onto her back and knelt down, straddling her wriggling, slim-hipped body and wrestling her flailing arms down to her sides.

The man had lowered his head to nuzzle the woman's neck, when he felt a tap on his shoulder. "Huh?" He whipped around. In a blur of motion, a rifle butt pistoned toward him, connecting soundly with his mouth, smashing his torn lips back against his teeth. Behind the man's fluttering lids, lightning popped and flashed. He fell back over the woman's head. Blood flowed from his gums and pulpy lips.

Between Navarro and the hardcase, the woman climbed to her hands and knees. Navarro reached down to help her to her feet. Meanwhile, Lee Luther scrambled out from behind another boulder and stopped a few feet away from the groaning, cursing hardcase. "I wouldn't do that if I was you!" the boy warned.

Navarro drew the woman to his side and looked down. The hardcase had clawed his .45 half out of his holster. He stared up at Lee Luther, blood washing over his lips and dribbling two streams down his chin. "You little son of a bitch!"

Navarro slammed his Winchester's butt against the man's ear, knocking him over on his side with an exasperated grunt. "Raise your voice again, and I'll knock you owlheaded!" He didn't want the man's partner knowing their party had been spoiled.

The man lay in the desert caliche, staring

up at Navarro, his beard bloody and flecked with tooth chips, his pale, egg-shaped head glistening with sweat. His brown eyes watered from the pain.

"Besides, the boy's just tryin' to save your life," Navarro said, keeping his voice low and extending his own Winchester out from his right hip, holding the woman's arm with his left.

The foreman cast a glance toward the wagon road, about thirty yards through the brush. Then he looked at the woman, who stood caressing her cheek. Keeping his voice low, Navarro said, "You all right, Hattie?"

"Been better, Tom. I'm obliged for the help."

"This is Lee Luther. Lee, Hattie Winters. Her and her husband and brother have a mining claim near here."

"Those chicken shits!" Hattie snarled, glaring back toward the road.

She was prettier from a distance — lean and hard-bodied, with small, high breasts pushing at the man's wool shirt she didn't bother to hold closed. The wind and sun had fried her hair and drawn the skin so taut across her face that her blue eyes bulged. Hattie and her husband, Homer, and her brother, Richard, had been farming rock near the Bar-V for the past three years.

"They just let those two bastards pull me right off that wagon without no fight at all. Homer took a graze. The way he's carryin' on, you'd swear he was gut-shot!"

Back at the wagon, Derrold Emory stood with his rifle trained on the sun-seared gents in the driver's box, one grimacing as he held his bloody arm. Emory glanced back where his partner, Hought Ellis, had dragged the woman. He shuffled his weight impatiently from one foot to the other.

"Come on, Hought — break a leg! It's my turn!"

He turned his head to tell the groaning man to shut up. Before he could get the words out, a rifle cracked from only a few feet away. Emory's low-crowned hat was torn from his head. His scalp burned where the bullet had parted his hair.

Startled, Emory staggered back, swinging his gun toward the source of the shot. "Wha— what the hell?" He stepped back to where he could keep an eye on the two men in the wagon while training his rifle on the area from which the shot had come.

From behind a boulder, blue smoke rose, fluttering on the breeze. Both mules brayed and jerked against the wagon brake. The off one turned slightly and kicked.

"Who did that, damn it?" the hardcase

46

called, his voice thick with worry. "Hought, was that you? Very funny."

A bird whistled in the desert to his left. The sun sank, and shadows grew.

"Did you see who did that?" he asked the men in the wagon.

"I didn't see nothin' — just a rifle," said the man holding the reins.

As Emory stepped slowly forward, he said tightly, "You two make one move, and I'll swing around and kill you both — understand? I got eyes in the back of my head."

The driver grunted acknowledgment over his partner's groans. Emory held his rifle straight out from his hip as he approached the rock. "Hought? If you're playin' a goddamn joke . . ."

Emory swung around the rock and thumbed back the rifle's hammer. Something moved up from down low on his right, and before he could aim his rifle at it, a brass-plated rifle butt connected soundly with his mouth. His finger pressed his Winchester's trigger, but he'd raised the barrel as he flew backward off his heels, and the rifle discharged skyward.

Emory released the gun as he hit the ground on his back, feeling as though every tooth in his mouth had been smashed to bits. Blood poured from his mouth, which was full of broken teeth. He looked up to see gray-blue eyes in a granite-hard, sun-seared face staring down at him coldly.

The man was tall, late forties, early fifties, with steel gray hair under a high-crowned black hat with a snakeskin band. He wore a dusty range shirt and denims with ponyskin seat and inner thighs. High cheekbones. Firm, cold mouth. Uncompromising gaze.

Taos Tommy Navarro.

"What the . . . ?"

"Don't cuss," Navarro snapped, reaching down, grabbing Emory's rifle and deftly removing the short-barreled .38 from Emory's holster.

It didn't seem fair. When Emory and Hought had seen Navarro at the Butterfield station, they'd decided to ambush *him* one day. But here he'd gotten the drop on *them.*

Navarro levered the shells from Emory's rifle, punched the pills from the .38's wheel, and tossed both weapons into the brush. He picked up his own rifle and, stepped back, glancing at Hought, whom Lee Luther was holding his Spencer on.

"You boys head on back to your ranch and explain those smashed mouths to Grant Sully."

Hought stood with his hat hanging down his back, his bullet-shaped head slick with sweat, his cinnamon-beard glistening crimson. "You had no call, Navarro."

"Shut up and fog it out of here!"

Not looking at his partner, Hought walked west along the wagon trail, no doubt toward his and Emory's horses. Spitting blood and teeth, Emory slowly, heavily gained his feet. He stared hard at Navarro. "Think you're real funny." He turned, spat more blood, black as a tobacco quid, and followed his partner down the trail.

When Hought and Emory had mounted their horses and headed northeast through the chaparral, Navarro helped Hattie Winters onto the wagon. She took the reins from her brother, Richard, and berated both him and her husband for their cowardice, then turned to Navarro.

"Be careful, Tom. Those two are mean enough to have a reserved seat in hell. I've seen 'em in this country before. If they know who you are, you got double trouble."

"I know where they ride."

Hattie released the wagon's brake and slapped the ribbons against the mule's backs. "Thanks again, Tom . . . and Lee Luther!" she called behind her. The iron-shod wheels sent little ribbons of red dust to the gravelly trail. "I'll be sendin' these two over to the Bar-V for man lessons."

She turned back around and dusted the team over a rise.

"Ah, it weren't nothin'," Lee Luther called.

Navarro looked at him and cocked a brow. The boy flushed, turned, and began walking back for their horses.

CHAPTER 4

At the Rancho de Cava, full dark had fallen over the patio, with several stars kindling brightly in the dry velvet sky.

Vannorsdell and the old don had taken their chili con carne in the house's main dining hall, where they were served by Doña Isabelle and her mother, the taciturn Doña Henriqua. The ranchers returned to the patio for *queso de tuna,* a traditional Mexican dessert made from the prickly pear cactus, more brandy, and one last cigar. They'd smoked only half their cigars when Don Francisco sagged back in his chair, his heavy eyelids fluttering shut.

Vannorsdell set his half-empty glass of sangria on the table, stood, and placed his right hand on de Cava's left. "You are tired my old friend, and so am I," the rancher said quietly.

De Cava's eyes opened. He jerked forward.

"I'll vamoose," Vannorsdell said. "Shall I call Doña Isabelle to take you inside?"

The don's eyes slowly focused. He looked up at his neighbor. "*Madre Maria.* I have fallen asleep on you."

"It's getting late."

"It can't be ten o'clock. We used to stay up later than this in Tuscon — and ride back to our ranchos in time for morning coffee!"

"That was a few years ago, amigo." Vannorsdell patted the old Mexican's long, rope-scarred hand. "*Muchas gracias* for your hospitality. I'll see you next month at the Bar-V."

"*Con gusto,* but wait." The old don leaned back in his chair and clapped his hands. "Isabelle!"

Sandals clapped on the tiles, and the girl appeared in the arched doorway. In Spanish, de Cava told her that he wanted his black stallion, El Morzillo, saddled and ready to ride in ten minutes. When the girl quietly protested, he assured her that he was still man enough to ride his horse after dark and that he wished only to accompany his dear friend to the top of *Bala Caballete,* or Bullet Ridge.

With another helpless shrug, the girl padded away.

"Francisco, don't you think you're a might

fagged for a ride this late?"

Shaking his head, the don took his unlit cigar in his left hand and held out his right. "We must talk . . . away from here."

Vannorsdell took the man's hand and gently helped him out of his chair. Together, they strolled through the dark house, hearing pans clattering in the distant kitchen, glimpsing distant lamps flickering down darkened halls. At the front door, Don de Cava grabbed his high-peaked black sombrero off a wall hook near a shimmering silver sconce and donned it with a *caballero*'s tilt.

They waited five minutes, finishing their cigars, before Vannorsdell's Appaloosa and the old don's black Thoroughbred were led up to the house by two hatless charros in ratty ponchos and dirty white pantaloons. The drovers' eyes were rheumy in the light from the entrance tapers, and Vannorsdell smelled the *chicha,* corn alcohol, on their breath.

Apparently, the don did, as well. He berated both men, balling his hands into tight fists and puffing out his cheeks. The men grumbled, *"Sí, sí, jefe."* They muttered Spanish curses, turned, and wandered heavy footed back toward the bunkhouse, from where the soft strains of a guitar rose amid the laughter of reveling vaqueros.

Wrapping his pistol belt around his waist, Vannorsdell stared after the two men disappearing into the shadows, silhoutted against the bunkhouse lights. He set his jaw with anger, but said nothing to Don Francisco. No need to embarrass the old don more than he already was. Before Vannorsdell could walk over and help the man into the silver-trimmed saddle of his big black stallion, Francisco toed a stirrup and hauled himself up with little effort. Angrily, the Mexican reined away from the *casa* and trotted off into the darkness.

"As you can see, my friend," he grumbled ten minutes later, as he and Vannorsdell rode stirrup to stirrup along a grassy bench, smelling the sharp pinion and peppery sage, "I command little respect around Rancho de Cava these days."

Vannorsdell chewed his cold cigar. "What happened?"

"Alejandro and Real. They have taken over the hiring and firing from Guadalupe. Unofficially, of course, but they run off every good vaquero Guadalupe adds to the role, bring in pistoleros they find in Tucson or south of the border. *Revolucionarios. Bandeleros.*"

Vannorsdell chewed the cigar. So what

he'd heard was true — the two de Cava sons had turned to outlawry. There had been a couple stage robberies in the past year: Butterfield coaches run down by masked gunmen, most dressed like charros but sporting weaponry like those of Sonoran bandits.

Da Cava struck a match on his stirrup fender and crouched to light his cigar stub. "The wilder the colt, the better the horse. That is what I always thought. Now I see that my wild colts have become *mestenos . . .* and I am no longer much of a *mestenero.*"

"Don, I don't know what to say."

A few minutes later, when they had climbed into dense pines near the boulder-strewn crest of Bullet Ridge, Don Francisco reined El Morzillo to a halt. When Vannorsdell stopped the Appaloosa, the don turned to him, the short stogie glowing briefly between his lips.

He took the cigar in his black-gloved fingers and exhaled the aromatic smoke. "You have in the past offered to purchase Rancho de Cava."

Vannorsdell lifted his head and squinted through the shadows.

The don continued. "I refused your offer, and you were noble and polite not to press the matter. I, however, have reconsidered. If I do not sell Rancho de Cava, I am afraid that when I am gone, my house and my range — granted to my grandfather by King Carlos of Spain nearly a hundred years ago — will become nothing but a bastion for *bandoleros.* They will bring dishonor to the de Cava name."

"I can help you root those sonso'bitches out, Don." Vannorsdell lowered his head and spoke sharply. "With the help of my riders, I'll toss a hooley-ann loop over Alejandro and Real and have 'em both shivvied back to the cavvy in no time. Those boys'll be holding their hats when they speak to their father."

Vannorsdell saw the old don's lip twitch a smile. Francisco took another drag off his cigar and blew the smoke into the pillared black shadows of the pines. "It is too late. I have little time." He straightened in his saddle, stuck his chest out proudly, and announced, "Rancho de Cava is yours, my good friend, if you still want it for the price you offered me last month."

Vannorsdell didn't say anything for a minute. He felt heavy and depressed. Welling in him suddenly was a deep sadness for this gallant, good man he'd known through the hardest years of his life. Acquiring the holdings of Rancho de Cava would make him one of the largest landholders in southern Arizona. But the reasons for his acquiring it — the defeat and infirmities of an old friend — made it a bittersweet trophy. He felt as predatorial and seedy as the don's own sons.

"It is how it is," the don said now, leaning across and giving Vannorsdell's shoulder a reassuring pat. "One must accept things as they are. Knowing that you, *mi amigo,* will be running Rancho de Cava will ease my passing."

Vannorsdell sat quietly, listening to an owl hooting behind him. Starlight glistened on the pine needles. "I'll talk to my bank," he said, turning back to his friend with a nod. "I'll send a rider with word of the loan's approval. If there are papers to sign, we'll sign them at the Bar-V over supper next month."

The two men shook hands.

"Buen viage!" Don Franciso sat the big black stallion for several minutes as Vannorsdell booted his Appy up and over the ridge.

Don Francisco finished his cigar, shredded it, and let the breeze take it. He reined the big stallion back down the ridge, toward the lights of Rancho de Cava.

Riding along, feeling relief but also a deep sadness at the passing of his years and his inability to raise sons worthy of his name, the old don threw his head back and sent the first few lines of an old Spanish dirge toward the stars.

He didn't hear the shot that went through his left temple, exploding his brain plate and whisking him out of his saddle.

El Morzillo heard it. With a scream, the big stallion ran, buck kicking, toward the hacienda.

Behind the horse, Don Francisco lay sprawled across a sage shrub, half his head splattered in the rocks and manzanita grass.

Earlier, just before the sun sank behind Mount Lemon, Navarro and Lee Luther were following a horse trail up the last ridge to the Bar-V headquarters, when a shrill whistle sounded from the ridge's rocky crest.

"Now what?" the boy said, lifting his weary gaze. He hadn't been reluctant to voice his fear of being late for supper. Being low man on the totem pole, he doubted the contrary German cook would offer him anything but a dipper of water. Navarro usually made his own meals in his own cabin or ate up at the big house with Vannorsdell — "the boss," as the old Dutchman was called by his men.

Navarro's hand was on his pistol butt as, keeping the claybank moving, he snapped a look up the ridge. Fifty yards or so right of the trail, a cream Arabian stood up on its rear legs, flailing its front hooves skyward, milky mane rippling.

Reins in her right fist, long hair falling from beneath her cream plainsman toward the horse's rump, the female rider threw up her left hand.

Navarro grimaced and slid his hand off his pistol butt. "Shit."

The girl brought the horse back to all fours. She reined the gelded Arab off the ridge and into a high-stepping gait through the rocks and barrel-cactus partially hidden by early-evening shadows.

"She sure can ride," Lee Luther said, watching with open admiration as Karla Vannorsdell jogged toward them.

"You've already got a date for Saturday night."

"Oh, I know. Besides, Miss Vannorsdell ain't said five words to me since I been here. I figure she's set her hat for some other rider on the Bar-V role — just haven't figured out who it is yet."

"Hello there, gentlemen," the girl said as she rode past them on the trail's right side.

The horse leapt a sage bush slightly

behind them and hit the trail with a snort. Karla turned the mount back north and booted it up on Navarro's left side, her heart-shaped, suntanned face flushed from exertion, hazel eyes bright with excitement. "How was everything at the Butterfield station?"

"You're gonna break your neck comin' off a ridge like that," Navarro warned.

"Not on Diablo here," Karla said, leaning down to run a hand down the cream's arched neck. "He's as sure-footed a mount as I've ridden at the Bar-V."

"You've only been here three years."

"Don't be cranky," Karla said. "How was the ride?"

Navarro shrugged. When the foreman offered the girl nothing more, Lee Luther, riding to Navarro's right, told her about the two men who'd jumped the prospectors and tried savaging Hattie Winters.

Karla listened intently across the neck of Navarro's claybank. Her eyes acquired an ironic cast. "Did Taos Tommy add another couple notches to his belt?"

Navarro scowled at her.

"There it is again — Taos Tommy," Lee Luther said. "How'd ye get that handle, anyway, Mr. Navarro?"

Tom turned to Karla. "You know, we were

having a nice, quiet ride."

"Come on, Mr. Navarro. Everyone knows except me."

"Yeah, come on, Mr. Navarro," Karla said. "Everyone knows except him."

Navarro reined the clay to a halt, leaned his left wrist on his saddle horn, and turned to Lee Luther, his blue eyes slitted with irritation. "When I was a little bit older than you, I cut down on a couple men in Taos. We were spinning the roulette wheel. They were riding me. Real hard. They were gunslicks, but I didn't know it at the time. Well, I'd been practicing with my old Dragoon, and it turned out, when they threw down on me, that I'd been practicing more than they had. Get the picture?"

As the kid stared at Navarro with parted lips, the older man continued. "To my everlasting regret, a newspaperman dubbed me 'Taos Tommy' Navarro. That old moniker has haunted me ever since, attracting would-be gunslicks no older than you, with the intention of adding a 'Taos Tommy' notch to their belts."

"Holy baloney," Lee Luther said, his eyes widening in awe. "You're a gunslinger!"

Navarro had heeled the clay ahead, but the horse had taken only two steps when the foreman stopped it again and swung an angry look at the kid behind him. "Gun-slingers, boy, go out of their way to look for trouble. I go out of my way to avoid it. Now let's cut the palaver and go eat." He booted his claybank into a trot.

Behind him, Lee Luther turned to Karla. "He's a rather proddy individual, ain't he?"

Karla stared up the trail as Navarro crested the ridge and disappeared down the other side, salmon dust sifting behind his silhouette.

"Tom Navarro is many things," the girl said thoughtfully. Three years ago, she'd come to her grandfather's Bar-V ranch from Philadelphia, when her parents had been killed in a train collision. Since then, Tommy Navarro had been many things to her, indeed — having taught her how to ride, track, avoid Apaches, and survive in the desert . . . not to mention his rescuing her from slave traders in Mexico. Yet, despite their age differences, she yearned for so much more.

"And, yeah" — Karla smiled as she glanced at the boy beside her — "I guess you could say proddy is one of them."

She and Lee Luther booted their mounts into Navarro's still-swirling dust.

CHAPTER 5

Guadalupe Sanchez, segundo of Rancho de Cava, had just lain down to read when he heard the distant rifle crack. The old vaquero's ears were not as good as they once were, but he could still recognize the report of an old-model saddle gun from two hundred yards away.

Sanchez lowered the heavy Bible to his lap, removed his round-rimmed spectacles, and canted his head toward the outside wall of his room. He listened for nearly a minute, hearing nothing but the boisterous din of the vaqueros playing blackjack beyond his closed door and ribbing José Rincon about his affections for Don de Cava's daughter, Lupita.

"You should ask her out to a dance sometime, José," said the don's oldest son, Real, who often slept in the bunkhouse when, addled by drink, he imagined the hacienda was haunted by the ghosts of long-dead ancestors. "A man with *guevas* like yours might just melt the old *zunga*'s heart."

Chuckles and laughter sounded amid the jingle of coins and the light thumps of cards tossed down on the table. One of the charros was softly strumming a guitar.

Sanchez sighed and threw back his blankets. He set the Bible on his night table, beside the three candles flanking the framed picture of his mother and a small wooden crucifix. Standing, he pulled his work jeans over his wash-worn underwear and stomped into his boots. He wrapped his cartridge belt and .44 Russian around his bony hips, then opened his door and moved through the smoky main room, between the bunks where a dozen vaqueros and pistoleros lounged, past the table where five more smoked, drank, and gambled beneath a chuffing lantern.

"Hey, Guadalupe," Real de Cava called, kicked back in his chair, a fat stogie stuck between his teeth, "where you going so late, uh? You got a big-titted, old *puta* hidden out in the wood pile?" The mean-eyed, prematurely balding lad, with a giant mustache and two big pistols on his hips, made a lewd gesture with both hands.

Guadalupe, was it? Not *el segundo* or *jefe* or even Senor Sanchez anymore. Sanchez should do the lobo's father a favor and drill a .44 ball through his belligerent sons's heart.

Not wasting a glance on the young coyote, Guadalupe moved to the door and stepped outside. He drew the door closed behind him, stepped away from the lamp-lit windows, and peered toward the star-capped western ridge, from where the shot had sounded.

Probably only one of the nighthawks pot-shooting a coyote or a mountain lion, but as long as Don de Cava lived, Guadalupe Sanchez was still segundo of this brand. When a shot was fired, it was his job to learn the cause.

"If the old cayuse's going out to take a piss," a vaquero intoned in a voice slurred from drink, "he won't be back till dawn."

Inside the bunkhouse, more drunken laughter rang out.

Hardening his jaw, Sanchez walked westward across the yard. Listening intently, hearing only distant cattle, coyotes, nightbirds, and the faint breeze rustling the grass, he strolled through the main gate and west along a secondary trail.

When he'd walked a hundred yards, two more shots rose in quick succession — one after another, as if a signal.

A man shouted, "Trouble! Come quick!"

The shots had flashed on the flank of the hill ahead and right of Sanchez. Grabbing his pistol from his holster, the old segundo left the trail and ran up the hill, breathing hard, stumbling over sage and galetta grass clumps. Forty yards ahead, a shadow moved. Sanchez stopped and extended his pistol, breathing so hard that he doubted he'd be able to hit anything, if it came to shooting.

"Name yourself!"

"It is me, *jefe*! Rodriguez!"

Sanchez lowered the pistol and continued trudging up the hill, pushing off his knees. He stopped where Rodriguez crouched over a figure sprawled in the grass and sage.

"What the hell happened?" the segundo said, wheezing.

Rodriguez's broad sombrero lifted, revealing the old rider's gaunt face. Starlight glittered in the vaquero's eyes. "I heard a rifle and rode over, *jefe.* I found him here, just like he is."

Sanchez hunkered down on his haunches, placed a hand on the dead man's skinny shoulder. The body faced away from him, but Sanchez saw the dark mustache mantling the upper lip, the impossibly black hair shining faintly in the starlight. The weeds around the old don's head glistened with fresh blood and brain matter. When the segundo rolled de Cava onto a shoulder, half-open eyes stared up at him glassily, rotten teeth showing faintly between his lips.

The segundo's heart leapt. The night spun around him. He looked up at Rodriguez kneeling across from him, reached over, and grabbed the man's shirt in his fist. "Who did this, Enrique?"

"I saw no one, *jefe*. I only heard the shot. A half hour ago, I saw the *hacendado* ride over the ridge with Don Vannorsdell."

"Vannorsdell," Sanchez repeated thoughtfully. The Yankee wanted Rancho de Cava, true enough, but Paul Vannorsdell was not a killer. Sanchez released Rodriguez's shirt and glanced around. "Take a look up the ridge. Perhaps the assassin is still around."

"*Sí, jefe!*"

When Rodriguez had mounted his horse and galloped over the rise, Sanchez peered down at the old don. Tears dribbled down his cheeks and his breath fluttered in his throat. "Rest easy, *amigo,*" he whispered thickly, running his thumb and index finger over the dead eyes, gently closing the lids. "You are home now."

From behind Sanchez, hoof thuds sounded and tack squeaked, growing in volume as a horse and rider moved toward him. It was too soon to be Rodriguez. Turning, Sanchez grabbed the butt of his Russian.

"Who comes?"

"It is Lupita. What is all the shooting about?"

Sanchez removed his hand from his gun as the woman rode over the brow of a cedar-stippled hill on a long-legged Thoroughbred. Her long coal black hair spilled down from the low-crowned hat thonged beneath her chin, bouncing on her tasseled black cape.

"What the hell is going on?" the woman demanded, slipping a boot from the stirrup and swinging her right leg over the horse's rear. "Who's been shot?"

As she came around the horse, Sanchez stepped into her path, blocking her view of the body. "Senora, Don de Cava is dead."

Her full-lipped mouth opened and her eyes widened, regarding Sanchez gravely. She brushed past him and, shoulders taut, walked to her father lying sprawled in the sage. She stood over the don and raised her hands to her face. Slowly, she dropped to her knees, placed one hand on the old man's chest.

After a long time, she looked up at Sanchez. Her voice cracked, brittle with outrage. "Who did this?"

Before the segundo could respond, yells and hooffalls sounded on the trail below the hill. He turned to see the silhouettes of six riders, riding both single file and abreast, curving around the butte's base.

"Up there!" one of them yelled.

As one, they reined their horses off the trail and ascended the hill, stirrup to stirrup, the horses cat hopping around shrubs and boulders. Starlight winked off rifles and revolvers gripped in the riders' hands.

Fifty yards from where Sanchez stood with Lupita, Real de Cava yelled, "Who's there?" The ratcheting click of a hammer being drawn back sounded faintly amid the thudding hooves and squeaking tack.

"Put up your guns," Sanchez ordered.

Real rode toward him, pistols flapping on his thighs in their tied-down buscadero holsters. The other riders, having dressed quickly, were missing shirts or hats, but they were all armed. They whipped nervous gazes about, no doubt expecting rustling trouble or maybe an Indian raid, though Don de Cava had made peace with the Apaches several years ago.

Real de Cava scowled down at the segundo. "Who the hell was shooting up here, Sanchez?"

Before the segundo could respond, Lupita said, her angry voice quaking, "Your father's been murdered, Real. You should be very happy!"

The young de Cava booted his mount forward, until he was sitting directly above his sister and his father's body. He stared down for several seconds, his shoulders rising and falling slowly as he breathed. It was too dark for Sanchez to see the expression on his face.

Real looked from Sanchez to Lupita and back again. "Who did this?"

Lupita snapped her eyes at him, and in the nebulous light, her face was streaked with tears. "As if you didn't know!"

"Shut up, hag. If I was going to murder my father, he'd have been dead long before now." He glared at Sanchez. "Answer me — who killed my father?"

"Your guess is as good as mine," the segundo snarled, the firebrand's haughty tone chafing him worse than ever. Like Lupita, Sanchez suspected Real, the older of de Cava's two sons. But Real had been in the bunkhouse when Sanchez had heard the shot.

What about Alejandro, Real's younger brother? Was he down at the roadhouse, like he normally was this time of the night, or hiding somewhere in the hills, with a smoking long gun?

"He left with Vannorsdell," Lupita said sharply, glaring at her brother. "Not an hour ago." She jerked her head at the ridge. "Be a man for a change and catch your father's killer."

Sanchez swung toward her. "Senora, Don Vannorsdell would not have killed your father. They were friends."

"Bullshit," she spat. "He wanted the ranch."

"How could killing Don de Cava possibly —"

"You're right for a change, you old hag," Real said through gritted teeth, reining his horse in a broad circle around the other riders. "Sure enough, it had to be Vannorsdell. That bastard!"

Sanchez followed the man with his gaze, balling his hands into tight fists. All they needed on top of the don's murder was a war with the Bar-V. "Real, it was someone else."

"Who?"

When Sanchez didn't answer, Real turned to the other men sitting their saddles grimly around him. "Paco, gather the other vaqueros. Summon Alejandro from the Wells.

Meet us at the fork of Bullet Creek before dawn."

"*Sí, jefe!*"

When Paco had galloped off toward the ranch, Real turned his impassioned gaze to Sanchez. "Are you riding with us, old man?"

"You're a fool, Real. You'll only get yourself killed, and you'll ruin Rancho de Cava!"

Real booted his horse toward Sanchez, halted it only a foot away from the older man, and stared down. His hand slid toward the pistol on his hip.

"Real!" Lupita admonished.

The hardcase's hand stopped, slid back down his thigh. Filling his lungs with a deep breath, he said to Sanchez, "I'll deal with you when I get back."

He reined the steeldust around and galloped up the ridge, urging his horse with shouted commands. The other riders cast fleeting glances at Sanchez — a few sympathetic or neutral but most defiant — and, holding their rifles across their saddle bows, booted their mounts after de Cava.

Sanchez wheeled to Lupita standing over her dead father. "You are making a big mistake, senora. Stop them!"

She glanced at the old segundo, then stepped away from her father, grabbed her reins, toed a stirrup, and swung onto the

Thoroughbred. She rode up beside Sanchez, canted her gaze downward. "Get a wagon and haul the don down to the hacienda for burial preparations. Since you've chosen to stay home while the real men go after my father's killer, you can get started on a coffin."

She swung the horse around and booted it down the hill. For a moment, starlight glittered on the stock of the old Springfield snugged down in her saddle scabbard. Sanchez stared after the young woman. He'd known her all her twenty-six years, but how well did he *really* know her?

Was she so eager to accuse Vannorsdell of killing her father only to detract attention from herself?

Sanchez had started down the hill when Rodriguez rode up on his right and reported he'd seen no sign of the killer. "What has happened, *jefe*?"

"Trouble," said Sanchez.

Tom Navarro's private dwelling, the Bar-V's original brick adobe with a brush roof and sagging front porch built of stone and rotting planks, sat off in the chaparral, a good fifty yards from the other buildings. A dry wash fronted the place, sheathed in desert willows and palo verdes.

A rocky canyon lay behind, filled with greasewood, yucca, boulders, ancient Indian ruins, and Mojave green rattlesnakes. Tom liked being out here with just the brush and the ghosts and the snakes, where, on nights like these, he could sit under the stars and imagine he was the last man on earth.

Where trouble, at least from other men, was a long ways away . . .

Sitting in a hide chair on the porch, he poured whiskey into the tin cup from which he'd drunk coffee with his supper, then cut it with branch water from a stone pitcher. The water was fresh from his well, the original well that had never dried up and kept offering the best water on the ranch. He sat back in his chair, sipped the whiskey and water, set the glass on the small barrel beside him, then picked up his makings sack.

He was rolling a smoke when the slow clomp of hooves sounded from the wash.

"It's me, Tom." Vannorsdell's burly, raspy voice lifted from the silvery shrubs. The rancher knew that Tom always smoked and drank whiskey on his porch after supper. He also knew that Navarro wasn't a man to vary his habits much.

"Well, well, well," the foreman said when Vannorsdell appeared on the path angling up through the bushes, his horse sweating from the long mountain ride. "If it ain't the tinhorn who likes to ride alone in 'Pache country."

"Oh, hush. It's 'Pache country no more. Nandash is dead, in case you hadn't heard."

"Yeah, I heard." Actually, Navarro had been nearby when the old Apache bronco was killed by scalphunters atop Gray Rock in the Dragoon range. Navarro had been trying to rescue Karla from Nan-dash's marauders when the marauders themselves were marauded by the slave-trading scalphunters, making Tom's mission even trickier.

He'd lost two good friends that night, and had had to track Karla and the scalphunters deep into Mexico, where he'd met Louise Talon and Mordecai Hawkins, who were tracking their own girl, Billie, nabbed by the same slave-trading scalpers who'd nabbed Karla.

"But the Chiricahuas are playing hopscotch with the reservation boundaries. And there's always the border bandits and the outlaws down from the Rim."

"Shut up and pour me a drink."

"You want it straight?"

"Is it rotgut?"

"Some of the worst I've ever tasted."

"Cut it." Vannorsdell had dismounted and

tied his horse to the porch, and was mounting the steps heavily, fatigued and sore from the ride. "Why do you always buy the worst whiskey in the Territory?"

"Twenty-five cents a bottle, and it's not bad when you cut it."

Vannorsdell picked up the glass and sat heavily in the squeaky hide chair on the other side of the barrel from Navarro. "Aw shit, I feel bad, Tommy."

"Learn you to insult my liquor."

"The old don's on his way out . . . and he's offered me Rancho de Cava."

Navarro turned to the rancher sharply. "No shit?"

Vannorsdell raised his glass, sniffed the whiskey, made a face, and drank. "God, that's putrid crap!"

"You've been wantin' to get your hands on Rancho de Cava for as long as I can remember."

"I know, but hell, you should've seen the sorry son of a bitch. The whole place has gone to hell in a handbasket. His boys have become owlhoots and his daughter — who doesn't even bother to greet me anymore — has become an angry old spinster at twenty-six. The headquarters is practically in ruins. Half his range has been overgrazed and half his creeks muddied up, because the vaqueros his boys hire aren't really vaqueros but border toughs. You should hear the way they talk to the old man!"

"Good water and grass over there, though. You've been wanting to bring in more white-faced bulls to breed with your longhorns. And if you start raising quarterhorses like you've been talking, those high meadows above Bullet Creek would be just right for foals. What do the don's boys have to say about it?"

"That's where I got this." Vannorsdell jerked up his jacket sleeve and raised his elbow, showing the torn sleeve with dried blood.

"Might get worse than that."

The rancher nodded. "The boys won't let Rancho de Cava go without a scrap, I'm afraid."

"What'd you tell the don?"

"That I'd talk to my banker tomorrow. I'll be ridin' into Tucson."

"So you're gonna buy it."

Sipping his drink, Vannorsdell squinted his eyes and shook his head. He set the drink down beside him and swallowed. "Hell, I don't know what I'm gonna do. On one hand, I feel like a buzzard pickin' the old man's bones before he's even in his grave. On the other hand, if I don't buy the ranch, we could have an army of *banditos* for neighbors."

"Could get bloody, tryin' to move Real and Alejandro off the place, not to mention Lupita . . ."

Vannorsdell shook his head and finished off his drink, making another face. "Christ, are you sure that ain't some Injun remedy for the pony drip?"

With a curse, the old rancher stood, slipped the reins from the porch rail, and mounted his horse. "By the way, my granddaughter told Pilar she's in love with you." Pilar was the rancher's Mexican housekeeper. "What are you going to do about that?"

"Nothing."

"Good." Vannorsdell rode through the shrubs, into the wash, and away.

Navarro poured another drink.

CHAPTER 6

The next morning, as usual, Karla Vannorsdell woke at the first wash of dawn. And, as usual, she dressed for the trail in her duck riding slacks, lime green blouse, leather vest, and low-heeled riding boots.

She brushed out her long chestnut hair, gathered it into a ponytail, then set her man's cream Stetson on her head. The Stetson was a birthday gift from Tom, because, riding as she did nearly every day in the desert sun, she needed a broader brim than those offered by most women's hats. He'd had it specially made in Prescott, with rawhide stitched around the brim.

Karla opened her door, padded quietly through the still-dark hall of the big house's second story, down the stairs, through the vast sitting room with its heavy masculine furniture and field-rock fireplace, and onto the broad front porch.

She paused at the edge of the porch and

glanced around.

Morning, with the freshness of the grease-wood and sage, the lavender mountains rising in all directions, the last stars fading in a vast green bowl. Across the sloping yard, smoke curled from the bunkhouse chimney, tinging the still air with the smell of burning mesquite and the coffee, eggs, and side pork of the drovers' breakfast.

When Karla had first come here from Philadelphia, she thought the Sonoran Desert as ugly and hellish a place as she'd ever seen. She'd been through some bad times in it, namely her capture by the slave traders when she'd gone chasing after the young vaquero she'd fallen in love with and whom her grandfather had sent away. She'd come upon Juan's tortured body buried in an anthill by Apaches, only his head protruding, and she'd shot him to put him out of his misery.

Bad times . . .

Still, she couldn't imagine living anywhere else but this high desert plateau, with its bald barrancas, hidden springs, bewitching sunsets, and vast moonscapes spiked with greasewood and saguaro. Her grandfather had grumbled about possibly sending her back east to a finishing school, but somehow she'd have to talk him out of it. She and

Vannorsdell had had their difficulties, but their skirmishes had grown more and more amicable.

Karla crossed the yard to the stables, saddled her Arabian while talking gently in El Diablo's ear, making him nicker and lower his head, bashfully squinting his eyes. She removed her pistol belt from a wall peg near El Diablo's stall, and wrapped it around her waist. The desert around the ranch was relatively safe, but there was always the threat of rattlesnakes and mountain lions.

Urging El Diablo to take one more drink from his stock trough, Karla mounted up and rode off through the chaparral behind the stables and corrals in which nearly a hundred mustangs milled, staring toward the bunkhouse, ears like cones, awaiting the stable boys and breakfast.

"Come for a morning ride?" she said when she brought the Arab in front of Navarro's squat cabin.

The rangy foreman was splitting wood in his denims and gray undershirt. A cigarette angled from the right corner of his mouth, spats hanging loose at his thighs. His short silver hair, still tufted from sleep, was set off by the shadows and his mahogany features, cheekbones sharp as carved wood.

He was fifty, but he had the body — long-muscled, heavy-shouldered, and taut-bellied — of a much younger man. That wasn't why she loved him. She didn't know why. His courage? His strength? The way his eyes twisted up at the corners when he rarely smiled?

Navarro brought the mallet down cleanly through an upright mesquite log. "Some folks have chores."

"Your men haven't even had breakfast yet."

"Neither have I."

"You can eat with Pilar and me when we get back."

Navarro shook his head and held the mallet in both hands. He glanced at the girl, sitting there atop her high-stepping Arab with its cocked tail and the regal U formed by its neck. Karla's slacks were drawn taut across muscular thighs and a round bottom, and pulled snugly over the tops of smooth brown boots with stars dyed into the leather where the toes tapered toward points. The girl filled her blouses right nicely these days, and she had a subtle, coquettish air that drew looks from even the surly German cook. She enjoyed being the only female about the place, aside from her father's rotund Mexican housekeeper, Pilar.

The corners of Karla's mouth drew back, dimpling her cheeks. She regarded Navarro with that wry, candid look that always made him squirm a little.

He needed to talk to her about what she'd told Pilar, but where would he find that brand of eloquence? Maybe he'd have Pilar talk to her. She had to shed those silly ideas. First setting her hat for a vaquero who could barely speak English and now for him, a man old enough to be her father.

"Your last chance," she said, broadening the smile a little, narrowing her eyes.

"Be careful."

Her lips shone now as the lips drew back even farther, and she patted the short-barreled pistol on her hip. "I'm packin'." She ground her heels against the Arab's ribs, giving the horse what it had been waiting for, and bounded off through the brush, heading west between the canyon and the wash.

A quarter hour later, she put the Arab through a cut between two steep, boulder-strewn banks, about to trace a horseshoe route back toward the ranch headquarters. Down the grade ahead of her, from behind the right bank, two men in serapes and high-crowned sombreros stepped into her path. Both wore pistols on their hips. They held rifles across their chests with a menacing air.

The one on the right — stocky and broad-shouldered, with a malignant grin on his round, mustachioed face — was Real de Cava. She'd seen him only once, when she'd ridden over to Rancho de Cava with Navarro and several other Bar-V riders, with a wagon load of feed. He wore two engraved pistols butt-forward, gunslick-style.

Karla halted the horse ten yards before the two men. They broadened their smiles, but there was no benevolence on either face. Her heart beating rapidly and the short hairs prickling beneath her collar, Karla slid her right hand toward her .38. Another hand closed over hers, stopping it.

As Karla whipped her head around, she caught a glimpse of another vaquero a split second before the man shucked her pistol from its holster, tossed it into the brush, then reached up and grabbed her by both arms. He whipped her down from her saddle so quickly that her stomach bounded into her throat, making her head spin.

She found herself standing in the middle of the trail, the indignant Arabian pitching around to her right, facing the vaquero who'd unseated her. He stood two heads taller than she, grinning down at her lewdly.

Her face heated with outrage. "What the hell do you think . . . ?"

"Well, well, what do we have here?" someone said behind her.

She whipped around. Still giddy from her unseating, she nearly lost her balance. Real de Cava moved toward her. "Senorita Vannorsdell, you have joined us at a most opportune time!"

Laughter rose, and she shunted her gaze to see at least twenty more sharp-eyed, unshaven Mexicans standing off in the shadows between the boulders and greasewood shrubs, rifles clutched in their fists.

Tom Navarro and Paul Vannorsdell were drinking coffee in wicker chairs on the big house's front porch, a map spread out on the low table before them. They were discussing the best places to dig more stock wells, a job they'd begin after roundup later in the autumn when the summer's severe heat abated.

Navarro had set his cup down and was about to draw an X in the crease between Navajo Basin and Rattlesnake Bench, when the sentry atop the house yelled suddenly, "Rider comin' hard!"

The Arizona Territory was still a generally lawless land, with Apaches still wild as mustangs, so Vannorsdell kept a sentry posted atop the house at all hours of the day.

"Who is it?" the rancher yelled, lifting his chin toward the porch roof.

"A Mex . . . and a cream Arab! Looks like Miss Vannorsdell's horse."

Navarro and Vannorsdell rose quickly. The rancher reached to set his coffee cup on the railing but missed. The mug hit the stone tiles with a pop. Ignoring it, Vannorsdell followed Navarro down the porch steps and into the yard, both men gazing toward the open front gate, hands on the butts of their holstered pistols.

Beyond the gate, dust rose along the curving desert trail. The thud of hooves grew louder. The rider galloped around a clump of pines — a tall Mex in a red calico shirt and high-crowned sombrero. Behind him, trailing on a lead line, loped Karla's cream Arab, twitching its ears angrily, shaking its head and fighting the bit. The rider jerked on the rope as he checked his own mount down to a trot and came on through the gate, crossing the yard and drawing back on his bridle reins as he approached Navarro and Vannorsdell.

"Where's my granddaughter?" the rancher asked sharply.

The Mexican turned his horse quarter-wise to the house and threw the Arab's lead at Vannorsdell, who swatted at it halfheartedly and missed. The Mex had Indian-dark features and a thin, patchy beard. Sweat streaked his cheeks. "Real de Cava sent me. You want your granddaughter back, ride alone to the top of Hatchet Butte in one hour. Even exchange, you for her. Remember, come alone. Do not wear a gun."

The vaquero reined his horse around and was about to boot it back toward the gate when Navarro reached up and grabbed the man's left arm. Tom gave the arm a hard pull. With a surprised grunt, the Mex tumbled off the horse's left hip and hit the dust with a thud. He clamored onto his hands and knees and jerked his head up, his nostrils flared, his eyes pinched with outrage.

Reaching for the ivory-gripped Russian revolver strapped butt-forward on his left thigh, he wailed, "Son of a —"

Tom rammed his pistol barrel into the Mex's open mouth, drove the man to the ground. On one knee, Tom thumbed the big Colt's hammer back and stared flintily down into the Mex's startled, frightened eyes. "That wasn't quite enough information, you son of a bitch."

The Mex stared up at him, the sun glistening off his small black eyes. When he'd let his arms fall to his sides, Navarro removed the pistol from his mouth but held the barrel an inch from his lips.

The Mex turned his gaze to Vannorsdell standing over Tom's right shoulder. "He killed Don de Cava!"

Vannorsdell crouched beside Navarro. "What the hell are you talking about?"

"You know!"

"If I knew I wouldn't be askin' you."

"We found the old man with half his brains blown out last night after he rode off with you."

Navarro turned to Vannorsdell, who met his gaze, frowning. Turning back to the Mex, Vannorsdell said, "Francisco's dead?"

The man glared up at him around Navarro's cocked Colt.

"Must've happened after I left him," the rancher said, returning his gaze to Navarro. "I heard a shot behind me, on the other side of the ridge. I figured it was just one of the hands shooting a coyote."

No one said anything for several seconds. The Mex lay on the ground, chest and belly rising and falling sharply, shuttling his sun-bright eyes between the two men crouched over him.

"Real thinks you pulled the trigger," Navarro said.

"Obviously." Vannorsdell squinted his eyes and pursed his lips as he inclined his gaze to the Mex. "He must've nabbed Karla on her morning ride."

Bunching his lips with fury, Navarro turned back to the Mex, drew the pistol back toward his own chest, and angled the barrel slightly left. He pulled the trigger.

The pistol popped and bucked, drilling a smoky hole through the man's left arm, halfway between his elbow and his shoulder. Screaming, the Mex grabbed the hole with his right hand and rolled onto his left shoulder, kicking his legs.

"You shot me, you son of a bitch!"

"You can take a message to Real," Navarro said. "He touches one hair on that girl's head, there's gonna be more dead de Cava riders than rocks between here and the San Pedro." Navarro ratcheted back his gun hammer again, planted the barrel against the writhing Mexican's forehead. "You got all that?"

"*Sí,*" the man grated out through gritted teeth.

Navarro withdrew the pistol and looked around. Most of the Bar-V riders were out working the herd or cutting alfalfa along the river, but several, including the skinny German cook and the beefy half-breed blacksmith, who'd been assigned to headquarters chores, had gathered around Navarro, Vannorsdell, and the wounded Mex. Danny Torres had run down the Mex's horse. The half-Pima, half-Mexican drover now stood ten yards away, holding the mount's reins and watching the scene with wary curiosity.

Grabbing the Mex's pistol from the man's holster, Navarro stuck the gun behind his own cartridge belt and jerked the Mex to his feet by his collar. The man's sombrero hung from its thong down his chest. "Now get on your goddamn horse and fog it out of here!"

Navarro gave the man a swift kick in the ass, and the Mex stumbled forward, nearly falling. Clutching his bloody arm, he glanced at Tom, fury mixing with the pain in his eyes, then grabbed the reins from Torres and awkwardly mounted his horse. Torres backed to the horse's right hip and slipped the man's Spencer from the saddle boot and looked at Tom, who nodded with approval.

Before the Mex's horse had galloped ten yards from the front gate, Vannorsdell jerked his eyes at the men gathered around him in the sifting dust. "What are you waiting for? Saddle your horses." He singled out the middle-aged man who'd been sharpening the sickle rake with a mill file. "Oscar, take a fast horse and summon the others."

"What should I tell 'em, boss?"

Vannorsdell glanced sharply at Navarro, then wheeled toward the house. "Tell 'em we got gun trouble."

CHAPTER 7

Forty-five minutes later, Navarro, Lee Luther, and a rider named Dave Watts, who'd been a sharpshooter for Longstreet during the Fight for Southern Independence, trotted their sweating horses along a dry wash east of the Bar-V headquarters. They ducked through a wind-carved tunnel in a sandstone scarp and came out the other side, blinking against the harsh light.

Navarro reined his horse left, pushed through greasewood and willows, and halted the claybank between the wash and a sheer sandstone wall rising toward the brassy noon sky.

Dave Watts and Lee Luther halted their horses off Navarro's right stirrup. "What now?" Lee Luther asked quietly.

Navarro swung down from his saddle. "Now you stay here with the horses while me and Dave do a little mountain climbing."

The kid's eyebrows beetled with disappointment. "You mean, you just brought me along to hold the horses?"

"That's right." Navarro shucked his Winchester, jacked a shell into the breech, and off-cocked the hammer. "Count yourself lucky."

Watts had dismounted his blue roan mare and stood staring up the scaly, weather-pummeled, sun-blasted ridge. He was a slight, muscular man with thin, dark hair and a handlebar mustache. Many thought he resembled the famous tracker Tom Horn, who had helped ship most of the Chiricahuas off to Florida. While Watts was a good horseman who worked well with cattle, he had a lazy streak and couldn't be trusted around liquor. He could, however, shoot a june bug off a mill pond from a hundred yards.

"Mountain climbing? You didn't say nothin' about mountain climbing," Watts complained.

"Didn't I?" Navarro said, moving past Watts to the base of the ridge. "I must've forgot."

As Navarro slung his rifle over his shoulder and started climbing the ridge, using his feet as well as his hands, muscling himself up, Watts cursed and followed suit. The ridge wasn't as sheer as it looked from below, a fact that Navarro hoped was lost on Real de Cava's men gathered at the ridge crest. With luck, de Cava wouldn't expect anyone to climb Hatchet Butte from this side and direct all his attention to the north and west. To encourage him to do so, all the other Bar-V riders had been ordered to gather atop a low, unnamed ridge just north of Hatchet.

De Cava had told Vannorsdell to come alone, but the rancher and Navarro had decided that having the other men gathered nearby was a necessary ploy, while the rancher himself rode up to meet de Cava atop Hatchet Butte. Otherwise, the de Cava gang would most likely shoot the rancher on sight. They'd have no reason not to kill Karla, then, too.

It wasn't the most difficult of climbs, but Navarro had skinned his hands and knees plenty, and he'd lost his hat, by the time he'd rounded a bulge in the crumbling rock wall. He was ten yards from the crest when a hiss rose on his left. He turned his gaze to a shadowed nook. It took his eyes several seconds to adjust to the dim light.

The diamondback rattler, big around as a man's forearm, was coiled above a rocky scab — probably its nest. Its flat copper eyes riveted on Navarro, the rattle blurred with movement, neck tensed and ready to strike.

Knowing he had no options, Navarro dug his right hand into the wall and lashed at the striking snake with his left. The snake's head with bared razor fangs had traveled only a few inches from its coiled body when Navarro's left hand closed around its neck, squeezing.

Tom jerked the snake from the wall. The snake coiled furiously, its body a live whip in Navarro's left fist, as he thrashed it twice against the cliff face, then opened his hand. The snake fell, writhing. It landed in the scrub about twenty yards to the left of Lee Luther, who'd watched its descent wide-eyed, his lower jaw hanging.

When Lee Luther looked back up the wall at Navarro, Tom waved a hand, telling the boy to stay away from the snake, and glanced at Dave Watts, about ten feet straight beneath him.

The sharp shooter was grinning beneath the brim of his sweat-stained Stetson, showing all his teeth as he wagged his head.

Navarro grabbed a knob above with his left hand, dug his boots into the wall, and climbed the last few yards, then pulled himself onto a narrow ledge running along the ridgetop. He turned, pulled Watts up beside him, touched a finger to his lips, and sidled along the ledge, running his hands along the rock wall behind him.

He peered around the left edge of the scarp. Below, on another, broader, flatter level of the butte's crest, about twelve sombrero-clad vaqueros stood staring north and west, as Navarro had hoped. Behind them, Karla knelt in the scarp's shade, her ankles and wrists tied. She didn't appear to be too banged up, and her clothes weren't torn. De Cava's border roughs had restrained themselves.

From behind the rocks, a man cursed and yelled, "That *grande hombre* shot me, the son of a whore!"

Lifting his gaze northward, Navarro saw the fifteen or so Bar-V riders, mounted and lined up along the hogback a quarter mile away. They did nothing overtly threatening, just sat their mounts, holding their rifles skyward, staring toward the de Cava men, many of whom were taunting the whites with Spanish curses and broken-English tirades against their mothers.

One vaquero, staggering drunk, dropped his trousers and mooned the Bar-V boys. Tom was glad his men weren't provoked. From the smell of mescal wafting from below, most of de Cava's men were soused and, if riled, probably not above drilling a bullet through Karla's head.

Turned away from the Bar-V men, facing eastward, Real, Alejandro de Cava, and several other border roughs seemed to be watching someone approach beneath the line of Navarro's vision. Then the ragged leather hat, the wrinkled red forehead, and pinched, angry eyes of Paul Vannorsdell rose above the ridgeline. Vannorsdell's horse stopped where Navarro could see only its head above the ridge, and the rancher's head and chest. The chestnut rippled its withers and nickered, nervous.

"What the hell have you done with my granddaughter, Real?" Vannorsdell demanded.

Real looked down at him. He and his brother were half turned away from Navarro so Tom couldn't see their faces. "Told you to come alone, you murdering old bastard."

"I didn't kill your father."

"No? Then who did? You rode up the ridge with him. You were the last one to see him alive. We find him dead, his brains blown out."

"You want the *ranch,*" Alejandro said, holding a rifle down low across his thighs.

"I'd have to have some pretty big *cajones* to kill your father on his own land. And I'd have to be a pretty miserable friend."

Alejandro turned to his older brother, who was two or three inches shorter than him, but broader through the hips and shoulders. "Shoot him, Real. You do it or I will."

"No, no," Real said. He glanced at the low northern butte, where the Bar-V riders sat stiffly, watching. "We will take this old man back to Rancho de Cava. There, we will try him . . . and hang him." He looked at his brother. "Get the girl."

"With pleasure." Alejandro turned and, his bell-bottomed black pants swishing about his boots, stalked over to Karla. He grabbed his bowie knife from its sheath, cut her ankles loose, then pulled her to her feet and half dragged, half led her over to the edge of the ridge.

Her arms were still tied behind her back. By the heavy way she moved, Navarro could tell her feet were asleep. Alejandro positioned her between himself and Real.

"Turn her loose," Vannorsdell said.

Real raised his Winchester, aimed it at the rancher. "Not until you've climbed down from that saddle, and your men have vamoosed."

The vaqueros, sobered now, were lined out defensively along the ridge's northern lip. They held pistols or repeaters as they shuttled their gazes back and forth between the two brothers and Vannorsdell, and the Bar-V men sitting the butte on the other side of the willows and gravelly wash below. The wounded rider, still out of Navarro's sight, had fallen silent.

Over Navarro's head, wrens and swallows screeched. Seeing that none of the men were looking his way, the foreman stepped smoothly out from behind the scarp, crossing the six-foot gap in the wall and hunkering down behind a tall limestone column jutting directly over the de Cavas, Karla, and Vannorsdell.

He peered around the left side of the column, then turned to regard Watts. The sharpshooter had dropped to a knee where Navarro had just been and, holding his rifle barrel up in his right hand, stole a look around the scarp.

Navarro whistled softly. Watts looked at him. Navarro raised his hand high, to indicate height, then ran his index finger across his throat.

Watts nodded.

Navarro stretched another look around the column. Vannorsdell had dismounted. Scowling, he turned to the Bar-V riders gathered on the northern butte. "Fog it home, boys!"

Real whipped a look at the Bar-V men and shouted, "We see you on our backtrail, we keel them both!"

Real snatched the pistol from the rancher's holster, swung the barrel against the older man's head — a glancing blow across Vannorsdell's right temple, knocking his hat off. The rancher stumbled back, dropped to a knee.

Alejandro laughed and sidled up to Karla, wrapping his left arm around her neck and pulling her back from the ridge's lip.

Watts's rifle boomed.

Alejandro screamed and stumbled forward, throwing Karla forward, as well. The younger de Cava twisted around and landed on his back, groaning and clutching his right shoulder, blood oozing through his fingers.

Cursing, Real jacked a shell into his rifle's chamber and wheeled, crouching and spreading his feet, toward the Bar-V riders. "You killed them both, now, you gringo vermin!"

As Real wheeled back toward Vannorsdell, who was clumsily gaining his feet, Navarro's rifle spoke. A quarter second before he'd squeezed the trigger, his left boot slipped in the caliche, dropping the shot. The slug tore through Real's left calf, punching the hardcase's foot out from beneath him. Groaning loudly, Real dropped to his right shoulder, losing his rifle.

At the same time, Vannorsdell lunged forward, grabbed Karla, turned, and ran back down the gravelly, boulder-strewn shelf toward the rancher's chestnut. As Real leapt for his rifle, Navarro snapped off another shot, missing Real's head by inches, the bullet blowing up dust just over the man's right shoulder.

Ignoring the shot, Real lifted his rifle and aimed at Vannorsdell and Karla, who had dropped below Navarro's line of sight. Navarro was about to snap off another shot at Real, when two slugs, followed a half second later by a third, plunged into the rock column to his right.

Squinting against the dust and flying rock shards, Navarro pulled back behind the column. The gun wolves had opened up on him and Watts and, by the frantic pops and booms of rifles and pistols, on the Bar-V riders, as well.

After another round had ricocheted off the ledge to his right, scattering gravel, Navarro stole another look around the left edge of the column. The Bar-V riders had vacated the butte. Navarro couldn't see them, but the thunder of their horses and the cacophony of their revolvers and repeating rifles told the foreman they were heading toward the butte in a raging fury. The vaqueros were returning fire, shot for shot, the bullets spanging, reports echoing.

Navarro snapped a look behind the column at Watts. "I'm going down —" He stopped, the lines in his forehead planing out. Watts lay in the gap between the column and the broader scarp, folded over his rifle as though only resting. The blood on his head, arms, and rifle barrel glistened in the high, dry sunlight.

"Shit!"

Navarro lurched around the column, dropped to his haunches, then leapt off the shelf. It was a ten-foot drop. He landed behind a cracked black boulder and rolled to his left, transferring the impact to his hips and shoulders. His ankles ached, but he leapt to his feet and ran forward, quartering left, picking out vaqueros and levering one shell after another, the Winchester bucking in his hands.

After ten yards, he stopped, rolled behind another boulder and a twisted cedar, and came up on his right hip, extending his Winchester northward.

Fifty yards down the lower shelf, Vannors-dell and his granddaughter ran a weaving course around boulders and greasewood clumps. Thirty yards behind them, Real had stopped and dropped to his right knee. He raised his Winchester and aimed toward the fleeing pair.

Snapping his Winchester to his cheek, Navarro fired four quick rounds, the bullets blowing up rock shards and gravel around and behind de Cava. It looked like a twister was kicking up dust. Tom squeezed the trigger again. The hammer clicked, empty. Real flung himself forward and rolled behind a stone outcrop, dragging his bloody left calf.

Ducking the bullets de Cava's vaqueros were throwing at him, Navarro flung another westward glance. Running side by side with their heads down, Vannorsdell and Karla disappeared behind a volcanic dike sheathed in greasewood and mesquite, safely removed from the gunfire.

Navarro set his rifle aside and plucked his Colt Navy from its holster, thumbing back the hammer. Realizing that the gunfire had died, and that the vaqueros were yelling in Spanish somewhere off to the east, he stood slowly, glancing around. Seeing no one and hearing only a few scattered shots, he strode quickly down to where Real had taken cover, bolted around the rock with his pistol extended.

Real wasn't there. Just the twin indentations of his butt cheeks and trouser seams and blood-smeared dust near a spindly sage clump.

Navarro looked around. The deep impressions of undershot boots wended through the scrub brush and boulders, heading east, where the other vaqueros had apparently retreated. He glanced behind him and toward the ridge, where Watts had pinked Alejandro. The kid was gone.

Below the ridge, the gunfire had fallen silent. Men shouted. A horse whinnied.

Navarro walked slowly along the scarp, peering around boulders. Moving around a gnarled cedar growing up from a deep depression, he stopped. Alejandro lay on his side behind the tree, his right shoulder gushing blood. His chest rose and fell as he breathed, teeth stretched back from his teeth.

"Tom!" someone yelled from below.

"It's all clear!" Navarro shouted.

He took one more step when something moved in the corner of his right eye. He swung right, bringing up his Colt. Ten yards away, a hatless, bearded hombre, blood smeared on his forehead, extended an ivory-gripped Schofield over a flat rock. Chisos Gomez's drink-bleary eyes narrowed as he sighted down the barrel. The gun exploded, black smoke puffing, the heavy ball pounding into a boulder near Tom's left thigh. Navarro squeezed his own Colt's trigger.

The bullet thumped through the pistolero's forehead, punching him straight back against the towering sandstone wall.

"I think," Navarro added to his last sentence.

CHAPTER 8

It was a haggard, ill-tempered group that rode into the headquarters of Rancho de Cava two hours after the shootout, the tan dust sifting over the buffalo grass and peppering the cool, shallow waters of Bullet Creek.

The women of Rancho de Cava — Lupita, Isabelle, and Isabelle's mother, Henriqua — had heard the horses and stood now before the sprawling house, shading their eyes with their hands.

Henriqua, longtime maid of hacienda de Cava, stood small and gray and sullen in her black uniform, her silver-streaked hair pulled severely back from her pinched face and secured in a bun behind her head. She stood behind Isabelle, her work-gnarled hands resting protectively on the girl's shoulders, giving her dark eyes to the men crossing the yard toward the stables.

Beside her stood Lupita — tall, beautiful,

and severe in her dark mourning dress and mantilla, her black hair brushed to a high shine and falling down her shoulders. Even the somber, shapeless mourning dress, which she'd inherited from her mother, who had died twelve years ago from consumption, could not camouflage the exquisite, high-breasted, broad-hipped figure underneath.

"Real!" Lupita called, an angry, anxious edge in her voice as she noted the absence of her younger brother, Alejandro, as well as several other men who'd ridden out last night with the group. Several who kicked up dust on their way to the stables — hatless, sweaty, dusty — sat hunched in their saddles, blood glistening from bullet wounds, a few using silk neckerchiefs as arm slings or bandages.

Real glanced at his sister, cursed, and swung his horse up to the house, stopping the steeldust a few feet from the women. He'd wrapped his neckerchief around his wounded left calf. "They bushwacked us," he snapped at his sister, anticipating her deprecation.

"Where is Alejandro?"

"I thought he was behind us. We weren't far from home when I realized he'd dropped back." Both statements were lies. In fact, he'd been so disoriented from the bullet in his calf and the corn whiskey and mescal that he and his men had found in a line shack last night, on their way to the Bar-V, that he'd simply forgotten about his younger sibling.

Lupita figured as much. The smell of rancid alcohol sweat hung about her brother, two years her junior, like a haze.

"Coward!" she yelled, stepping forward in her black canvas shoes, holding her shawl closed across her heaving bosom.

Staring up at Real, who sat slumped in his saddle, mustachioed lips stretched back from his teeth, she yelled, "You are a drunken coward. You cannot bring to justice the man who butchered your own *padre*! And you leave your brother with the *enemy*!"

"Shut up, hag! If I did not have this bullet in my leg, I would dismount and slap you silly!" Having kicked out his bad foot, he grimaced against the pain that lanced upward into his thigh. Behind Lupita, Henriqua pulled her daughter two steps back toward the courtyard wall, covering the girl's ears with her hands.

"I will send riders back for Alejandro, *puta*!" Real shouted, leaning out from his saddle, forked veins swelling above his nose.

"And after the dust has settled, I will avenge my father if that means killing old Vannorsdell *and* that *hombre grande* Navarro with my bare hands!"

"Navarro?" Lupita laughed. "Is that who sent you running home like ass-whipped schoolboys? He is an old man."

"Old, yes, but he still has a few tricks up his sleeve. Do not worry. I have a few of my own. Now suppose instead of insulting me, you go down to the bunkhouse and help dress the wounds of my men?"

Real began to rein away, stopped, and shuttled his glance toward the low, grassy hill rising north of the hacienda. Along the base of the hill, old pecan and peach trees reached up from the untrimmed yellow grass.

In the trees, a man appeared — a short, lean, gray-haired man in a silver-trimmed, low-crowned black sombrero. Guadalupe Sanchez walked along through the trees, trailing his sleek pinto mustang by its reins, the segundo canting his head low as if closely studying the ground.

"What the hell is he doing now?" Real asked, sneering. "Picking peaches?"

"He built your father's coffin and helped us prepare the body," Lupita said coldly. "So far, that is more than you have done!"

Real spat in the dirt near his sister's feet, then cursed and spurred his tired horse across the yard. Before the open stable doors, where the other riders and the stable boys were unsaddling the sweat-glistening mounts, Real swung down and hopped on his good foot to a stock tank.

He sat gingerly down on the tank and ordered a twelve-year-old stable boy — the bastard son of one of the ranch's field workers — to saddle a fresh horse. The boy, holding a saddle by its horn in one hand, a 'dobe-decorated bridle in the other, slid his eyes from Real's bloody calf to his face, frowning curiously.

Real berated the boy to do as he was told or take twenty lashes to his backside.

As the boy hustled back into the stable, Real tightened the neckerchief he'd wrapped around the wound, then rolled a cigarette. He glanced up to see the segundo, Sanchez, riding his mustang southwest along the base of the hill and disappear into the willows along Bullet Creek.

"Crazy old bastard," Real growled, licking the brown paper quirley closed and striking a lucifer to life on the stock tank.

When the boy had saddled and led a mouse-colored mustang down the stable's long, sloping ramp, Real stepped gingerly into the saddle. He clucked and reined the horse around, spurring it with his right heel, and in ten minutes he was galloping down through the southeast stables and implement barns and the remains of the land grant's original stone dwellings, long since destroyed by Apaches.

He rode hard for another ten minutes, traversing the irrigated hay fields along the river, over a pine-studded rise and into a shallow valley, where three peons in white pajamas swung long-handled sickles in waist-high manzanita grass. The field was bordered by pines and joshua trees, and the hills rose up beyond the river, smoky green with mesquite and greasewood.

He approached a girl in a doeskin skirt, mocassins, and a blouse of canvas sacking cut low to reveal her hard, suntanned chest and shallow cleavage. La Reina Fimbres was leading a donkey pulling a cart piled high with mesquite and ironwood sticks.

"Real!" the girl exclaimed as the vaquero approached at a full gallop, the mustang kicking up grass tufts and dirt.

He checked the horse down. She stared up at him, feet spread shoulder width apart, full lips pursed, wide-set eyes narrowed. A deerhide thong secured her long, sunburned dark hair behind her neck.

She said, "We heard you rode after . . ."

He extended his open right hand to her. "Climb up."

She hesitated, casting anxious glances toward the fields where the peons toiled. "I have to take these sticks to the barn for Papa. Then —" She gave a low shriek of surprise as he leaned down, grabbed her hand, and swung her lithe, muscular body up behind his saddle. He put the steel to the mustang, and he and the girl rode up and over a low rise and into the yard of a thatch-roofed, sun-bleached adobe around which red horn-toed chickens pecked at melon rinds.

Two mongrel pups, tied in the shade of a narrow stable of unpainted pine slats, ceased their frolicking to regard the horse and two riders with raised ears and cocked heads. Scattering chickens, Real booted the mustang up to the adobe's covered porch, lifted his right boot over the horse's neck, dismounted, then reached up and brusquely pulled the girl down, as well.

"What happened to your leg?" she asked, as he hopped up onto the porch and ducked under the door as he entered the cabin.

"A Tucson whore bit me," Real growled, stopping just inside the cluttered adobe, which smelled strongly of chili peppers, garlic, and mesquite smoke, looking around. His gaze lingered on a mat on the floor to his left, where a shirtless, long-boned young man snored softly on his back, a straw sombrero tipped over his eyes. "What the hell is he doing here?"

Looking down, the girl's almond-shaped eyes squinted angrily. "Pepe! Just what do you think you are doing, young man, sleeping when you are supposed to be hunting?"

The sixteen-year-old boy had jerked his head up with a start. He rubbed his eyes with the heels of his fists. "I just laid down for a little nap," he complained, annoyed at the disturbance.

"Have you shot a deer?"

Pepe shook his head and yawned. Seeing Real, his eyes snapped wide. His face quickly acquired a sheepish cast.

"Then you get out there and don't come back until you've shot a deer for the stew pot, you lazy goat!"

Moving quickly now and shooting embarrassed looks at Real, Pepe stood, grabbed an old Burnside rifle from beside the rock fireplace, and stumbled out the door, his sandals slapping the hard-packed earthen floor.

"Before you go, loosen my saddle cinch," Real called to the boy. "I'll be here awhile."

De Cava had doffed his hat and rolled onto a cot on the opposite side of the room, kicking a chair out from the small eating table and resting his wounded leg on it. Nodding at the bloody calf, he said to La Reina, "Work your magic, senorita. Pop that pill out of my leg."

La Reina glanced at the leg, pursing her lips with disgust. Then she retrieved a dark purple bottle from a cupboard and handed the bottle to Real. From another cupboard she produced a long, thin folding knife and a tin basin. When she'd filled the basin with water from a stone pitcher and sterilized the knife with a match, she knelt down before Real, who was well into the bottle of sangria. She expertly removed the bandage, cut the slacks away from the wound, examined it closely, and set to work, probing the wound for the slug.

Real cursed and jerked his leg several times, taking several long pulls from the bottle. The sangria dribbled down his chin and onto his sweat-soaked white shirt.

"You only come when you are frisky or when you want me to remove bullets from your hide," the girl accused, pouting, as she worked the knife's slender blade.

Real winced and tensed the leg, took another hard pull, swallowed, and sighed.

"Don't I give your father money and san-gria?" He raised the bottle as if for proof. "Don't I give you plenty of frilly dresses and" — he smiled lewdly — "*mucho felici-dad* between the sheets?"

The girl flushed, her cheeks dimpling and her eyes narrowing. Her tone softened. "*Sí.* But it would be nice if I had a reason to wear the dresses. A trip to Tucson, say, or Nogales. Not so far . . ."

Before he had a chance to reply, she stuck her left fingertip into the hole with the knife. *"Holy Mother, you're killing me!"* Real ex-claimed, rising up on his elbows and arch-ing his back.

The girl removed the knife and held the small, round bullet between her bloody thumb and index finger. "Got it!"

When she'd cleaned the wound and wrapped the calf in white cloth, Real took another long pull from the sangria and wrapped his right arm around La Reina's neck, pulling her down to him. "Now your reward, my little peasant queen!"

A half hour later, she got up and gathered her clothes. Watching her dress, Real chuck-led. "You almost made me forget my main reason for coming here. Tomorrow morning I want you to send Pepe out for your brother, the *pistolero.*

Standing silhouetted before an open window, her hair gilded by the waning afternoon sun, La Reina turned to him quickly. "Cayetano?"

"*Sí.*"

"You know my father has disowned him!"

"*Sí,*" Real said, reclining with his hands laced behind his head, grinning as he watched the girl's long fingers smooth the sack blouse across her breasts. "But I need a man with Cayetano's gun savvy" — he winced against the pain spasming up his leg — "to teach some gringos a lesson they won't soon forget."

An hour after dark, Gundalupe Sanchez left the bunkhouse and walked across the yard of Rancho de Cava, oddly silent in the wake of the vaquero's shootout with the Bar-V riders, and entered the big house's front courtyard. The gate squeaked as he closed it behind him, latching it with a ring, then traversed the stone tiles to the broad oak doors.

Tapers smoked on either side of the entranceway, casting bizarre-shaped shadows across the brown adobe. There was the faint smell of the lemon oil the women had used to cleanse the don's body for burial, and of mesquite smoke. The segundo paused before the door, studying the iron knockers and large strap hinges.

Should he knock now that the don was gone, throwing his own position here into question, or go on in without knocking, as he'd always done?

Sanchez decided to knock.

After a minute, the door was opened by young Isabelle, who nodded formally as Sanchez, nodding in return, his sombrero in his hands, stepped around her, and walked inside. He followed the dimly lighted corridor through the smoking parlor smelling of Spanish brandy and Havana cigars. Continuing through a broad, arched entrance, he stepped into a wood-beamed sitting room, at the end of which a fire burned in a massive stone hearth. Candles flickered in gold sconces set upon two square tables covered with white linen cloths.

Between the tables sat the coffin Sanchez had built with his own hands last night and early this morning. In the coffin lay the don in a brushed black suit with a crisp white shirt and an elaborately embroidered wine-colored tie. In the don's hands, resting upon his flat belly, was a broad-brimmed, low-crowned sombrero with red, green, and silver threads in the traditional de Cava pattern of a tiger swiping at two diving hawks.

The don's black mustache had been combed and waxed, the wax glistening in the light of the fire. From the position of the don's head, you could not tell that half his brains were missing.

In one of the several folding chairs arranged before the coffin sat the slender, sullen maid. Dressed in black, with a lace shawl shrouding her head, Henriqua crouched over her Bible and rosary, muttering prayers. Nearby sat one of the rancho's peon families, a father, mother, and three children, their heads bowed in prayer.

As the segundo began making his way toward the coffin, the man and his family stood and shuffled slowly up the aisle. The woman and her children were appropriately quiet, their eyes downcast. When the man passed Sanchez, his eyes were puffed and rheumy with tears. His gaze briefly met the segundo's, the farmer's right eye narrowed with emotion. He gave a phlegmy sigh and his head a single, bereaved shake, then followed his family out of the room.

His hat in his hands, Sanchez continued up to the coffin and cast his weary gaze upon the don. They'd spent so many years together, holding the ranch against the blistering desert heat, bandits, and Indians. Once, vaqueros from long lines of cattle-

118

men rode proudly upon this land. Drinking was outlawed except during the rodeo, and the only shooting was restricted to snakes, coyotes, and marauding Indians.

Now drunkards and pistoleros scurried about this formerly noble grant — vermin on saddles, spending as much time wreaking havoc south of the border as they did at Rancho de Cava, tending cattle or perfecting their roping and riding skills.

A few years ago, Sanchez would have sobbed. A jaded old man who'd seen this coming for years, he simply placed a gnarled hand on the don's, squeezed, muttered a prayer, and turned away.

He'd passed Henriqua, her head still bowed over her beads, and was nearly to the end of the room when Lupita stepped out of the shadows. Light from a nearby wall sconce flickered cinnamon light across the regal planes of her face. Lingering around her was the faint smell of brandy.

"Come to pay your respects, Senor Sanchez?"

"*Sí,*" he said and bowed gravely. "I am deeply saddened by your loss."

Lupita said nothing, but her eyes softened slightly.

Filling the silence, Sanchez said, "I have

packed my bags, and tomorrow I shall take my —"

"What is your hurry?" Lupita gathered her cloak about her shoulders and leaned against the arched doorway. "This is your home, is it not?"

Sanchez looked at her, careful how he formed his words. Her own words of last night still bit him. "It was —"

"When the war with the Bar-V is over, we will have a ranch to run. Obviously, my brothers cannot do it. You are segundo, you will remain segundo. I will talk to Real and Alejandro — if Alejandro still lives."

"Senora, I am a vaquero. The men your brothers have hired are not vaqueros. They will not take orders from me."

Her voice hardened with anger. "They will if I tell them they will!"

The old segundo lowered his gaze to the frayed brim of the hat in his gnarled hands. Anger welled in him, but this was no place, no time to vent it.

Also, where else would he go? He'd been raised by Pimas, all dead now. He'd learned very young how to ride and rope and to gentle *mestenos*. There was little else he could do. In spite of the desecration, Rancho de Cava was his home.

There was always the possibility, however

120

slight, he could thwart this war that Lupita, Real, and Alejandro were bent on waging with the Bar-V, and help turn the ranch back the way it used to be, when he and the don were young.

He wondered what the don would want him to do. Leave and die alone in the Sierra Madres, with only a gold pan and a burro to his name? Or swallow his pride and stay at Rancho de Cava and weather the coming storm?

"Please. I will see." Sanchez stepped past her, heading into the shadows toward the front of the house.

"Guadalupe?"

He stopped and turned back around.

"What were you doing in the north orchard this afternoon?"

His right eye narrowed slightly, and the bull-hide of his face darkened along the knobs of his cheeks. Momentarily, his heart picked up its beat, then steadied and slowed. "I was just musing, the way old men muse, senora." The old segundo's leathery face broke into a brief, phony smile. He bowed again and walked away.

CHAPTER 9

Earlier, when the Bar-V riders had returned to the headquarters, they wasted little time burying Dave Watts in the cemetery atop the rocky rise flanking the main house. Bodies didn't last long in the desert.

Like most Bar-V men, Watts had no family — at least, none he'd stayed in touch with. What few belongings he had would be distributed among the other men, his tack and weapons going to whoever needed them most.

Paul Vannorsdell said a few words over the rough pine coffin the blacksmith had hammered together and nailed a lid on. When the ranch owner was through, he donned his hat and regarded the other men standing grimly in a semicircle around the grave.

Zopilotes circled, the shaggy buzzards executing lazy figure eights against the blue-green sky.

Vannorsdell said, "There's no use mincing words — we're at war, boys. Stay armed at all times and watch your backs." He looked at Navarro. "Double the pickets around the headquarters — night and day — and post extra men with the cattle. They'll no doubt try to melt away our herds."

One of the riders said, "Want we should still deliver those steers over to Lordsburg tomorrow, boss, like we planned?"

"No, we'll wait on that," the rancher said. "No one crosses the de Cava range till this thing is resolved.

"Several o' those *charros* were pistoleros, boss," another man piped up, packing his pipe. "I seen some of 'em down Mexico way. Looks like Real's done hired him an army."

Vannorsdell glanced at Navarro darkly. "I saw 'em. You boys just keep that in mind and stay out of their way. They were drunk today, or we would have had a *real* fight on our hands."

The men donned their hats, grimly mounted their ground-tied horses, and rode down to the headquarters, their shadows long in the early evening light. Vannorsdell and Navarro walked together along the shoulder of the rise. Brooding, they wended their way amid the graves of other fallen

Bar-V men and that of the rancher's own wife, Dahlonega, killed in an Indian raid nearly twenty years ago, when she and Paul were still living in a dugout, with brush corrals and only a handful of scrubby longhorns making up their herd.

Vannorsdell stopped, dug a cigar from his pocket, and bit off the end. Gazing southeast, toward the de Cava grant just beyond a long salmon spine of pine-spotted andesite nearly fifteen miles away, he lit his cigar, turning the Havana and sucking the flame.

"It's a helluva note, Tommy. One of my best friends is dead, and his family blames me for his murder."

"It's a mite prickly, but you've been through worse."

"I was younger then, tougher and meaner. This breaks my heart. I may have to kill Francisco's sons. That's a helluva thing to take to my own grave." Vannorsdell drew deep on the cigar and stared at Blackstone Ridge bordering the de Cava grant.

"I'll have a talk with Alejandro when he comes around," Navarro said. They'd taken de Cava's younger son to the main house and posted a guard on him while the half-Comanche blacksmith, Three Feathers, who was also a passable medico, doctored his shoulder.

"Good luck with that firebrand. Probably either him or Real killed Francisco, but there's no way to prove it. No doubt they're blamin' me to distract attention from themselves." Vannorsdell shook his head. "I don't know, Tommy. This has land war written all over it. I truly loved that old don, but his sons are poison mean. I hate to think how all this is gonna play out." He drew on the cigar again, staring at the coal, pondering.

Navarro had been rolling a quirley. Now he lit it. Blowing smoke at that of Vannorsdell's cigar, the still air letting it linger, he said, "Let's try to keep a lid on the powder keg for the next few days, until I've had a chance to talk to my old friend Sanchez."

Vannorsdell blinked up at his tall foreman.

"If you noticed, Sanchez wasn't among the riders we swapped lead with," Navarro said. "That old vaquero's too sharp to pull a chuckleheaded stunt like that."

"You stay away from de Cava range, Tom. I don't need to lose my foreman on top of all this other grief."

"I'll meet him on neutral ground."

"Even if you two do smoke the peace pipe together, it wouldn't matter. Real and Alejandro don't listen to him anymore. They got their bristles up, and they're painted for war."

"I'll send him back with word that Alejandro's alive. That'll mean *something* to Real and Lupita. I'll set it up to turn Alejandro over to Lupita later. If she sees we saved her brother's life, she might listen to what I have to say. I've had some run-ins with Lupita myself, but I don't think she has it in her to kill her father."

"You've had run-ins with Lupita?"

Navarro flushed slightly and took a drag off his cigarette.

Vannorsdell studied him. "What kind of run-ins, Tom?"

Navarro turned and began walking down the hill toward his claybank silhouetted against a falling bloodred sun, cigarette smoke billowing around the foreman's head.

Wistfully puffing his cigar, Vannorsdell watched him mount up and ride off down the hill. "Damn, that had to been like makin' love with a rattlesnake."

Navarro stopped at the big house, its windows lit against the night. Finding the young Mexican unconscious in an upstairs guest room, with Pilar knitting in a chair beside the bed, and a guard posted in the hall, Tom returned his horse to the stables.

He ate with his men in the bunkhouse, issuing the next day's work orders and as-

126

signing picket riders. When he'd silenced the punchers' grumblings about riding out to the de Cava place and finishing the fight the de Cava men had started, he walked back around the stables and across the arroyo to his cabin.

He mounted the ramada, placed a hand on the door latch, and stopped. Facing the door, he heaved a long sigh. "One of these days you're gonna get yourself shot, lurkin' around my place."

"I'm not lurking."

"Oh? What would you call it?"

He turned left. Karla was a long, slender shadow reclining in his hammock, boots crossed, arms crossed behind her head. "Taking a break."

"From what?"

"Watching Alejandro. Three Feathers thinks he should be watched in case his temperature climbs. Pilar took over for a while." She swung her legs over the side of the hammock, planted her boots on the ramada's floor. "My grandfather can be a hard man, but he never would have killed Don de Cava. What's going to happen, Tom?"

Navarro turned to stare out over the ramada's three steps, into the night-cloaked arroyo. "I'm gonna set up a private pow-wow with Guadalupe Sanchez. Maybe he can talk some sense into Lupita and Real."

"If he can't?"

Navarro lifted a shoulder. "We'll dream up something else." Tom looked at her, sitting with her elbows on her knees and giving her troubled gaze to the arroyo. He moved to her, squatted down on his haunches, and squeezed her left wrist. "They didn't hurt you, did they?"

"Just scared the heck out of me. They took my gun and pulled me out of my saddle before I knew it. Guess I gave them a hand up there, didn't I?"

"It wasn't your fault."

"Got any whiskey?"

"No." He stood, opened the cabin door, and stepped into the musty darkness, redolent of candle wax, mesquite smoke, and gun oil, and fumbled with a table lamp.

Behind him, boots thumped on the ramada. He turned to see Karla moving into the open doorway, her disheveled hair swirling about her shoulders, her face drawn but alluring.

Navarro grabbed his wooden water bucket and disappeared through the back door. When he returned, she was sitting at his rough pine table, a brown whiskey bottle and a dented tin cup before her.

She sat sideways in a hide bottom chair,

her slender, well-turned legs crossed, one elbow on the table, resting her head against her fist. Her chestnut hair spilled down her arm to the bottle. A moth ticked against the lamp, its shadows playing over the table's cracked pine boards.

Navarro poured water into the enamel basin on the table. He set the bucket on the floor, dropped a sliver of lye soap into the basin, and began unbuttoning his shirt cuffs.

Staring at the floor, Karla said quietly, "Did you propose to Mrs. Talon?"

Navarro froze and beetled his silver brows at her, his ears showing red. "Who told y—"

"My grandfather told me you were thinking of buying some mares and stud horses from him, and heading north with Mrs. Talon." She dropped her arm to the table, swept her hair back from her left ear, and looked at him. Her eyes glistened in the lantern's buttery glow. "So did you?"

He dropped his gaze and rolled his left sleeve up his corded forearm. "In so many words."

"What was her answer?"

"Said she'd think on it."

Both sleeves rolled above his elbows, he lowered his head over the basin and splashed water on his face. He took the soap sliver, rubbed it briskly between his hands, and lathered his face. He felt her watching him but didn't look at her. He rinsed his face, then grabbed a towel off a hook, and dried.

When he lowered his hands from his face, her chair was empty. A warm, curving body closed on him from behind, her hands sliding around him and spreading across his chest as she canted her head between his shoulder blades.

She sighed luxuriously, rubbed her cheek against his shirt. "Hmmmm . . . *mucho hombre* . . ."

"Karla . . ."

"I know you love me, Tommy. You rode into Mexico to save me."

He tossed the towel on the table and turned, took her shoulders, and gently pushed her away from him. Ignoring his own, frustrated arousal, he put some steel in his voice. "Karla, I do love you — like a daughter."

"No." She shook her head.

"Do you know how old I'll be when you're thirty?"

"I can't live without you, Tommy. Even when I was with Juan, I thought of you. You make me feel safe. You make me feel like a woman."

She wrapped her arms around his neck,

rose up on her toes, pushed her heaving bosom up against him, and closed her mouth over his, kissing him hungrily. He felt the firm mounds of her breasts swell against his chest. Passion rose in him. In a moment, he found himself holding her, no longer resisting, but placing his hands on her back, returning her kiss . . . enjoying the silky-wet feel of her tongue probing his mouth.

He pulled back from her, his cheeks flushed, his heart pounding. His brain swirled. "I love Louise Talon."

Karla gazed up at him, her eyes soft and wanting. "You love *me*. I can stay with you, Tommy."

Navarro grabbed her left arm, led her to the door, pushed her outside. "This nonsense can't go any further. You have to stay away from me before something happens we're both gonna regret."

He shut the door in her tear-streaked face. Rubbing his hands through his close-cropped hair, he took two steps from the door and stopped. He listened, hearing her quiet sobs, silently willing her to leave.

After a time, footsteps sounded on the ramada. Then her boots crunched gravel, the sounds fading until they disappeared, replaced by the night hum of cicadas, lowing cattle, and yammering coyotes.

Navarro slopped whiskey into her cup and threw it back. He poured another jigger, took the cup to his cot, and sat heavily down.

He cursed and threw back the whiskey, then kicked off his boots and lay down with a sigh. He didn't wake until milky dawn light washed through the cracks in his shuttered windows. Rising, he stomped into his boots, washed, wrapped his pistol belt around his waist, and headed over to the bunkhouse to repeat orders and to check on the men who'd been wounded during the dust-up.

That done, he went up to the main house, where he breakfasted with Paul Vannorsdell, consulting the rancher on his plans to meet Guadalupe Sanchez at the Butterfield station to discuss the brewing war between their spreads.

"The Butterfield station?" the rancher said, one eye twinkling knowingly over the rim of his coffee mug.

Navarro shrugged a shoulder and looked off the porch, toward the stables, where the men were tacking up their horses. "Neutral ground."

Vannorsdell sipped his coffee, gray brows bunching with thought. Then he set the cup on the table beside him. His and Navarro's empty breakfast dishes were there, as well.

"You gonna pull out on me, Tom?" the rancher asked, looking off toward the corrals, the slats and snubbing posts turning salmon with the rising sun. Top-knotted quail twittered in the chaparral.

"I think so."

"When?"

"When this little misunderstanding has been resolved. If it's still good, I'll take you up on that offer to sell me some studs and dams."

"Where you goin'?"

"Since I can't go back to Colorado, I think I'll try Wyoming. I've been in this desert long enough. I hear there's still some good land up there."

Tom was wanted in Colorado Territory for killing two deputy U.S. marshals who'd had it coming.

"Well, I can't begrudge you that," Vannorsdell said with a weary sigh. "She say yes?"

"Not yet. I think she will when I give her a little more to hang her hat on."

"I think she will, too. I've met Louise Talon. She's a smart woman." He paused, then shot Tom a glance. "My granddaughter been pestering you anymore?"

"Nope." Navarro tossed back his coffee dregs and set the mug on his empty plate. "I best swap chair wood for saddle leather." Standing, he adjusted the holster on his hip and headed for the stables, Vannorsdell bidding good luck to his back.

Fifteen minutes later, Navarro rode off the mesa upon which the Bar-V headquarters sprawled, and put his claybank into a lope through the southern sage, greasewood, and cactus-studded hills. The sun climbed over the eastern peaks, its torchlike heat making his back and collar sweat and causing him to tip his hat over his left temple, to shield his face.

He'd just climbed out of a salty-white playa when a rider trotted out from behind a cedar-studded knoll about fifty yards ahead and right. Karla's long chestnut hair bounced on her shoulders as she reined her Arab on an interception course with Navarro. She waved.

The foreman cursed.

CHAPTER 10

Navarro kept his claybank moving along the faint horse trail as Karla approached from ahead, looking fresh in the morning light, wearing a red-and-yellow plaid shirt and, instead of jeans for a change, a slitted green riding skirt. Her pistol was snugged into a saddle holster just below the horn.

"Good morning," she said, smiling, eyes bright, hair blowing, as if nothing had happened between them.

"Mornin'."

"Come out to find me for a morning ride?"

"I'm heading to Tio Muranga's. You best mosey."

"Muranga's?" Karla turned her horse and fell in beside his right stirrup. "That's on de Cava range, isn't it?"

Navarro nodded. "I'm gonna send Tio for Sanchez. We're gonna meet at the stage station to discuss the situation."

"Oh, the stage station. Convenient."

Navarro ignored her sarcasm. "This isn't work for a girl. Skedaddle."

"Ske-*daddle*?" Karla said, wrinkling her nose skeptically. "I'm a little old for skedaddle, don't you think, Tommy?"

"No, and I don't think you're too old for a whipping, either, so run along before you get my back up."

"Let me ride along to the station."

Tom shot her a hard look. "No."

Karla held up her left hand, palm out. "I'd like to see Billie again. She's the only girl I know out here." When Navarro stared over his horse's ears, she said, "I promise not to do or say anything to embarrass you in front of Mrs. Talon."

"Karla, I'm not gonna tell you again."

She heaved an angry sigh. "You're a bastard, Tommy."

"Don't forget it." Navarro gigged the claybank into a gallop, his dust sifting over the girl sitting the cream Arab behind him, staring after him and trying not to cry.

Navarro forced the girl from his thoughts and put his mind to work on the de Cava problem. It was beginning to look more and more as though the old man's killer was another man riding for the de Cava brand. Which meant it could have been any of the thirty or so vaqueros and peons working the grant.

Which meant the Bar-V was in one hell of a pickle . . . unless Navarro could convince the three de Cava heirs they were sniffing up the wrong tree for their father's shooter.

To that end, Tom followed a narrow, spring-supplemented tributary of Bullet Creek to the *estancia* of Tio Muranga — a cluster of cracked, sun-seared adobes standing amid irrigated wheat, oat, and hay patches. He found the old peon feeding slops to his pigs while his dozen or so children wielded hand sickles in the hay patch south of the house.

When Navarro had apprised Tio of the situation and his dire need to confer with Guadalupe Sanchez, the old peon nodded expansively, muttering his understanding. "Anything to avert a war. Heaven forbid, Senor Navarro!"

Holding his horse's reins in one hand, Tom placed his other on the wizened old-ster's shoulder. "Tio, it's important that you speak to Senor Sanchez alone. No one must overhear."

"*Sí,* of course. I may be old and half blind with too many children and a fat, do-nothing wife, but I am no fool in most other ways."

Corncob pipe clamped in his teeth, Tio mounted his old mule named after the dearly departed *patron,* Francisco, and rode off toward the de Cava headquarters. Navarro wasn't worried about the old peon's abilities. He'd heard rumors of Tio's banditry during his younger days south of the border, and knew the old man still had some cunning.

Navarro drew up water from Tio's well, slaking his own thirst as well as the claybank's, then mounted up and continued on toward the Butterfield station, taking his time. There was no point in using up his horse when he didn't have to. Sanchez might not be along for several hours, and there was always the possibility — if Tio couldn't find him or it wasn't an opportune time for Sanchez to leave the rancho — he might not be along at all.

Navarro rode along a broad arroyo, heading southwest between two low, craggy ranges. A rifle barked behind him, making the claybank buck. The echoing report hadn't died when a man groaned.

Clawing the big Colt from his hip and thumbing back the hammer, Navarro reined the claybank hard left. At the top of a rock shelf twenty yards away, a man stood clutching his belly as his rifle fell from his hands and clattered down the slope. The man's chin dropped to his chest, his face etched with pain — the face of Derrold Emory, whose lips were still puffed and red from its impact with Navarro's rifle butt when he and Hought Ellis had attacked Hattie Winters.

Emory stumbled forward and fell head-first off the shelf, hitting the steep incline on his face then, rolling to the bottom, disappearing in rocks and dry desert scrub.

The rifle spoke again, echoing shrilly, thudding into dirt and rock to Navarro's left. Tom whipped his head that way.

Hought Ellis lowered his rifle and stumbled back from a low ridge, on the other side of the arroyo, his exclamations muffled by distance. Wincing, he ran over the lip of the ridge and down the other side.

Frowning, Navarro looked around for his guardian angel. Galloping hooves thudded and Tom turned his gaze to his backtrail. A long-haired rider galloped around a bend, the cream Arab shaking its head with excitement. Karla held a carbine across her saddle bows as she checked the Arab down a few feet away, her cheeks flushed and her eyebrows knit with concern.

"I got the first man, but I think I missed the other one."

"That was you?"

"I was taking the shortcut over to Indian Head Ridge when I spotted two men on your backtrail. Decided to follow along, see what they had in mind."

Navarro's face was hot with chagrin. Not only had he let himself get drygulched, but his life had been saved by a girl.

She must have read the expression in his eyes. Holding the Arab's reins taut in one fist, she said with a placating air, "It was you who taught me to shoot."

The patronization was only an extra twist of the knife, but he didn't have time for self-flagellation. He had to teach Hought Ellis a lesson about drygulching.

"Wait here," Tom said, unbooting his Winchester, cocking it one-handed and spurring the claybank into the arroyo.

He crossed the sandy bottom in five strides, put the horse up the opposite bank, and dismounted, dropping the reins. He scurried up the ridge, pushing off the ground with his left hand, loosing sand and rocks behind his slipping, scuffing boots.

Making the ridge, he stopped. He dropped the rifle's forestock to his left hand and, with his right index finger pressed firmly against the trigger, looked around sharply.

Directly below lay a steep gorge cluttered

with rocks, brush, and stunted pinions. On the opposite bank, about twenty feet down from the ridge, lay a log-framed mine portal jutting six feet out from the yawning black hole in the chalky bank and covered with dirt from which spindly brown grass and yucca grew. The rock tailings were strewn like jackstraws along the bank and into the gorge below.

Hought Ellis was climbing the tailings, scrambling over the rocks and broken shrubs, his rifle in his right hand, his grunts and gasps rising on the hot, dry air.

Navarro grinned, crouched, and holding the Winchester out from his right hip, pelted the rocks around Ellis with six quick shots. Ellis narrowly avoided a seventh shot by scrambling behind a boulder. When the echoes had died, he leapt the last ten feet straight up and scrambled into the portal, dropping his rifle and reaching out to quickly retrieve it.

Navarro cursed.

Ellis's throaty voice shot out from the mine entrance. "You had it comin', Navarro. You done broke all my front teeth, bottom and top!"

"Apparently you didn't learn your lesson, Hought."

A muzzle flashed in the gaping black mine

entrance. The rifle cracked as the slug spanged off a rock two feet to Navarro's right.

Glancing around and quickly deciding a course of action, Tom ran left, hurdling rocks and shrubs, until he'd wound around the gorge's steep ridge. He stood on a broad, flat boulder and gazed directly down on the dirt- and grass-covered roof of the mine portal, twenty feet below.

When he'd caught his breath, he scrambled down the slope, leaping off rocks, and stepped out onto the portal's roof, gently testing his weight. If he could distract Ellis by throwing a rock to the right, he could thrust his rifle over the roof's left side and pop a couple tablets into Ellis's sorry hide, voiding the possibility of future drygulchings and Navarro's need to be rescued by an eighteen-year-old girl.

Tom had taken two steps onto the roof when Ellis cut loose from below, firing into the ceiling, blowing up dust and making the roof shake under the dirt and cactus.

"I know what you're thinkin', Navarro. It ain't gonna happen!"

The drygulcher fired two more shots, one slug finding the crease between two ceiling logs and spraying up dirt and gravel. Three feet ahead of Navarro, a shrill hissing rose.

It took a couple seconds for Tom to distinguish the rattlesnake from the sand between a sage bush and a yucca plant at the roof's lip.

The snake lifted its flat, diamond-shaped head, its body coiling tightly, its sage green scales glistening, the rattle rising and vibrating.

Below, Ellis fired two more shots. A split second after the first shot, the snake struck at Tom, its head springing forward as the body uncoiled, its jaws opening and closing, reaching for flesh. It was a young snake, with more balls than savvy. The head landed two feet away from Tom's right boot.

As Ellis shouted another curse and loosed another shot, making the roof jump, Navarro slipped his rifle barrel underneath the snake, sweeping up and forward. The rattling, S-shaped viper disappeared over the roof's lip, landing on the portal floor with a light thud.

If Ellis was where Tom thought he was, he was no more than three feet from the snake.

Another shot. "Ahh!" Ellis cursed. Four shots popped, one after the other.

Silence.

"Oh, Jesus." Louder, shriller: "Jesus Christ, the son of a bitch bit me. I'm snake-bit. *Navarro, you son of a bitch, I'm snake-bit!*"

"Couldn't have happened to a nice feller," Tom said, turning back to the ridge and beginning to climb.

"Navarro, don't leave me here. That snake bit me twice on the leg!"

Tom rose upon the rocks, breathing hard.

Behind him, Ellis called, "Tom, goddamn it, I need medical attention."

"I'll send out the next doctor I see," Navarro called without turning as he crested the ridge and began moving back the way he'd come.

Walking down the other side of the ridge, he spied Karla waiting between two cacti, flanked by her Arab and Tom's claybank. The claybank watched him and nickered.

"The other one dead?" she asked as Navarro approached.

"No, but he's gonna wish he was in about one hour."

"Can I come with you now?"

Navarro chuckled and slid his Winchester into his rifle boot, then collected his reins. "That was indeed good shootin' girl, and thanks for savin' my bacon. But you turn around and ride home before I take you over my knee."

He mounted up, rode ten yards away,

stopped, then half-turned in his saddle. "Don't let me catch you on my backtrail."

Her lips curved a smile. "That whippin' might be fun."

He shook his head and booted the clay-bank into a gallop. In seconds, the chaparral had swallowed him.

CHAPTER 11

Forty-five minutes later, Tom trotted the claybank into the stage station yard, inhaling deeply the smells of coffee and venison stew on the mesquite smoke wafting from the chimney of the main cabin. As he reined the clay up to the hitch rack, Louise appeared in the cabin's doorway, the heavy timber door propped open with a chair in case a breeze should happen by.

Wiping her hands on her apron, Louise stepped onto the porch. Her hair was pinned up, but several strands flitted around her flushed, perspiring cheeks. "Two visits in one week — to what do I owe the honor, Mr. Navarro?"

Tom swung down from the saddle, loosened the saddle cinch, tossed his reins over the rack, and mounted the porch. "Trouble."

Dread darkened her eyes. "Indians?"

Navarro shook his head and told her

about the killing, Karla's kidnapping, and the dust-up at the Bar-V. He told her he'd sent for Sanchez, hoping to meet the segundo in neutral territory. He didn't tell her that he'd wanted to see her again, too.

"Do you mind?"

"Of course I don't mind. Is Karla all right?"

Remembering how the girl had saved his ass earlier, Tom said wryly, "She landed on her feet, as always."

"I'm always glad to see you, Tom. I've been alone all day. Mordecai and Billie went to Tucson for supplies." Louise squeezed his hands and smiled up at him, her brown eyes flashing in the afternoon light. "But I wish this visit were under better circumstances."

Tom leaned toward her and there was an awkward moment as he decided whether he should kiss her on the lips or the cheek, opting finally for the lips. He wasn't sure he'd made the correct choice until he began pulling away. She stopped him. Leaning toward him, she laid her hand against his cheek, prolonging the kiss.

When she pulled back and dropped her hand, she offered an intimate smile, which warmed him deeply.

"Come on in inside," she said, taking his

hand in hers and leading him toward the door. "I'm making stew for the next stage."

Inside she gave him coffee, stew, and two thick slices of buttered bread. The stew was thick and deftly spiced, with plenty of venison chunks and vegetables from Louise's kitchen garden, the best stew he'd tasted. He told her so, yelling into the kitchen, where Louise was knocking pots and pans around and making the range door squawk.

Tom spooned in another mouthful. "When we go north, you can cook for me full-time."

Suddenly, silence. Her head appeared in the kitchen door, flushed and beaded with perspiration. She smiled. "I'd like that."

"Pay won't be as good," Tom warned.

Her smile broadened. "Yes, it will." Blushing, she pulled her head back into the kitchen, and the clatter of pans and slam of cupboard doors rose once again.

Tom could feel the heat emanating from the stove, unrelieved by the open door through which no breeze penetrated. He could feel the heat in himself, as well. He wished suddenly that he and Louise were already married and heading for the spruce-covered crags of the northern Rockies and their own horse ranch nestled in a grassy, aspen-studded valley. To their own cabin, their own bed . . .

In his mind's eye he saw her again the way he'd seen her the first time, knee-deep in that Sonoran stream, long red hair dancing about her slender shoulders and full, pale, lightly freckled breasts. He'd come upon her by accident, as he'd rounded a bend in the stream, and she'd scared him nearly as badly as he'd scared her.

Now, unable to fully suppress a devilish grin, he finished his stew while casting expectant glances out the cabin's front windows, watching for Sanchez. Louise walked out of the kitchen, blowing stray wisps of hair from her face and carrying an empty cup and the big blue-speckled coffeepot by its wire handle.

Tom wiped all traces of the grin from his lips as she set the cup on the table across from him, replenished his coffee, then filled her own cup to the brim. When she'd returned the pot to the kitchen, she sat down across from him, smoothing the dress beneath her legs and taking a deep, weary breath, thrusting out her lower lip and blowing hair strands from her forehead.

They drank coffee and discussed the de Cava problem. When Tom had rolled a cigarette and was about to scratch a quirley to life on the table, he stopped and turned to the window. Outside rose a muffled yell and the staccato clatter of a heavy wagon.

"Oh, my gosh!" Louise exclaimed, placing both hands on the table and pushing herself to her feet. "The stage is early, and I don't have the food on the table!"

Tom waved out the match and dropped the unlit quirley into his shirt pocket. "I'll give you a hand."

"Oh, I couldn't ask you," she said, half running toward the open kitchen door.

Tom followed her into the kitchen, and in a minute, he was attempting to slice one of the six loaves set out on a cooling rack. When Louise saw that his hammy paws were squashing the bread, she told him to set the table instead. He went swiftly to work on that, setting out plates, cups, and silverware, then carrying out the butter bowl and a big stone plate piled with bread, the slices still curling steam toward the cabin's cottonwood beams.

He was bringing out the stew pot when the stage thundered into the station yard, the adobe-colored dust dripping from its steel-rimmed wheels, the driver leaning back on the reins as the horses stopped before the cabin, their heads drooping wearily. The sun glistened off the sweat coating their hides.

While Louise tended the stage crew and passengers — including two well-dressed couples, a young lady with a newborn baby, a cowboy, and two miners — Tom went out and switched the teams. That was normally Mordecai Hawkins's job, but since the hostler was off with Billie in Tucson, it would have been up to Louise if Tom wasn't here. The woman never ceased to amaze him.

As he backed the two fresh horses into the hitch and buckled the straps, he couldn't help wondering if he really deserved a woman like Louise Talon — an old saddle tramp and former gunslick like himself, who still had men wanting to punch holes in his hide.

He finished the switch just in time to refill coffee cups inside the station house and help Louise serve dried apricot pie with fresh-whipped cream. He even relieved the young mother of her eight-week-old baby boy, giving the young woman time to eat her pie in peace while Tom jostled the blanket-wrapped child on the front stoop.

The driver, a salty old Frenchman named Benoit, stood nearby, eating his pie and discussing the trail trouble he'd been encountering between here and Lordsburg — one holdup nearly every three weeks.

Though the owlhoots wore bandannas over their faces, the jehu knew they were de Cava riders by the brands their horses wore.

When the young mother took her baby back from Tom and crawled back onto the stage with the other passengers, Benoit released the brake and popped his black-snake over the fresh team. The stage lurched and rattled eastward through the chaparral. The shotgun messenger, biting a hunk from his tobacco plug, waved his shotgun high above his head. The rocks and cactus consumed the carriage, the dust sifting, the sounds of the thudding hooves gradually fading.

Navarro peered northeast, shading his eyes with his hands. Seeing no sign of Sanchez, Tom went back inside and helped Louise clear the table and wash the dishes. They'd had time to get to know each other on the ride back from Mexico last year, but now, talking while they worked, they began filling in the gaps between the stories.

When they'd finished putting the dishes away and gone back out to the main room, Tom made good on his urge to hold Louise and give her the passionate kiss he'd been dreaming about for a long time. He held her tighter than he'd ever held her, and she held him just as tightly, hands entwined behind his neck. Her mouth opened for him, their tongues pressing against each other.

Her lips had the texture of fine silk, the faint, sweet taste of orange-blossom honey. Clinging to him, she dug her fingers into his neck and moaned softly, her breasts swelling against his chest. He ran his hands down her sides to her waist and the womanly flare of her hips.

When someone cleared his throat, Louise gasped and stepped back. Navarro turned sharply toward the door, one hand slapping his pistol grips. Standing in the doorway, silhouetted against the bright station yard, was the diminutive, bandy-legged figure of Guadalupe Sanchez in a low-crowned, silver-trimmed sombreo and fringed shotgun chaps, a .44 Russian revolver mounted high on his right hip.

"Many pardons for the interruption, Senor Navarro," the segundo said in his dignified baritone, politely removing his hat and bowing to Louise. "Many pardons, senora."

He stepped back onto the stoop, turned, and moved off to his right. Presently, wicker creaked as the old segundo sat in one of the chairs positioned along the cabin's front wall.

Tom turned a wry look to Louise, shrugged, then strode out onto the stoop. Sanchez sat with his dusty hat in his lap, both boots on the floor, staring off across the station yard. Seeing Navarro, he rose and smiled warmly, holding out his hand, which Tom shook.

"Guadalupe, you look well."

"As do you, Tom," the segundo said, a baleful note in his voice. "In spite of our — how do you say? — dilemma."

"*Sí,*" Tom said, sitting in the chair to Guadalupe's right with a weary sigh, making the wicker creak. "I guess you probably know Vannorsdell had nothing to do with the don's murder."

His face the color of an old trail-worn saddle that hadn't been oiled enough, Sanchez stared across the station yard, at a small dust devil that rose on a sudden breeze, danced off toward the west end of the corral and a small hay pile with a pitchfork protruding from it, and collapsed. "Any other man I would suspect, under similar circumstances, but not Don Vannorsdell. I have known him long, almost as long as I have known Don de Cava."

"I'm sorry about your loss."

The segundo nodded, his wrinkled eyes narrowing slightly. His gnarled red-brown hands were laced over the buckle of his cartridge belt, moving with the slow rise and fall of his flat belly.

"Any ideas who pulled the trigger?" Tom asked.

Before Sanchez could reply, Louise stepped onto the stoop, carrying a tin cookie tray. On the tray were a bowl of stew, a small plate with two slices of buttered bread, and a tin cup of coffee. The food and coffee steamed in the shadows under the porch roof.

"Mr. Sanchez, I thought you'd be hungry after your ride."

Sanchez accepted the tray with gracious dignity. As Louise returned to the cabin, he sat back down in the chair and set the tray across his knees. He curled his callused fingers around the cup, brought the coffee to his lips, and shook his head. "I have no idea who killed the don. But . . ." He let his words hang there as he sipped the coffee, then set the cup back on the tray with a puzzled expression, absently brushing his left hand across his thick walrus mustache standing out against the dark hues of his face. "Whoever did it rode a horse with one shoe built up on the right side."

"You tracked him?"

"Only along the hillside, from the point

where the don was shot. The tracks disappeared in the arroyo east of the orchard."

"You ever see that print before?"

Sanchez shoved the second spoonful of stew into his mouth, chewing hungrily, a slice of bread curled in his left hand. He shook his head. "But I wasn't looking for it." He swallowed and dipped the buttered bread in the stew. "I am, however, looking for it now."

"You'll stay on at Rancho de Cava?"

"For a while. Until the don's killer has had his — how do you say it? — reckoning." Sanchez bit off a hunk of the stew-soaked bread.

Navarro opened his mouth to speak, but Sanchez raised his hand, cutting him off. "I know what you are thinking — that Real or Alejandro had a hand in their father's murder. Considering what they have become, your suspicion is understandable, my friend Tom."

"Do you think it's possible?"

Sanchez shook his head. "You see, I have lived with the boys nearly every day of their lives, and while they have become a blight on Rancho de Cava and will no doubt run the operation into the ground — and while I would break a stout oak branch over their heads — they do not have it in them to kill their padre."

"Not even for the ranch?"

Again, Sanchez shook his head. "It is not possible. It is a Spanish thing. It would be like pissing on a church altar before the admonishing eyes of a hundred saints. It cannot be done."

"What about Lupita?"

"Ah, Lupita," Sanchez said with a knowing half smile, swabbing his empty bowl with the second slice of bread. "She is another story. That one does not have a conscience. She could have pulled the trigger herself . . . or convinced one of the riders to do it."

Leaning forward in his chair, elbows on his knees, Tom nodded. Lupita could get nearly any man to do nearly anything, he knew, having been in her clutches one long, bewitching night in Tucson about fifteen months ago.

"We have Alejandro," he told the segundo now.

Sanchez looked at him sharply. "He is alive?"

"Took a bullet to the shoulder. He'll be down for some time, but it looks like he's going to make it. He shouldn't be moved for another week."

"I was hoping the little bastard had gone

to meet his Maker." Sanchez sighed and shoved the last bite of stew-soaked bread into his mouth, then wiped his mustache with the back of his hand. "It is just as well. His death would only fuel the fire."

"Want him back?" Navarro asked, fingers laced together and favoring Sanchez with a flat, wry expression.

The segundo shrugged. "Do I have a choice?"

He and Tom each rolled and smoked a cigarette. Louise brought out the big pot, refilled their coffee cups, and took Sanchez's tray back into the cabin.

Drawing deep on his cigarette, Tom said, "I'd like to bring the kid back myself."

Sanchez exhaled smoke, glancing at Navarro, a faint glimmer of curiosity in his old brown eyes.

"I'll bring him back in one week, under a white flag."

"It might be better if I ride over and pick him up, Tom."

"I'd like to talk with Lupita. If I bring her brother back alive, I might be able to convince her the Bar-V's back isn't up and that Vannorsdell didn't kill de Cava. In the meantime, can you keep Real off his warhorse?"

It was hard to tell with his skin so dark,

but Sanchez seemed to flush slightly with chagrin. His lips parted, then closed. The segundo stared northwest across the station yard, beyond the corral and the barn, his eyes narrowing and the muscles in his face drawing taut.

He sat frozen, staring, both hands resting on his thighs, cigarette stub smoldering in his right hand. His head moved slightly. His eyes slid across the ground before the cabin, to the right of the two horses tethered to the hitching post.

Navarro followed Sanchez's gaze. A conical shadow separated from the shadow of the cabin's roof on the hard-packed, hay-flecked ground, about twenty feet out from the porch. Straight above, the roof squeaked.

"A thousand pardons, Tom," Sanchez said, rising slowly from his chair, his right hand dropping the cigarette stub and moving to the stout Russian riding high on his right hip.

He drew the revolver and fired two shots into the porch roof.

The reports sounded like two quick thunderclaps as they echoed off the cabin and around the yard. Dust and wood slivers rained down.

Above, a man grunted and cursed in

159

Spanish. The ceiling shook, dust sifting downward, as a body hit the shingles. The man rolled over the roof's lip, following his high-crowned sombrero dangling from the thong around his neck, and hitting the ground before the porch with a solid thud.

"I believe I was followed," Sanchez finished.

CHAPTER 12

A second after the man had rolled off the roof, a rifle cracked in the yard's northwest corner, the slug slamming into the cabin over Sanchez's left shoulder.

As Sanchez returned fire, Tom spied movement in the opposite corner of the wagon yard. A bearded man wearing a straw sombrero and two cut-down holsters ran up from the rear of the corral. As he dove behind the stock tank by the front gate, Tom drew his revolver and fired three shots, two bullets plunking up dust around the tank and another slamming into the split-log rail before it.

As more guns opened up around the cabin, Tom leapt off the porch, untying both sets of reins from the hitch rack, then slipping both rifles from their saddle boots as the horses, frightened by the gunfire, bolted eastward into the chaparral.

Leaping up the porch steps, Tom tossed

Sanchez his old Spencer. The segundo caught the rifle one-handed. Holstering his big revolver, he cocked the rifle and pressed his back against the cabin as two bullets tore widgets from the porch floor in front of his boots. He extended the rifle and fired a shot toward the barn.

"Inside!" Navarro yelled from the cabin's open door.

He poked his gun out the doorway and fired three shots, covering the segundo as Sanchez bolted into the cabin. As Guadalupe ran to the west window, Navarro fired one more shot through the door, then pulled the door closed and barred it.

Navarro turned from the door, raked his gaze around the cabin. "Louise?"

As if in reply, a rifle shot sounded from the kitchen. Navarro ran through the kitchen door, stopping just inside the small room dominated by a black iron range. Louise stood before the open back door, a rifle raised to her shoulder.

Beyond her, a stocky Mexican had fallen to his knees, both hands cupped to his blood-soaked belly. In one hand he held a sawed-off shotgun. His face bunched with pain, lips stretched back from his gritted teeth, he began raising the barn blaster.

Louise cursed and, working the Winchester's lever, ejected a spent shell and jacked another into the breech. She aimed and fired.

Peering over her left shoulder, Navarro saw a round hole appear in the Mexican's left temple and blood spray out the back of his head. Both arms flying straight out from his sides, he flung the shotgun like a hot potato. He fell awkwardly, legs curled beneath him, and lay still.

Sensing Navarro behind her, Louise turned her head, her eyes meeting his incredulous stare. Louise kicked the door closed. "Friends of yours?"

"Not anymore," Tom said, setting his rifle against the wall.

He leaned into a heavy table on which bread, vegetable peelings, and a paring knife were strewn. Louise set down her rifle, hurried around the table, and helped Tom slide the table snug against the door.

Tom picked up his Winchester. "Any other ways inside this place?"

Sanchez's rifle cracked in the main room, sounding like thunder echoing in a narrow canyon.

"No."

Tom's gaze was hard and commanding, belying his anxiety. "Stay in here and keep down."

He hustled back into the main room as Sanchez, sidling up to the west wall and extending his Spencer through the window, snapped off a shot. The segundo quickly ejected the spent shell and slammed a fresh one into the Spencer's chamber.

A bullet cracked into the closed front door, jarring it slightly. The timbered door and stout pine walls had been constructed to repel attacks by bandits and Indians, and the slug didn't come close to going all the way through.

A man's voice rose beyond the front door. "Sanchez, come on out and meet your Maker, you traitorous dog!"

Saying nothing, the old segundo coolly aimed his Spencer's barrel and snapped off another shot.

Heading for the window on the other side of the room from Sanchez, Tom asked, "How many we got out there?"

"I counted four," Sanchez said, dropping to one knee. Two more shots pounded the cabin around the segundo's window. Sanchez snapped off another shot. Working the Spencer's trigger-guard loading mechanism and thumbing back the heavy hammer, his eyes bleak with shame at having been followed, he said, "De Cava riders."

"Don't beat yourself up." Navarro pressed

his right shoulder against the open shutter and scanned the chaparral about thirty yards out from the cabin.

A rifle cracked, the slug drilling into the casing a foot from Tom's head. He peered across the yard. Smoke wafted above a rocky, brush-sheathed knoll. A man in a sun-bleached straw sombrero lay atop the knoll, his rifle jerking as he cocked it.

Tom levered three shots, blowing up dirt and rocks and snapping shrubs around the knoll. Dust sifted as the man withdrew behind the knoll's lip.

Meanwhile, Sanchez swapped lead with two shooters on the northwest corner of the yard while another triggered slugs through the window right of the front door, the slugs plunking into the tables, shattering a fruit jar and scattering flowers. A lamp exploded.

As Louise moved into the main room through the kitchen door, a slug slammed into a tin washbasin hanging on the wall a foot from her head. The pan gave a bark and slid back and forth against the wall.

"Get under a table!" Tom shouted at her.

Cursing, his hard face flushed with fury, he rammed a fresh shell into the rifle's breech, ran to the front window right of the door, and edged a glance around the frame. A mustachioed Mex in a black-and-red-striped shirt and red sash crawled through the corral and ran toward the gaping barn doors.

Tom tracked him with the Winchester. As the Mex stepped into the barn's inner shadows, Tom squeezed the trigger.

The man grabbed his thigh, dropping his rifle and hopping back behind the barn's front wall. He lunged out from behind the wall, skipping on his good leg, grabbed his rifle, and retreated again behind the wall. Tom's second slug blew up dirt and hay between the gaping barn doors.

Navarro was about to fire again when slugs from both sides of the yard slammed into the windowframe, one cutting the air just above his head as it whipped through the window and buried itself in a wall.

The slugs kept coming, chewing and spraying splinters around the frame. Meanwhile, Tom used his rifle to close the shutter and lock it.

He turned to Sanchez, who fired through the west window, then withdrew and pressed his back against the wall. A bullet whistled through the window and drilled into a table.

"They mean business," the segundo said.

"I get that impression."

Sanchez spat wood splinters from his lips. "That's Augustin de Marcos out there. He's become very tight with Real. A pistolero much more than a cattleman."

Navarro moved to the front door. A pop behind him spun him around. Louise was at the east window, levering her Winchester behind a cloud of powder smoke.

Navarro's gut wrenched. "I thought I told you to stay down!"

Louise fired and levered another shell. "You give the orders on Bar-V range, Mr. Navarro." She aimed toward the knoll, pinning down the man in the sun-faded sombrero. "Here, you're under my jurisdiction."

Tom cocked an eyebrow at her and opened his mouth to respond, but changed his mind. There was no arguing with a woman like that. He'd better get used to it.

As Louise and Sanchez fired through their respective windows, Tom continued to the door, turned the knob with his left hand, and threw it open. He dropped to his left knee in the doorway, picked out a man hunkered down behind a hay mound just left of the barn, and fired three quick rounds.

The bullets hit nothing but hay.

Cursing, Navarro bolted back behind the doorframe as two shots ripped into the wall before him, making it shake, one shot shattering the dry mud chinking between the logs. When the man behind the hay mound paused, Navarro bolted across the open door, snapping off two shots, again hitting nothing but hay as the shooter ducked behind the mound.

"Slippery sons o' bitches."

The man on the east knoll drilled a round into the open door, scraping a couple layers of skin from Tom's left forearm. He felt as though he'd been touched by a glowing skillet. Shooting from the east window, Louise barked a slug off the shooter's rifle, sending up sparks and evoking a shriek.

Sanchez fired intermittently into a gully arcing around the yard's west edge, trading shot for shot with the man grounded there in the mesquite shrubs and cholla. The frantic whinnies of the stage horses rose from the corral.

Tom stepped back across the door as the man with the bullet-burned thigh opened up from between the barn doors, hammering the cabin's front doorframe. Tom was about to poke the Winchester out the front window and silence the man in the barn once and for all, when Sanchez said, "I think we have more guests."

Tom looked at him. The old segundo had stepped back and was squinting at something in the western distance. "Wagon dust."

Tom turned to Louise, who had turned away from the east window, her rifle smoking in her hands. "Another stage?"

"Oh, my God." Louise's voice was pinched with dread. "It's Mordecai and Billie."

Tom went over to Sanchez's window and slid a glance around the frame. A hundred yards away, a scarf of red-brown dust rose above the thick desert scrub. The faint clatter of iron-rimmed wheels rose above the intermittent gunfire and shrieks of ricocheting lead.

A bullet plunked into the outside frame. Tom withdrew his head and muttered a curse. "They're gonna parade right into our shindig."

Louise stiffened, then began to move toward Tom. Remembering the window and the man behind the knoll slinging lead through it, she stopped and stepped back against the wall. Her face blanched. "We have to stop them!"

Tom slid his eyes about the room, thinking. Sweat streaked his face, carved runnels through the dust on his neck. "No one's covering the back. I'll slip out the back door, and try to flank 'em. If I can surprise one or two, the others might hightail it."

He bolted past the window, heading for the kitchen.

■ ■ ■ ■

Fifteen minutes before Sanchez saw the dust, Billie Brennan, sitting on the wagon seat right of Mordecai Hawkins, looked up from the dress she was sewing and heaved an exasperated sigh. "Doggone, Mr. Hawkins, do you have to hit every chuckhole in the gall-blasted trail? My fingers feel like pin cushions."

Hawkins glanced at the girl, whose long, light brown hair hung straight down from her floppy-brimmed farmer's hat. "If your fingers feel like pin cushions, little miss, it's through no fault of mine. Fool's work, tryin' to sew in a moving buckboard wagon."

"I've always done perfectly fine in the past, because you haven't tried to hit every chuckhole in the road."

Wrinkling his thick red nose and pitching his voice high, mocking the girl's supercilious tone, Hawkins said, "I ain't been tryin' to hit *every* chuckhole in the road. There just so happens to be *more* chuckholes in the road after last week's gully washer. If I tried to avoid 'em *all* so you could sew some fancy pretties on your dress to impress that young puncher from the Bar-V, we wouldn't get back to the station till after dark."

170

"They aren't fancy pretties — whatever fancy pretties are," Billie said, returning her eyes to the dress sprawled across her lap. "It's diamond lace I bought in Tucson. I just want to look nice for the dance" — she glanced up at Hawkins, squinting one brown eye — "*not* for Lee Luther." Turning back to her work, she added with less vigor, "I hardly know the boy."

Hawkins chuckled. "I saw the way you two were makin' eyes at each —" The old mountain man stopped and peered straight ahead, scowling. What had sounded like a distant rifle shot had risen from the direction of the stage station, now only about two miles away.

"What was that?" Billie asked, sudden tension drawing her voice taut. As if in answer, another shot rose, then another.

Holding the ribbons high in his hands, Hawkins stared over the two mules' bobbing heads. He told himself that the shots — if they *were* shots — could be those of cowpunchers hazing calves from mesquite thickets or honing their aims on snakes or coyotes. Nevertheless, Hawkins's heart increased its beat, and small goose bumps rose across his shoulder blades, chilling him like a fall breeze over the Bighorns.

"Hold on, girl!" Hawkins shook the reins

across the mules' broad backs. Braying, the heavy beasts shook their heads and manes and lunged into a shambling run.

Billie stuffed her sewing under the seat, snugged her hat down low, wedged her low lace-up boots against the dashboard, and held on to the seat with both hands. The wagon fishtailed around curves in the meandering trail. It bounced over rocks and potholes and the furrows made by recent rivulets. Spindly desert scrub and sunbaked rocks flew by, the mules' dinner-plate shoes pelting Billie's face with dust and fine pebbles.

When the cabin shuttled into view above the scrub, Hawkins jammed his mule-ear boots against the dashboard and hauled back on the reins, stopping the mules under a sprawling sycamore and giant cactus. Gunfire rose clearly, a staccato, angry fusilade just around the last bend in the trail. Slugs slammed into logs with resounding thumps and spangs.

Smelling the faint tang of gunsmoke on the eastern breeze, Hawkins leapt down from the box. His brows anxiously furrowed, he grabbed his Henry rifle from under the seat and ran around the rear of the wagon, ambling under the weight of his sagging belly.

172

Indians or bandits, no doubt. It sounded like Louise was putting up a good fight from the cabin.

Hawkins leaned his rifle against the front wheel and extended his arms to Billie, whose hands gripped the seat so tightly her knuckles were bone white. "Come on, girl!"

"What are you gonna do?" Billie cried as a gun cracked sharply in the station yard. Her eyes were tear-glazed, bright with terror as she peered down at Hawkins.

He lifted her down, jerking her hands loose, then grabbing her right hand and pulling her along behind him as he stalked into the chaparral. Under a cottonwood, he stopped and squatted before her, peered into her stricken eyes. "Stay here. Don't move a muscle or make a sound."

He shoved her down on a rock, pulled his old Smith & Wesson from his holster, and extended it to her, butt-first. "Take this. When I come back for you, I'll whistle twice. Anyone else comes . . . well" — he nodded at the gun in the girl's trembling hand — "I taught you how to shoot."

He tramped back to the wagon, picked up his Henry rifle, and headed into the chaparral. He followed a narrow dry wash through mesquite and desert willows, tracing a lazy curve toward the northwest corner of the station yard.

Shots resounded before him, cracking and echoing, occasional slugs spanging off their targets with angry shrieks.

He left the narrow wash, pushed through mesquite shrub, and hunkered down beside a rock. He was at the northwest corner of the station yard, the barn ahead and left, the cabin fifty yards ahead and right.

"Come on out, Sanchez!" a man yelled in Spanish from the other side of the barn. "You're only prolonging it!"

Smoke puffed from behind the barn's far wall. A rifle was thrust through the open front doors, and two shots popped.

The horses in the far corral whinnied and screamed and jostled the corral with wooden knocking sounds. The gate latch creaked and snapped.

Another shot rose sharply to Hawkins's left, indicating another shooter in the gully running close against the cabin's west side. The slug plunked into the casing around the window.

Hawkins's blood pumped. The goose bumps had been replaced by an angry heat.

Three men. He'd take the one in the barn first, then the one on the other side. Last, he'd see about the man in the gully.

He began to move left, rising . . . and

pressed his head against a pistol barrel. He jerked with a start and froze when the pistol's hammer clicked back.

He turned his head slowly, running his gaze up along the long, silver-plated barrel of a Colt .45, aimed at his head, to the grinning face of the mustachioed Mexican behind it.

CHAPTER 13

Navarro shoved the table away from the back door, sidled up to the knob, and turned it. Sensing someone behind him, he looked over his shoulder. Louise stood just inside the kitchen, her rifle held low across her thighs, her eyes bright with beseeching.

"Be careful!"

His gaze met hers. "Shove the table back when I'm gone."

He opened the door a crack and peered into the backyard, where the hombre Louise had shot lay under a wavering, buzzing cloud of flies, the spilled blood glistening in the angling sunlight. Seeing no gunmen nor hearing any shot on this side of the cabin, he slipped outside and drew the door closed behind him. Inside, the table barked across the puncheons as Louise slammed it against the door.

Keeping his back pressed to the cabin's rear wall, Navarro sidestepped to the southwest corner and slid a look around the protruding ends of the hand-adzed logs. The man who'd been shooting from the gully was still there, shooting toward the window from which Sanchez returned fire with his Spencer.

Beyond the gully, Tom saw no dust rising along the trail, which meant the wagon had stopped somewhere back in the chaparral. Tom fingered his rifle, hoping the shooters hadn't seen the dust. It was hard to tell, but so far it appeared that all four were still slinging lead at the cabin.

Navarro raked his gaze around the yard and the gully. The yard was barren and level right up to the gully's lip. There was no sure way to get around the man hunkered there without being seen. Turning, Tom stole along the cabin and snuck a peak around the opposite corner.

A man was still triggering lead from behind the knoll. Tom watched him. The man emptied his rifle and withdrew his head behind the knoll's lip as Louise's Winchester blew up widgets of dust and sand around him.

Navarro studied the terrain. There was more sage on this side of the cabin than the other, and two fairly large rocks and a stubby pipestem cactus offering cover from both the knoll and the barn. He got down and swiped his hat from his head.

Dragging his rifle along in his right hand, he snaked eastward across the yard, wending his way through the sage clumps, the heels of his hands and his knees picking up several sharp goatheads. Climbing to his knees, he crouched behind the pipestem. Smoke puffed from behind the knoll straight ahead and twenty yards away, the rifle barking loudly.

Navarro ran crouching into the chaparral and circled around behind the knoll. The shooter appeared before him, hunkered belly down near the hillock's crest. The man fired over the lip, then drew his rifle back, casually ejecting the spent shell, which clattered tinnily over the rocks.

He, like the others, was taking his time. This was probably more fun than chasing de Cava cattle or digging wells. Besides, if the shooters didn't kill Navarro and the others before dark, they could gain the cabin under cover of darkness and set fire to the roof.

Drawing deeply on the brown paper cigarette dangling from his lips, the man rammed a fresh round into his rifle's chamber. He lifted the barrel to the knoll's lip. A shot from the east window blew up sand

and shrub branches, causing the man to jerk the rifle back down. He grinned gamely, removed his cigarette, spit sand from his lips, then stuck the quirley back in his mouth and set his rifle between two sage clumps atop the knoll, aiming at the cabin.

Tom stopped at the base of the knoll, six feet from the man's tooled boots with shining, razor-edged Chihuahua spurs, and grunted, "You've been flanked, amigo." The man's back tightened; he swung the rifle around.

Tom shot him twice in the chest, one smoking hole appearing beside the other on either side of his breastbone. His head slammed back against the knoll; grunting, he dropped his rifle, which slid to the knoll's base, coming to rest against Tom's left boot. The man exhaled loudly, his legs relaxed, and his eyes closed.

Not giving the man a second glance, Navarro wheeled and headed toward the corral.

"Hold your fire, amigos," a Spanish-accented voice called loudly from across the yard, stopping Tom in his tracks. "I have a pretty girl and an old man here, and I do not think you want to see them hurt." The man chuckled loudly.

Navarro turned toward the yard and

pushed through mesquite shrubs as the voice rose again. "Senor Sanchez, Mr. Navarro — are you listening? I am going to kill these two if you do not come out and face me like men, amigos."

Tom knelt between a boulder and a barrel cactus, and angled his gaze across the stage yard. Mordecai Hawkins and Billie Brennan stood between the open barn doors, slumped and dirty, as though they'd rolled in the dust. The girl's blue plaid gingham dress was torn off one shoulder, and her long auburn hair was mussed. Hawkins's wasn't wearing his hat; a rivulet of blood ran down his cheek from his right temple.

Behind and between them, using them both as shields, stood a stocky Mexican in a black-and-red-striped shirt and gaudy black sombrero. Partly cloaked by the barn's shadows, he held a pistol in each hand, one pistol aimed at Hawkins, the other at Billie. His teeth shone white between his parted lips.

Navarro whipped back around, then hurried over to the man he'd just killed. He and the dead man were of similar sizes, with similar frames. What the hell? It was a long shot but it was the only chance he had of getting close to Hawkins and the girl.

Leaning his rifle against the knoll, he

crouched down and pulled the man's head up by his collar, and jerked the ragged poncho over his head. Letting the dead man fall back against the knoll with a thud, Navarro draped the poncho over his own head, ignoring the blood splotches. He stood, grabbed the man's sombrero off a nearby sage clump, and snugged it down on his head, the horsehair thong dangling beneath his chin.

"Amigos, I am growing impatient," the Mex yelled from the barn. "Do I have to kill the old man to show that I am serious?"

Navarro picked up his Winchester and, holding it low in his left hand, pushed through the shrubs and walked purposefully, almost cockily across the yard, heading in the general direction of the barn. He made a show of keeping a watchful eye on the cabin, as if worried about getting shot, but kept his right eye skinned on the north side of the yard, where another Mex knelt behind the corral gate, grinning through the slats while fingering the hammer of the repeater in his hands.

Spying movement straight ahead, Tom turned his gaze that way. The man who'd been shooting from the gully had emerged and was walking slowly sideways toward the barn, keeping his Sharps carbine trained on the cabin. The Mex in the barn rapped one of his pistols against Mordecai's head.

"Goddamn it, you are making me angry. I give you three seconds, and I keel the old man! One. . . ."

Navarro stopped. If he got much closer to any of the four shooters, he was bound to be recognized.

Which one should he shoot first? The man behind Hawkins and the girl was out of the question.

He raised his rifle quickly toward the man from the ravine, who stood about thirty yards straight across the yard, and fired. He saw the man's knees buckle and heard him grunt as, jacking another round and wheeling sharply right, he took quick aim at the man in the corral, who'd whipped a wide-eyed gaze at him.

The man hadn't even started bringing his rifle up before Navarro triggered a shot. The round slammed into the rail before the man's head, the concussion making a hollow *thwack*!

Ramming another round into the chamber while keeping the rifle's butt snugged against his shoulder, Navarro dropped the barrel slightly and fired as the man began rising off his knees, his hands tightening around his rifle. Navarro's shot caught him just above his left hip, spinning him around with a surprised shriek.

Tom swung his gaze to the barn, where Mordecai had done what Tom had hoped — thrown himself into the Mex. Triggering both pistols into the air, the man fell backward, Hawkins throwing himself on top of him, his hands flailing after the guns.

Navarro was sprinting toward them when a shot popped, echoing across the yard. The slug burned across Tom's left shoulder blade, throwing him down hard on his left hip.

Disoriented, Navarro glanced around, saw the man in the corral extending his smoking rifle over the top slat, fury in his bunched lips and brown eyes, long hair brushing across his cheekbones. The rifle stabbed smoke and fire, the slug tearing into the ground six inches to the right of Tom's right hand, the twanging sound of the ricochet echoing across the yard. The man lowered his rifle, levered another round.

As he brought the barrel across the slat, Tom gained his knees and extended the Winchester. He squeezed the trigger a half second before the other man triggered his Spencer, the bullet burning a furrow across Navarro's upper left arm. Tom's own slug drilled the man through his right shoulder, swinging him half around before he dropped to both knees. One of the milling horses — a big bay with a white Z across its face — gave a screeching whinny as it trampled him.

Tom jerked his head left. Between the barn doors, the Mex had pushed to his knees and was aiming his right pistol at Hawkins, down on all fours and regarding the Mex with fury in his eyes.

Left of the Mex, cowering on her knees and staring at the Mex and Hawkins, Billie screamed. A rifle cracked behind Navarro — two quick, furious shots, one slicing across the Mexican's right temple, the other slicing through the slack of his shirt under his raised right arm.

He swung around toward the cabin, eyes snapping so wide Navarro saw as much white as iris, and gaining his feet, both cocked pistols extended straight out from his shoulders, bolted toward the cabin.

The rifle behind Navarro spoke again, drilling a small, round hole through the Mex's neck. The man stopped, a dull groan seeping up from his throat as a bright blood drop appeared on the lip of the hole. He stood frozen, wide eyes blinking slowly. The eyeballs rolled back in the man's head as the rifle cracked again, and another hole appeared high in the Mexican's striped shirt, simultaneous with the whack and crack of the slug through the man's breastbone.

As the man stumbled back between Billie, who had thrown herself facedown on the ground and covered her head with her arms, and Mordecai, who was climbing to one knee, Tom turned to the cabin.

Sanchez stood on the stoop, just before the wide-open door. The wizened, old man still wore his sombrero. His feet were spread, knees bent, his Spencer rifle snugged to his shoulder. A wisp of gray-blue smoke curled from the barrel as the segundo, staring at the dead Mex now lying prostrate between the barn's open doors, slowly lowered the rifle to his hip.

Louise's anxious face appeared in the shadows behind him, the woman tall enough to peer over the segundo's right shoulder. Looking around and seeing that the threat was gone, she pushed passed Sanchez, leapt off the porch, and sprinted across the yard to the barn. With a glance at Navarro, who remained on his left hip in the middle of the yard, sucking air through his teeth and feeling as though a grizzly had tried making a meal of his left shoulder, Louise knelt and took Billie into her arms.

Sanchez started down the steps to Navarro, but stopped suddenly when he spied movement inside the corral. He lifted his gaze beyond Tom, seeing through the corral slats that the man Tom had wounded was crawling through the fear-milling horses toward the corral's far northeastern corner.

Navarro followed his gaze, then cursed and climbed to a knee. Sanchez planted a firm hand on Navarro's shoulder.

"I will get him," the segundo snapped out through gritted teeth, breaking into a run.

Sanchez rounded the corral's front corner and ran heavily on his old legs due north, following the man whom he recognized as Pancho Tangoria, shambling off through the chaparral. In a shade patch, Tangoria stopped suddenly and turned toward Sanchez, swinging his revolver around, triggering off a shot.

The slug plunked into a corral post, scattering slivers. Sanchez stopped, raised his Spencer, and fired at Tangoria's crouched, retreating form. The gun clicked empty.

Cursing and watching his quarry disappearing into the desert's spindly foliage, Sanchez set his rifle against the corral post, unholstered his big Russian .44, and walked slowly into the chaparral, swinging his gaze from left to right, listening, wary of an ambush.

The segundo couldn't let the man return to Real with the news that Sanchez had met Navarro. If he did, Real would consider Sanchez a traitor, and there'd be nothing more the segundo could do to stop the war.

Sanchez moved across a shallow wash and pushed through spindly desert willows, bending the branches back with his left hand. Ahead and right, heavy thuds sounded. Sanchez crouched and raised his pistol. Mounted on a sleek cream mare, Tangoria thundered off through the brush, then was swallowed quickly by the rocks and greasewood.

Sanchez holstered his pistol and sprinted toward the cottonwood to which the other four horses were tied. He untied a dun Arabian, heaved himself into the saddle, and rammed his spurs against the horse's ribs, the dun leaping northward into an instant gallop.

He and the Arab dashed through the desert for maybe fifty yards, following his quarry's sifting dust, when the cream came into view straight ahead along a swale. Sanchez unsheathed his .44 and snapped off a shot. Startled, the cream jerked slightly left, throwing the slumped rider off its right shoulder.

Tangoria clawed at the saddle horn,

missed it, and hit the ground on his right shoulder, his right foot hanging up in the stirrup. He was jerked around and dragged on his butt for several feet before the boot slipped free, and the man piled up against a boulder.

The cream gave a whinny and galloped off, its reins whipping.

Sanchez slowed his horse. Revolver extended, he stopped the dun ten feet from Tangoria, slumped back against the boulder. The man's face was a sweating mask of pain, blood splotching his shirt, his right leg hideously twisted.

"Madre," he grunted, raising his anguished gaze to the horse and rider shading him. "Help me. My leg is broken!"

Sanchez didn't say anything. His dun lowered its head and shook, making the bridle chains clatter.

Tangoria studied Sanchez, lips puffed and bloody from the fall. He had a thumb-sized mole at the right corner of his mouth. It quivered as he glanced down at his empty holster. Looking back up, he swallowed hard. "You wouldn't shoot an unarmed man, would you, Sanchez?"

The segundo's face was a leathery mask, eyes like coal. Snapping the Russian's hammer back, he raised the gun, squinted his left eye, and aimed down the barrel.

"No!"

Sanchez drilled the man through his open mouth, the desert valley causing the pistol shot to sound little louder than a snapping branch. The man's head bobbed and fell.

CHAPTER 14

"You sure you should go back to Rancho de Cava?" Navarro asked Sanchez.

They had draped the dead attackers belly-down across their saddles. It was late afternoon, and the dusty stage yard was all shadows and ocher light. The horses, tied tail to tail, snorted and stomped disapprovingly at the heavy copper smell of blood.

"I must go back and find out who killed *el patron,*" the old segundo said, standing beside his pinto, reins in his gloved right fist. "If not for him, I would be an old bandit living alone in the mountains."

"I imagine these fellas have a few friends back at the rancho who might not like what happened to 'em," Hawkins speculated, glancing at the dead men humped beneath their own saddle blankets. Flies hovered over the bodies in thick clouds.

"I have a few friends left myself." Sanchez turned out a stirrup and stepped into his saddle with unusual grace for a man of his years. "Not many but a few." The segundo thought of Lupita, who only last night had asked him to stay on at Rancho de Cava. He reached down from his horse, shook Hawkins' hand, then Navarro's.

"I'll bring Alejandro home Monday afternoon," said Navarro.

"*Sí,* but it is a risk."

Navarro bunched his cheeks in a wry expression. "Yeah, and I reckon you and me haven't had much luck avoiding trouble so far."

"If I am — as you say — still *kicking,*" Sanchez said, "I will cover your ass."

"*Gracias,* old friend." Navarro pinched his hat brim and stepped back beside Hawkins as Sanchez gigged his pinto forward, leading the grisly procession out of the station yard and eastward into the chaparral, where quail and cactus wrens flitted and chirped amid the greasewood.

Casting glances after Sanchez, Navarro and Hawkins walked across the yard and mounted the cabin's porch, where Louise and Billie stood, soiled and weary. "Why didn't you bury the men out here?" Louise said, staring into the desert where Sanchez's salmon-tinted dust sifted over the pale green chaparral. "Why is he taking them back?"

"Guadalupe's got his own way of doin' things," Tom said.

Louise shuttled her gaze from the trail to Navarro and Hawkins, both men bloody from the scrap. "Let's get you boys inside so I can tend to those wounds."

Nearly an hour later, when the sun had set behind the western crags, Sanchez reined his pinto to a halt on the lip of a shallow gully. He freed the horses and led them, two by two, into the gully and let them drink at a small spring bubbling up from mossy stones. The run-out was little more than a muddy cup sheathed in Mormon tea, but the day's heat lingered, and the horses needed any water they could get.

He was leading the last two horses into the gully when he spotted a peculiar print in a sand drift still scalloped from the spring rains. He stared at the print, then led the horses to the spring, dropped their reins, and walked over to the track, pulling his trousers up at the thighs and hunkering down for a look.

It was the same print he'd seen in the pecan orchard, near where the don had been shot.

Frowning, Sanchez stood and moved across the gully, finding several more prints with the same built-up shoe, some half obscured by cattle and wild horse tracks, before losing them altogether in a rocky flat on the other side of the gully.

He stared across the flat for several minutes, pondering the terrain, realizing that even if he had more light, the tracks would be impossible to pick up again in the rocks. Pensively chewing his mustache, he returned to the spring, gathered up the reins of the two horses he'd left there, and led them up the bank to the others.

When he had all the horses tied tail to tail, he mounted the pinto and led off again toward the de Cava headquarters, nestled in the darkening hills to the northeast. When the headquarters appeared, only a hundred yards ahead, he removed his big Russian from its holster and filled the chamber he usually kept empty beneath the hammer.

He chuckled. What would an extra bullet do if Real's thirty or so riders turned on him? Still, if they sent him to the saints, it would be comforting to send six to the devil.

He rode into the yard, threading around the outbuildings, scattering the goats that had not yet been penned up for the night. The long, L-shaped bunkhouse lay before him, its shutters thrown back from the lamp-lit windows, its heavy doors standing wide. Several vaqueros milled around the veranda, some holding coffee cups, others whiskey bottles. Two were tossing bowie knives at the side of a hay wagon parked nearby, the thuds loud in the still desert night.

Hearing the slow clomp of Sanchez's horses, a man on the veranda turned drunkenly. "Hey, what do we have here?"

The others turned, as well. The knife throwers stopped their game to turn and gawk as Sanchez reined up beside the wagon, the packhorses stretched out in a long line behind him, the lamplight showing on the blankets.

The segundo tossed the lead rope at one of the knife throwers. Dull with drink, the man didn't grab for the rope until after it had bounced off his chest. "Better bury these drygulchers before they attract wildcats," ordered Sanchez.

A couple of the vaqueros had peeled back the blankets to peer at the cadavers then regarded the segundo, their eyes narrowed with incredulity. "Sanchez, you shot these men?" asked a tall man named Theron. "All these men?"

A stocky form stepped through the bunkhouse's open door, playing cards fanned out in his right hand, a fat stogie in his teeth.

Real's large-roweled spurs chinged on the veranda floor. He stood silhouetted in the doorway for several seconds, staring toward Sanchez and the horses lined out behind the segundo, hanging their heads after the long ride.

"What do we have here?" Real growled, removing the cigar from his teeth.

Other men from the veranda were looking over the bodies, clucking with amazement. One of the knife throwers turned to Real, his voice pitched with awe. "Sanchez killed them: Raoul, Pablo, Valdez, Tangoria, and de Marco!"

Real stiffened slightly when de Marco's name was recited, his nostrils flaring. He turned to Sanchez, his brows arched skeptically.

"I do not like being shadowed by your broncos," said Sanchez. "In the morning, why don't you have your men do something worthwhile, like hazing those yearlings down from the Cordova Flats? It is time we all got back to work around here, don't you think?"

With that, Sanchez gigged the pinto forward. Real stared after him, frozen.

The hair of one of the dead men gripped in his fist, a wiry half-Comanche gunman named Cortozar turned to Real. "Do you really think . . . ?"

"Shut up," Real said, sticking the cigar back in his mouth and thoughtfully puffing smoke. "Get rid of them."

"Bury them?"

"Just get rid of them."

Fifty yards away, Sanchez halted the pinto beside one of the rancho's several corrals, which was connected to a sprawling adobe stable. The segundo unsaddled the pinto, turned it into the corral, and was forking hay into the slatted crib when footsteps sounded behind him. He dropped the pitchfork and spun, clawing the .44 from its holster.

"Stop — it's Lupita!" came the female voice. The silhouetted figure moved toward him in the darkness, a black shawl draped around her head and shoulders. She stopped a few feet away, glanced down at the pistol in Sanchez's hand, and curled her lip. "You are faster than I would have thought. Maybe more willing, too." She paused. "I was walking by the well when you rode in with the dead men."

Depressing the hammer, Sanchez holstered the .44. "I didn't kill them all." He looked around, making sure they were alone. "I had help from Tom Navarro."

Lupita glanced around quickly, then

stepped toward him to hear him more clearly, hissing, *"What?"*

"Tom and I met at the stage station to discuss the don's murder. Those five followed me."

Lupita's whisper was shrill and accusing. "What were you doing with Navarro?"

"I told you, senora. We met to discuss —"

"Surely you wouldn't believe anything *he* has to say!"

"Navarro is an honorable man."

"He works for a murderer." Lupita narrowed her eyes. "What of Alejandro?"

"He is alive. When he is well enough to travel, Tom will bring him home."

A curious mix of emotions crossed her face. Sanchez wondered which name had caused it: the Bar-V foreman's, her brother's, or both.

Lupita's right eye twitched again with anger as she said, "Real will kill him. He works for a murderer."

Sanchez shook his head. "Senora, do you really think Senor Vannorsdell would be stupid enough to kill the don a kilometer from the hacienda?"

"In a moment of rage, with my father stubbornly refusing to sell to him? Why not?"

"They were friends. They held this country

against the Indians."

"Don't be a fool, Guadalupe. You know what this land would be worth to Vannorsdell."

Sanchez studied the woman for a time. She had been his primary suspect, but that was changing. Maybe she was much softer within than without. Seeing that her eyes were not as certain as her words, he fashioned a knowing, lopsided smile. "Who are you trying to convince, senora? Me or you?"

Angrily, she wheeled, her skirts swirling. She stomped a few yards away and stopped, facing the hacienda rising on the slope beyond her.

She wheeled back to him. "If not Vannorsdell, who?"

"One of our own, I am afraid."

"Why?"

"If we knew that, we would have our killer."

There was a pause. Lupita's expression was thoughtful as she held Sanchez's gaze. "One of Real's gun wolves?"

Sanchez was happy that she had opened her mind to possibilities beyond Vannorsdell, but the mystery remained. "Perhaps."

Lupita drew a long breath through her nose, her shoulders jerking. "My father *must* be avenged!"

"Sí."

Lupita heaved another exasperated sigh, then turned and started toward the hacienda. Sanchez had turned back to the hay crib when her voice rose behind him again. "You better move into the hacienda. You have few friends in the bunkhouse."

He turned back to her, opening his mouth to object. Lowering her eyes demurely, she cut him off. *"Por favor, el segundo.* You are the only one who can help me find my father's killer."

Sanchez stared at her probingly, taken aback by the statement. As uncomfortable as bunking in the house would be, she was right. He couldn't avenge the don from his own grave. He inclined his head. "Of course."

"You can have the room beside the don's." With that, she turned, her low boots crunching gravel as she climbed the slope to the house.

When Sanchez finished forking hay, he stowed his tack in the stable, then walked over to the bunkhouse, holding his rifle down low in his right hand. The horses bearing the dead men had been led away, and only two men sat on the veranda, smoking and passing a crock judge back and forth between them. They stopped talking and drinking to stare curiously as Sanchez mounted the veranda and strode past them and into the bunkhouse.

Stopping just inside the door, the segundo surveyed the room. Only about half of Real's men appeared to be here, gambling or lounging about their bunks under a thick haze of tobacco smoke. The others were probably running horses up from Mexico or hitting banks in small Mexican towns. Real was playing five-card stud at one of the two round tables, chewing a stogie, his eyes bright from the sangria one of the farmers had brewed.

Spotting Sanchez, Real did a double-take, then removed his cigar and grinned. "*El Segundo,* won't you join us?" He extended his right hand, indicating an empty chair with a mocking flourish. He knew the segundo did not gamble.

"I am moving out," Sanchez said, striding down the aisle between the bunks, the smoke so thick he could barely make out the faces of the men lounging on either side of him. Some read magazines or old newspapers. Others played solitaire, cleaned and oiled weapons, sharpened knives, or simply drank by themselves, brooding. José Horan's pet rat sat on his chest. He fed the rat bits of crackers, coaxing the rodent onto its back legs as it nibbled the cracker from between the pistolero's fingers.

A pudgy, round-faced hombre with a thin black mustache and a hideously scarred nose looked up from a bowl of beans as Sanchez passed his bunk. "Did you really kill those men or was there divine intervention?" Several other men snickered.

Sanchez unlocked the door of his private room, stepped inside, set his rifle in a corner, and lit the lamp on his table. From the main room, someone yelled, "The next game is for *el segundo*'s quarters!"

Sanchez trimmed the lamp's wick, then stooped to retrieve his saddlebags from beneath his cot. He stopped when something moved under the cot's single wool blanket, up near the pillow.

Watching the thing move around ever so quietly, Sanchez grabbed an edge of the blanket and threw it back. The thick stone-colored diamondback coiled up tight as a wheel hub, gave Sanchez its flat-eyed, evil glare, and rattled loudly. The forked tongue shot out of the arrow-shaped head, and the rattle, big around as the barrel of a .45, was a quivering blur.

Sanchez stepped back, palmed his revolver, and fired two shots, severing the head and spraying blood across the cot. The body spasmed, whipping. In the main room, guffaws shook the rafters.

Sanchez holstered his .44 and grabbed his saddlebags out from under the cot. When he'd stuffed his few possessions into both flaps, including his old Bible, he slung them over a shoulder, grabbed his rifle and his brown wool poncho and rain slicker off a hook by the door, and left the room, leaving the door wide behind him.

In the main room, the men were still snickering.

"Go ahead," Real said as Sanchez stepped through the bunkhouse door. "Let the women protect you!"

More guffaws sounded as Sanchez strode up the hill to the crumbling hacienda shrouded in darkness.

CHAPTER 15

Later the same night, Doña Isabelle slipped fully clothed out of her bed, picked up her shoes, and opened the door of her private sleeping chamber, which was just right of her mother's, down a lonely wing of Hacienda de Cava.

She peered both ways down the silent hall penetrated by several shafts of pearl moonlight angling through high, arched windows. She stepped out, closed the door behind her, and padded lightly past her mother's door, bare feet tapping almost silently on the cracked stone tiles.

Outside a few minutes later, she climbed over a low rock wall, paused to step into her shoes, then, holding a black shawl about her shoulders, crossed her mother's small, neat vegetable patch before descending a long, gentle slope through high grass and oak trees. She crossed the creek at the bottom of the slope, skipping across the stones, arms thrown out for balance, and climbed the bank on the other side.

The boy waited for her at the lip of the slope — a tall, slender silhouette in a frayed serape and straw sombrero, the horse beside him cropping grass, the low munching sounds audible beneath the crickets' metronomic chirp. He hunkered down on his haunches, placed two fingers in his mouth, and whistled softly, beckoning. She ran to him, threw her arms around his waist, pressed her face to his chest.

He gave her an affectionate squeeze, then pushed her away from him and turned to the horse, his voice a raspy whisper. "Quickly. Real has posted more night guards. Fortunately, the two on this side of the house are drunk in the creek bottom."

Chuckling to himself, the boy leaned down and laced his hands together. Isabelle thrust her left foot into the makeshift stirrup, and Pepe straightened, smoothly hoisting her onto the worn Mexican saddle with its big horn and cracked cantle and stirrups.

He leapt up behind her and clucked to the mustang. Then they cantered down the hill, the girl in the saddle, the long-limbed boy riding behind her, his arms around her, the reins in his hands. They dropped down from the low ridge and headed southeast into desert scrub and shallow canyons, where the night was as black as a burial shroud.

They rode for twenty minutes, threading their way through the canyons, the boy, having grown up here, knowing every rock and cactus along the paths, every knoll and precipice. They crossed a low plateau, then dropped into another, deeper canyon. About them, the eyes of nocturnal hunting beasts burned in the darkness, the brush cracking beneath padded feet, soft snorts lifting the fine hairs along the girl's spine.

At the base of a rocky cliff, Pepe stopped the horse and pushed himself straight back off the horse's rear, both sandaled feet hitting the ground at the same time. Dropping the horse's reins, he lifted Isabelle down from the saddle, his hands tightening around her waist as he nuzzled her neck from behind.

"Pepe!" she laughed, pushing him away.

Chuckling, the boy loosened the saddle cinch, shucked his old Burnside rifle from the sheath, and took the girl's hand. He led her up the long slope through the rocks and cracked boulders. The goat herder's shack huddled at the slope's base, shielded by rocks and dry scrub.

Pepe paused, dropped to his knees by a

spring-fed pool in the rocks, and cupped water up for the girl. She knelt, held the boy's hands in her own, and drank.

"More?" the boy asked.

She shook her head, licking the water from her lips. "That's enough. It's good."

"It's the best anywhere at Rancho de Cava. No one else knows about it but the Apaches, of course."

"And the creatures," Isabelle said, glancing at the tracks and scattered droppings etched by starlight around the spring. A shudder ran through her.

"Don't worry," Pepe said, holding up the old but well cared-for rifle in his right hand. "I have this. The creatures respect me, as do the Apaches."

"Oh, the Apaches respect you now, too?" the girl said, good-natured mocking in her lowered voice.

"They better," the boy said. "I killed two broncos just last month, over there on the other side of these rocks. I was resting here after a long hunt, and they were trying to sneak up on me. Only two shots — *pow, pow*!" He grinned broadly and lifted his chin. "They're up there now, on the ridgetop — what's left of them after the birds have had their fill!"

Holding her shawl tightly about her shoulders, shivering against the chill, the girl beamed at him admiringly.

Pepe took another sip from the spring. "When we're married," Pepe said, "I'll dig a well and shore up the sides with rocks, and we'll have all the water we'll ever need."

"But not here. I don't want to be so close to the Apache trail."

"No need to worry about Apaches," Pepe said confidently, "but no, not here." The boy's smile was bright and cunning in the darkness, the starlight glittering in his eyes. His long, thick, Indianlike hair, to which dust and plant seeds clung, hung down around his face with its flat cheekbones, broad mouth, and sharp chin. He was missing a tooth, but otherwise he was a handsome young man and was filling out nicely, his legs muscled from riding and hunting. "Ten miles south and west. Is that far enough? There's better grass over there, and the water is nearly as good."

"That should be far enough," Isabelle said. "Can we go inside now? I'm cold."

Pepe lowered his head and drank, then rose and took Isabelle's left hand in his right, and led her the last few yards to the hovel, which boasted four walls but no roof. Over the low door Pepe had hung a deer-hide stitched with talismans for keeping out witches and evil spirits.

"Wait here," he said, releasing the girl's hand.

He walked into the pale boulders right of the rock house and returned a moment later with a rusty lantern. He set the lantern on a flat rock, fished a box of sulfur matches from a pocket of his trousers, lifted the mantel, and lit the wick.

When he'd trimmed the wick, he turned to the hovel's door. His rifle in one hand, the lantern in the other, he swept the door aside and raised the lantern, peering into the hovel's deep purple shadows.

He stepped inside, let the flap fall behind him. A moment later, he swept it back, poked his head through the door, and extended his hand to Isabelle, fingers splayed.

"It is safe."

Inside the roofless hovel, by the lantern light, Isabelle prepared a pot for tea at the rough pine table Pepe had found in an old mining shack. From an abandoned army post, he had also scavenged two chairs and an army cot covered with a dusty green blanket and a pillow. A stack of neatly split firewood and kindling stood beside the hovel's fireplace, built into the rock wall. In it, Pepe laid a fire.

Stars glistened in the purple sky above the hovel's stone walls. Vagrant breezes curled over the rocks and nudged the smoky flames.

When the fire was crackling and the teapot was sighing on a rock wedged into the mesquite sticks, Pepe grabbed Isabelle brusquely around the waist, nuzzled her neck for a time, then led her over to the cot. They sat on the edge and kissed passionately, Pepe holding her tightly in his arms, Isabelle running her hands up and down his back, breathing deeply. She always liked the musky, slightly wild odor of him — his own sweat mixed with the smell of horse and the desert.

"I have missed you so much," Pepe whispered between kisses. "I think about you all the time."

"And I think about you, Pepe," Isabelle groaned.

Pepe brushed her hair back from her face as he kissed her, then pulled her down beside him on the cot, resting her head against the pillow. Nuzzling her neck, he set his left hand against her right breast, gently squeezing. After a while, he began unlacing the front of her lace-edged dress.

"No," Isabelle said, pushing his hand

away. "We mustn't tonight, Pepe. It isn't right."

The boy gently forced his hand back up, continuing to unlace the silk ties as he kissed her.

"Pepe, no!" Isabelle said sharply, pushing his hand away, sliding out from under him, and sitting up. She threw her mussed hair back from her face.

Propped on an elbow, Pepe looked up at her, his hair tangled, his face flushed. He ran his right hand along her shoulder, down her back. "I brought the sheepskin . . . like before." He began digging in his pocket.

"No, leave it!" She turned to him gravely. "Pepe, Don Francisco is dead."

He stared at her, his heavy black brows beetled over his deep-sunk eyes.

"Making love now isn't decent," Isabelle said. "Can't we just be together?"

Pepe's eyes flashed darkly. "He's dead and buried. He doesn't know." Pepe laid his hand on her upper left arm, tugged gently. The girl remained rigid. "Isabelle, we've met every week for the past four months. You're all I think about."

"It's a very tragic thing," she breathed, quickly crossing herself. "We shouldn't be here like this after such a thing."

Pepe's gaze grew suspicious. "I didn't

know you were so broken-up about it."

She blushed faintly, looked down as she absently fingered the emerald-studded Spanish brooch around her neck — a gift from the don. Pepe watched her. "He gave that to you, didn't he?"

Isabelle shot him a scowl. "You know he gave me things." The scowl deepened, the blush rising into her heart-shaped face. "Don't look at me like that. He regarded me as a daughter."

Pepe sneered. "He wanted you."

"Stop." She paused, looked at the brooch in her hands. "His death is very tragic."

In his mind's eye, Pepe watched the don move into Isabelle's sleeping chamber at Hacienda de Cava. Isabelle was standing naked in her copper bathtub, water dripping down her long, olive-skinned body with its pert breasts and finely turned thighs. He wasn't sure what expression Isabelle had on her face, watching the don amble toward her. He hadn't imagined that part yet. He didn't even know if any part of the vignette had actually occurred, or was just the product of his jealous imagination, but his instincts told him it, or something very similar, had happened. Or *would* have happened, had the don continued living.

"I won't be singing any dirges," he muttered.

Her eyes narrowed. "What?"

"He molested you."

"He didn't." Isabelle turned away. "Just that once, when he'd had too much brandy, and he put his hand on my breast. I shouldn't have told you."

"He wanted to marry you!"

Isabelle laughed. "Look at you. You're jealous."

Brows furrowed, again Pepe looked away. "You probably would have married him, bore him some heirs. Your mother wanted you to."

Isabelle looked at Pepe again, her eyes owning that patronizing cast they always acquired whenever she tried to soothe his jealousy. He didn't like it. It made him feel like he was being played like a musical instrument.

"Don't be so harsh," she crooned. "He was a lonely old man. It drove him to crazy thoughts of marrying me and having more children, to replace those who turned against him."

Pepe held her gaze with a probing one of his own. "You enjoyed his riches, didn't you, Isabelle?"

"Those are jealous words," Isabelle said,

leaning toward him and gently pressing her hand over his mouth. "Don't you know I would never let anyone come between us? It's you I love." It was true. There, at that moment, she loved no one more than she loved Pepe.

The teapot was whistling. Isabelle stood quickly and put her back to him, before her eyes could give away her troubled, furtive reflections. She moved to the fire. With a rawhide swatch, she stooped, removed the tin pot from the flames by its wire handle, set it on the table, and into the steaming water shook some tea leaves from a small tin container. She had been ashamed of the thoughts that flitted through her head — the wealth offered to her as the wife of the old don, whose body had disgusted her. Would it have been better than an impoverished life on a dusty horse ranch with a young man whose passion inflamed her?

"Who do you think killed him?" she said, standing at the table and staring down at the teapot.

"Vannorsdell," Pepe said irritably. "Who else?"

"It can't be. They were good friends. I've heard them talk and laugh together. They never argued."

Pepe ran his left hand across the blanket,

sighing fatefully. "Maybe they were friends only so long as the gringo thought the don would sell the ranch to him. You know how the Americans are."

Holding the shawl about her shoulders, Isabelle returned to the cot, but instead of lying down beside Pepe, she sat on the cot's edge, staring pensively across the room. "Everything now is so uncertain."

Pepe ran his hand along the girl's back. "What do you mean, my love?"

"The future of Rancho de Cava. Mama and myself. It isn't yet certain that we'll stay on here. We were here mostly for him. Lupita told Mama there may not be enough money to support us."

Pepe swung his legs to the floor, sitting up beside Isabelle. "You cannot leave Rancho de Cava — at least not until we can be married and have a ranch of our own."

"What about Mama?"

Pepe shrugged. "I suppose she'll live with us, no? You'll need help raising our babies."

Isabelle turned to him, laid her hand on his smooth-skinned cheek. "You're so kind, Pepe." But in her mind she was regarding the look on her mother's face when she announced she wished to marry a peon and move with her mother into a thatch hut, after all their privileged years in the sprawling Hacienda De Cava.

Before her expression could betray her thoughts, she stood, poured tea into two dented tin cups on the table. She gave one to Pepe and, with her cup in her right hand, sat down on the cot and slowly sank back against him. She took her cup in both hands and sipped.

"Don't worry, Isabelle," Pepe said, stroking her hair. "I'll take care of you. We'll have a dozen children. Together, we'll raise many mustangs and become very rich."

"Do you really think so, Pepe?" she asked, her mind far away.

"Why not? When a man works hard, the world is his. That is what Papa has always said, and it makes sense, no?"

"Yes," Isabelle said. "That is what Mama has always said, as well."

They sipped their tea, staring into the fire. Pepe draped his right arm around the girl's shoulders. When they were through with the tea, Pepe set their cups on the floor, then placed his hand on Isabelle's chin, directing her face toward his. They kissed for several minutes, until Pepe again placed his hand on her breast.

"No, Pepe," Isabelle said sharply, removing his hand and sitting up. "It's not right."

Pepe was exasperated. "More of this non-sense?"

"*El patron* is dead. How can you be so nonchalant? Your future is as much in the air as mine!"

"I thought you loved me."

"I do love you. If you loved me, you wouldn't pressure me this evening."

"But I'm going to be gone for a couple of days," he beseeched her with more than a trace of melodrama, "and I wanted to take the memory."

"Where are you going?"

"Real wants me to fetch Cayetano," the boy announced proudly, "the best pistolero around."

"Cayetano?"

Isabelle thought about it, a perplexed expression on her face. "So there really will be a war with the Bar-V, then, won't there?"

"Call it a war if you wish." Pepe grinned, showing his missing tooth. "But with Cay-etano, it will be more like a massacre. Good riddance to the gringos, I say!"

"Pepe, take me home now, please."

"What's the matter? Talk of battle too much for you?"

"I'm tired, and I want to go to bed — my bed."

Pepe chuffed with disgust. He returned

the tea, cups, and pot to the single board shelf beside the fire.

"Must you bring him, Pepe?" she asked, gazing up at him beseechingly.

"Of course I must. On Real's orders."

"The great Real."

Silently Isabelle followed Pepe outside and stood near the hovel as he filled a rusty tin bucket with water from the spring. He took the bucket inside and presently the hiss of the doused fire rose. Sweeping aside the deerhide flap, Pepe reappeared, tightened the saddle cinch, and slid his rifle into the boot before lifting Isabelle onto the horse's back.

As he did, her right foot touched something hard against the horse's side. She glanced down at the rifle in the soft, worn saddle scabbard beneath her right leg, the gray stock protruding. The greasewood oil that Pepe had rubbed into it glistened in the starlight.

Pepe carried the old rifle wherever he went. Priding himself on his hunting prowess, he provided game for many peons at Rancho de Cava, and often for the hacienda. He was a crack shot. Isabelle had seen the rifle often, but for some reason she found herself staring at it now, as Pepe mounted and batted his heels against the horse's ribs.

The horse trotted off into the darkness of the canyon. Her hair flopping against her back, her rump jouncing in the saddle, the brooch bouncing across her bosom, Isabelle felt a strange unease. She wasn't sure what had caused it, and she unconsciously decided not to examine it too closely. Wasn't everything turning out the way she had planned?

CHAPTER 16

Two days later, Lee Luther and Ky Tryon were riding along Horseshoe Gulch, looking for strays. It was late in the afternoon and both riders were sweaty, tired, and looking forward to day's end, when they could ride back to the Bar-V headquarters for supper and, afterward, gas with the other riders till bedtime.

Tryon halted his horse on the lip of a narrow cut choked with mesquite brush and tossed a heavy stick he'd picked up earlier. He whistled shrilly as the stick hit the brush, then, standing up in his stirrups, gave a few sharp bellows. No calves spooked from the cut.

"Huh — that snag's usually good for a couple quitters." He turned his claybank back toward Luther, who rode slowly along the cattle trail, hunkered over a small tobacco pouch and cigarette papers.

"Jumping Jehosaphat!" Tryson said,

chuckling as he came abreast of the boy. "What on earth are you doin'?"

"What's it look like?" Lee Luther said with a concentrated air, staring down at the makings on his right thigh. "Rollin' a smoke."

The lanky Tryon laughed. "You don't smoke!"

"I'm about to start."

"It's a bad habit. After a few years, your lungs feel small, and you don't have enough wind to hoof it across a barnyard."

Lee Luther had the paper troughed between the first and second fingers of his right hand. He was trying to roll it closed but the tobacco was sliding off the paper and onto the saddle between his thighs. "You boys do it," he said. "Hell, everybody in the bunkhouse smokes 'cept me."

"For Chrissakes, why are you tryin' to roll a smoke on horseback, if it's your first time?"

"Navarro does it. I see him do it all the time, like it weren't no more trouble than swattin' a fly. Sometimes he'll even roll a smoke while he's trotting."

Again, Tryon laughed, enjoying the break in the afternoon's monotony.

"Damn!" Lee Luther said, giving up in frustration and letting a sudden breeze sweep both tobacco and paper from his hands. "Almost had it that time!"

Jerking back on his horse's reins, Tryon leaned over and snatched Lee Luther's tobacco pouch from the boy's lap. As Luther halted his own horse, Tryon removed his right glove and poked two fingers into the pouch, producing a piece of brown wheat paper. Peppering the paper with tobacco, he quickly, expertly fashioned a smoke, grinning proudly and holding it up for Lee Luther's inspection.

Lee Luther grabbed the quirley and growled, "Yeah, but can you do it while you're ridin'?"

He stuck the cigarette between his teeth and reached into his shirt pocket for a match. Feeling a bit self-conscious and hoping he wouldn't cough his lungs out like the last time he'd attempted to smoke a cigarette, he glanced at Tryon.

The rider had turned to stare straight ahead along the trail. From his expression — one eye squinted, his sunburned skin stretched taut across his cheekbones — he didn't like what he saw. His fingers frozen in his shirt pocket, Lee Luther followed Tryon's gaze and felt his back muscles bunch along his spine.

Four swarthy riders astride high-stepping Arabians, wearing sombreros and serapes and holding rifles, approached from about thirty yards away. They rode loosely in their silver-trimmed saddles, heads canted to one side or the other, lips stretched back from their teeth in sneering grins.

Lee Luther's right hand began moving toward his holstered Colt.

"Keep it there unless you wanna snooze with the snakes," Tryon said, barely moving his mouth, keeping his gaze on the Mexicans. "They got us dead to rights."

Tryon heard Lee Luther swallow. "Should we try to run for it?" the boy asked.

"Like hell."

The four riders checked their horses ten yards away and stood staring at the Bar-V men. The man second from the left twisted a phony smile and said, "*Buenas tardes, amigos*. And what brings you to Rancho de Cava?"

"What're you talkin' about — Rancho de Cava?" Tryon snapped with unfettered animosity and disgust. "You're on Bar-V graze, hombre."

"Bullsheet," said the Mex.

Tryon slowly lifted his left hand, making no sudden moves, and pointed into the distance behind the de Cava men. "See that line of hills yonder? That's your line."

"What hills? Those there?" said the vaquero sitting left of the first man who'd spoken. "I think you have that wrong, gringo. The boundary is those buttes over there . . . behind you, uh? That means you are a good kilometer off your home ground."

"Now, under normal circumstances, we would not have a quarrel," the first man said. "We would simply share a smoke and a laugh and go our ways." His expression hardened as he brought the barrel of his Winchester down, aiming at Tryon's chest. "But after the other night, when your *jefe* killed ours, the penalty for trespassing became death."

"Our *jefe* didn't kill your *jefe,* you fool!" Tryon barked, rising in his stirrups.

"And we ain't trespassing," added Lee Luther, a fearful trill in his voice.

Sneering, the Mex thumbed back his Winchester's hammer.

"Hold it," a voice sounded from Tryon's left, on the other side of Lee Luther. "First man who slings lead buys a bullet from me."

Tryon looked left across Lee Luther's saddle horn. Two men hunkered on the lip of a low hill, cheeks snugged up to rifle stocks. A third peered out from behind a rock, behind and left of the de Cava men. Tryon felt a slight sense of relief. Ward, McGraw, and Sharpe, all of whom had been working the area called the Shadows with Tryon and Lee Luther, had the Mex riders in their rifle sights.

The de Cava men turned slow looks at the hill, the sneers leaving their faces. No one said anything. The cicadas hummed and the crickets chirped. A finger-sized, olive-colored salamander regarded the horseback riders from a nearby rock, its throat contracting and expanding, its eyes like two tiny black Indian beads.

Tryon grinned at the first Mex.

"Perhaps . . . we crossed the line without knowing," the man said tensely, shuttling his gaze between Tryon and the hill.

He raised his Winchester slightly, and drew back on his Arabian's bridle reins. The horse backed up two steps, nudging the one to its right and quartering around in the trail. The other Mex riders followed suit, looking around confusedly, brows beetled with alarm.

"I'd say you got it wrong, all right," Tryon said, slowly removing his Schofield from its holster, thumbing back the hammer. "We at the Bar-V, though, like to let bygones be bygones. You boys hightail it back to where you came from, we'll call it an even score."

"Sí, un marcador igualado," the first man said, his mount sort of side stepping back along the trail. The others were holding their reins tightly, backing their horses away, shunting their exasperated gazes among Tryon, Lee Luther, and the other three Bar-V men on their right. "Until next time!"

His last word had no more passed his lips than the man swung his rifle sharply toward Tryon and pulled the trigger. The slug whistled just left of Tryon's head. Ky raised his revolver at the shooter and fired, but his crow-hopping mount caused the slug to sail wide. Losing his grip on his reins as his horse bucked with a shrill whinny, Tryon flew back off the horse's right hip and hit the ground on a shoulder, hearing the snap of his gun arm across a rock.

Gunfire rose, and horses whinnied. Men were shouting in both English and Spanish.

When Tryon tried to lift his hand still gripping the pistol, pain shot through him and dropped a red veil over his eyes. The broken arm wouldn't budge. He cradled it gently in his other arm and, ducking away from the prancing horses trying to bolt away from the staccato gunfire, crawled back from the trail.

Two shots punched the rocks around Tryon. He turned behind one of the rocks and, wincing against the searing pain in his broken limb, switched the gun to his left hand, and thumbed back the hammer.

Peering into the trail over which smoke hung in a gauzy, sifting cloud, he saw Lee Luther sitting in the trail, knees bent before him, squinting into the dust and smoke and clutching his right arm while shooting with the other hand. Blowing a sombrero off a head, he pulled the gun back and thumbed back the hammer, yelling, *"Yeah!"*

Tryon aimed his Schofield at one of the rifle-wielding Mexicans returning fire to the hilltop, but before Tryon could trigger the gun, the man's shoulder popped open, spurting blood. The man tossed his rifle over his head. Bearded face bunching and eyes widening, he fell back onto the butt of his rearing mount, lost his grip on the reins, and crashed down the right side.

His horse lunged sharply left, swinging the man around like a kid falling off a merry-go-round, and his boot caught in the stirrup. The horse whinnied and lunged off down the trail, heading for de Cava range, dragging the screaming rider alongside, bouncing him off the rocks and cactus.

Lee Luther yelled with jubilation, the boy's six-shooter dancing and roaring in his hand.

Tryon ducked another shot and returned fire. His shot sailed wild as his target wheeled his mount and, seeing that he and his compadres had caught the skunk by the wrong end, galloped back toward de Cava range. The men on the hill snapped off a few shots in the man's wake, then silence fell with dust over the trail.

Cutching his broken arm, Tryon looked around. The Mex riders had left one man behind — dead in a dusty, bloody heap on the left side of the trail. The man's rumpled sombrero lay half on his back, half on the trail.

Still sitting with his boots before him, Lee Luther laughed and hooted and extended his gun eastward. The hammer fell on an empty cylinder, giving an anticlimactic click.

"Shit," the boy said, scowling at the gun.

"It's all over, Junior . . . for now." It was Frank Sharpe, moving down the hill toward the road, Hacksaw Ward to his left. Short-legged, potbellied Ace McGraw had stepped out from behind his rock and was staring after the de Cava men while thumbing fresh shells into his carbine's loading gate. Blood dribbled down his jaw from a nasty burn on his cheek.

"You boys all right?" asked Ward, tall and rangy with a thin gray beard streaked with brown. He wore nondescript range garb except for a cream sombrero he'd won from a vaquero in a Tucson poker match. The braided thong dangled beneath his chin.

"The kid's hit," Tryon bit out, lips stretched back from his teeth. Clutching his right arm, his red-checked shirtsleeve bulging grotesquely just below the elbow, he rocked back on his butt and cursed.

Ward knelt beside Lee Luther and began inspecting the boy's bloody left arm. As if realizing for the first time that he'd taken a bullet, the kid said with a mixture of shock and awe, "I'm hit, I reckon. Sure enough. I never been hit before. It don't hurt too bad."

Meanwhile, Ace McGraw crossed the trail to Tryon. "You take one, too, Ky?"

"Ever set an arm before, Ace?"

"Heck, no."

"Well, hand your rifle to Frank, plant your off foot against my chest, and give my arm a good, sound jerk with both hands."

"Ah, hell, Ky!"

"No cause for foul language. Just do as I say and I'll buy you a drink once we're back to the bunkhouse . . . if I'm still conscious."

Grumbling, McGraw handed his rifle to Frank Sharpe, who was standing beside him and staring down woefully at Tryon. McGraw shook his head, rubbed his hands together briskly, then reached down, gently took Tryon's right hand in both of his own, and lifted the misshapen limb from Tryon's thigh.

Ky sucked air through his teeth, a pained hiss.

McGraw released the hand like a hot potato. "You sure about this?"

"Do it, Ace!"

McGraw picked up the hand, planted his right boot against Tryon's shoulder, and jerked the arm straight out. The arm gave a crunching sound as the broken bone went together, the bulge flattening.

Tryon screamed. The blood ran out of his face. His eyes rolled back in his head, and he fell straight back in the dirt.

CHAPTER 17

"Keep his head down!" Navarro yelled to the young cowboy seated in the hurricane deck of the bucking paint stallion. "Keep him away from the fence!"

Navarro and Paul Vannorsdell sat atop the Bar-V's round pen, peering at the horse and rider within, both a blur of motion as the mustang tried to shake free of the young Mexican buster.

"Keep your boots away from his ribs!" Vannorsdell instructed, cupping his hands around his mouth, a cigar smoldering between the thumb and index finger of the right one.

As the horse whipped hard to the right and kicked savagely, his rear hooves rising as high as the top corral slat, the rider flew out of the saddle like a feed sack flung from a moving train.

As the boy careened over the horse's lowered head and hit the ground flat on his back, limbs akimbo, Navarro and Vannorsdell cursed.

To Navarro, the rancher said, "Where'd you find this kid, anyway?"

"I didn't. You did." Navarro gave a wry grin. "That's Pilar's nephew from Las Cruces. She talked you into adding him to the role."

Vannorsdell cursed and flicked ashes from the stogie. "That boy's gonna see stars till dinnertime tomorrow. If he ever wakes up, put him on wood cutting."

Hooves thumped on the trail beyond the ranch yard. The sentry posted at the front gate yelled, "Our men. Trouble!"

Navarro and Vannorsdell climbed off the corral and were moving toward the gate when the six riders cantered into the yard, a couple bloodied, the others mussed and looking owly. Ky Tryon hunkered low in his saddle, his right arm in a sling he'd fashioned from his neckerchief.

"What the hell happened?" Navarro asked as the men reined up before him.

"De Cava riders." Tryon grimaced. "Caught me and the kid with our pants down. Ace, Hacksaw, and Frank shook us free but not before Billy Bonnie there took some lead." Tryon indicated Lee Luther, sitting the gold-eyed pie on his left. "We stopped the clock of one, probably two. Billie here thinks he wounded another."

"What happened?" said a girl's voice.

Navarro looked past the riders gathered before him and Vannorsdell. Karla was striding toward the group from the big house. She wore tight dark blue denims and a crisp white blouse, the tails tucked into the jeans. Twin braids gave her a girlish look in spite of the amply filled blouse and rounded hips.

"Shoot-out," said Lee Luther importantly, sitting up a little straighter in his saddle and canting his head toward his wounded arm.

Karla's voice rose with alarm. "Lee Luther, did you get shot?"

"Just a scratch. No need to fuss, miss."

"Gotta admit," said Hacksaw Ward, "the lad gave as good as he got."

"You men better get over to the bunkhouse. Have Three Feathers look you over," Navarro said.

"He's in the house, checking on Alejandro," Karla said, wheeling and heading back the way she'd come. "I'll fetch him."

Later, when the wounded riders were being treated by the half-Comanche blacksmith who doubled as the ranch medico, Navarro, Vannorsdell, and Karla filed out of the bunkhouse, leaving the door open behind them. Inside, the cook was serving up his stew and biscuits, and the air from the rock chimney filled the cooling, early-evening air with cedar.

"Might be best to fire back right away, first thing in the morning," Vannorsdell said. "They need to know we're not going to take this sort of thing sitting down."

"They know that," Navarro said. "That's no doubt why Real's given them orders to hit us wherever they find us."

"He'd like nothing better than for our men to venture onto their range painted for war," Karla told her grandfather with a chastising air.

"Listen, young lady," Vannorsdell said, flushing with anger, "I don't take lightly my men being ambushed on my own range!"

"Neither do I," Navarro said. "But they have us outgunned."

"What would you suggest?" Vannorsdell snapped at his foreman, crossing his arms on his chest.

Navarro was about to respond when Frank Sharpe stepped through the door, a square white bandage covering his left cheek. "I hate to add to your troubles, boss."

"Let's have it, Frank."

"Out in that shadow country, our tally was comin' up far shorter than what we expected, especially with the good calving season we had."

His face turning a deeper shade of red and his small eyes slitting, the rancher turned to his foreman. "I'll go down shooting my very last cartridge before I let Real's coyotes rustle me out of a ranch, Navarro. Have all able riders ready to —"

"Wait," Navarro said. "Let me play a wild card first."

Vannorsdell stared at him, eyes intense.

"At first light, Alejandro and I'll take us a ride. I'll have a talk with the lady of the house. Lupita's always had pull with the old man. Maybe she has the same pull with the boys."

"At least, being a woman," Karla said, "she has more sense. But you riding over there is crazy, Tom."

"For once, I agree with my granddaughter," Vannorsdell said. "The first de Cava rider to spot you will shoot you so full of holes you won't hold a thimbleful of cheap liquor."

"Not if I have Alejandro. If I can get to Lupita, she'll hear me out."

"You're gambling, boss," Frank Sharpe said.

Vannorsdell chuffed sarcastically at Navarro. "Just because you and Miss de Cava have had . . . run-ins . . . doesn't necessarily mean she'll listen to your defense of me — if any more than your head even gets to her, that is."

Tom was aware of Karla's incredulous glance. Ignoring it, he said, "I'll take that chance. Seems to me, I don't have a choice."

Vannorsdell sighed, studied his foreman. "I suppose it wouldn't be right, sending the men to war without exhausting all our options." He nodded and started toward the house. "We'll go over the details at breakfast."

When he'd left and Frank Sharpe had gone back into the bunkhouse for supper, Karla cocked an eyebrow at Navarro. "Lupita de Cava?"

Navarro shrugged. "It was a slow night in Tucson, and the firewater was flowing freely."

"I was about to wish you good luck tomorrow," the girl said tonelessly. "Alejandro will be ready to ride at first light. Good night, Mr. Navarro."

Navarro watched her walk away from him, her back stiff with anger. "Good night, Miss Vannorsdell, ma'am." He pinched his hat brim, turned, and started toward his cabin.

Ten o'clock the next morning, Navarro lay

atop a rock scarp fingering out from Blackstone Ridge, training a pair of field glasses on the rocky flat below, where five vaqueros were hazing a small herd of cattle along a dry creek bottom. From this distance, Tom couldn't see much through the ocotillo and ironwood but the rising dust, golden brown in the midmorning sun, and glimpses of sombrero crowns and horse heads and tails, or a man's arm waving a coiled riata.

He had a feeling that if he could tighten the focus down to the left rear flank of one of the beeves, he'd see the Bar-V brand scorched into the hide.

With a wry snort, Navarro stood, walked back across the rock finger, and down the grade to where Alejandro de Cava sat his zebra dun, his good hand tied to his saddle horn, high-topped boots tied to his stirrups. The slender youngster, with his thick brown hair and his tight-fitting, flare-cut slacks and red and gold sombrero, sat slouched in the saddle. His right arm hung in a sling that Three Feathers had fashioned from a pillow case. The youth had lost some weight over the past few days he'd been recovering in Vannorsdell's spare bedroom. He'd lost some color, as well. But beneath the pain in his eyes was bald animosity. His frail, unshaven jaw was set tight.

"What do you see?" he snapped, leaning forward as the zebra dun cropped grass. "Is death coming for you, Navarro?"

"I wouldn't be too cocky," Tom said, snatching both sets of reins off an ironwood shrub and grabbing his saddle horn. He swung into the saddle. "If it comes for me, it comes for you."

"You are badly outnumbered."

"Been there before."

"Even if you make it to the hacienda, do you really think my brother and sister will believe your lies?"

Navarro turned to him, his blue eyes hard. "Maybe not. Maybe I should stick my pistol in your mouth and leave you here for the buzzards." He paused. "Your old man should've done as much a long time ago and saved himself some grief."

Navarro reined the claybank around and gigged it down the deer path they'd been following since sunup. When they came to a low brushy area stippled with cedars and cottonwoods, Navarro turned the claybank off the trail, ducking under low branches and swerving around bullberry thickets, jerking the young de Cava's dun along behind.

"Where are you going?" the kid complained, the branches knocking his sombrero down his back. "You are off the trail, Na-varro. Are you drunk?"

Ducking under the branches, Tom kept riding between heavy brush on his right and a crumbling rock wall on his left.

"Mierda!" Alejandro cursed. "These trees are jarring my shoulder!" He ducked under a sycamore bough, crouching low against the dun's neck and gritting his teeth as the branch tore his hair. "You will pay for this, you son of a sow!"

Navarro stopped both horses, swung down from his saddle, and tied the mounts to a flame-shaped juniper. Removing his bowie from the belt sheath on his left hip, he cut the ropes binding Alejandro's hand and feet to the saddle and pulled him off the horse a little less gently than he should have, given the kid's bullet-shattered shoulder.

Alejandro cursed, suggesting Navarro do something physically impossible to himself. Tom grabbed a coiled rope from his saddle-bags, slid his rifle from the boot, then shoved Alejandro back the way they'd rid-den.

"What tricks do you have up your sleeve? You're too old for this kind of foolishness, Navarro. Why don't you give up and ride out of here while you still can?"

"Just keep walkin', Junior."

"Vannorsdell killed *mi padre,* and he will pay with his life and his ranch!"

Tom just kept walking, kicking the kid along ahead of him.

"Navarro, I am serious. I think my shoulder is bleeding. I am weak!"

"Keep walkin', Junior, or you're gonna be a hell of a lot weaker."

When they got to the brushy open area they'd traversed a few minutes ago, Navarro pushed the kid down against a gnarled oak growing near the base of the boulders and secured him to the tree with the rope. Ignoring the kid's protests, he tied his feet together, then gathered dry brush and green branches and built a smoky fire about ten feet from the kid's boots.

Savvy to Navarro's intentions, Alejandro threw his head back and called for help.

Navarro produced a neckerchief from his back pocket and picked up a pinecone. As the kid sucked in a deep breath and opened his mouth to give another yell, Navarro thrust the pinecone into his mouth. He extended the neckerchief across the kid's face, slid it like a bridle bit into his mouth, and tied the ends tightly behind his head.

The kid's slitted eyes flared. He grunted and gagged and jerked his head around, beside himself with rage.

"You fight the gag, you'll choke on it," Navarro warned, straightening and throwing more branches onto the fire.

Great clouds of snow-white smoke billowed straight up in the breezeless air, which smelled like green leaves and sap.

Navarro waited until the fire was going good, crackling flames licking at the green sycamore and oak branches, curling the leaves. He added another large branch to the fire, rolled a smoke, and sauntered westward through the brush.

When he came to the edge of the ridge, he dropped to a knee. Quirley in his teeth, he shaded his eyes with his left hand and peered southwest, where the de Cava men had been hazing the Bar-V cattle. The men had worked the herd a little farther southeast along the dry water course. Two were fully visible, sitting along the north bank of the course, probably smoking quirleys, taking a break from their labors. They seemed to be looking this way.

Navarro glanced over his right shoulder. The smoke billowed up from the brush and low tree-tops, tattering and tearing only after it had risen a good two hundred feet above the growth.

Tom turned back to the riders. He sucked on the quirley and waited. After a few minutes, a third rider joined the first two, and they sat their mounts abreast, staring this way.

"Come on," Navarro said, exhaling cigarette smoke. "Better check it out."

One of the men turned toward the water course. A faint whistle rose. When two more men had joined the three on the bank, the five began moving toward the ridge, reining their Arabians through the sand sage and brush carpeting the rocky playa.

Navarro took another drag off the quirley, stubbed it out in the sand, shoved soil over it with the heel of his hand, and rose. *"Muchas gracias, amigos."*

Carrying his rifle down low on his right side, he walked back to the fire, where Alejandro sat wide-eyed and still, no longer fighting the gag. His gaze met Navarro's with unbridled animosity.

"I know," Tom said, moving around to the other side of the fire and tossing another green branch onto the flames. "I'm the son of a lowdown dirty sow. Been called worse by better hombres than you, Junior."

Alejandro made several low grunting sounds, barely audible through the pinecone and the neckerchief. Navarro moved to the cracked granite wall and began climbing, pulling himself up one-handed by the cracks, holding his rifle in his left hand. It wasn't a hard climb, but on top, he sat back against the cliff, wedged into a little nook around which some brush spiked, huffing and puffing as he tried to catch his wind.

Cursing his tobacco habit, he rolled and smoked another cigarette. Watching the smoke from the fire rise before him and gradually thin, he waited.

CHAPTER 18

Below the ridge upon which Navarro waited, Alejandro de Cava sat against the tree, breathing through his nose and trying to remain calm so he wouldn't gag on the pinecone. His heart thumped in his ears. Before him, the fire burned down until only a few thin smoke wisps rose, tattering on drafts.

Birds chittered in the brush.

After what seemed like hours, the crunch of a footstep sounded on his left. He turned toward the sound.

A vaquero whose name he couldn't remember appeared, walking slowly into the clearing, a cocked pistol in his left hand. When the man saw Alejandro, he stopped, stared at the kid for a moment, then rolled his eyes around the clearing, not moving his head.

Another man appeared on Alejandro's right, a shorter man named Toribio wearing a blue bandanna around his forehead. The bandanna shone brightly beneath the brim of his stovepipe hat. A long yellow grass stem protruded from between the man's teeth, bouncing as he moved, swinging his Sharps rifle from left to right and back again. He, too, stopped when he saw Alejandro.

The kid grunted through the gag, jerking his head and eyes up, trying to indicate the ledge above and left. Both men looked at him, frowning.

A third man appeared, then two more, all wielding rifles or pistols, moving into the clearing, crouching and jerking their heads this way and that. Alejandro canted his head back, and one of the men backed toward him, swinging his rifle around.

When the man turned and crouched beside the kid, slipping two fingers beneath the bandanna just left of the kid's mouth, Navarro's head appeared just over the lip of the ridge. Alejandro tensed.

The foreman snugged his cheek against his rifle butt and sighted down the barrel. He'd positioned the sun behind him, so all Alejandro could see was a silhouette against the gray cliff behind him.

Alejandro's heart skipped a beat.

"Freeze," Navarro said.

The vaqueros wheeled toward him. Seeing Navarro cheeked up to his rifle, three of the five froze. Two raised their weapons. Navarro's rifle blasted one through the left temple, the other through the belly. The second man fired his Spencer into the ground as his knees buckled. With only a single quiet grunt, he fell forward and rolled onto his side, holding his bleeding belly with both gloved hands.

Navarro worked his loading lever, a two-syllable, metallic rasp in the clearing's silence. He raised the rifle again to his shoulder, swinging the barrel around as the three vaqueros stood gawking up at him, red-faced.

"We're gonna do this nice and orderly," Navarro said. "You all throw the guns you're holding over here to the base of the ridge."

The three stared up at him, eyes glinting savagely beneath their broad hat brims. He doubted they were fluent in English, but their eyes betrayed their understanding.

"Vamos!" he shouted.

One jerked with a start, then lowered his rifle and swung it underhanded to the cliff's base. It landed with a thud. The other two complied at the same time, their pistols clattering together in the brush near the rifle.

Navarro trained his rifle on the man with

the stovepipe hat, standing beside Alejandro. "You, Mr. Lincoln, remove all your other weapons. When I come down there and frisk you, you better have gotten rid of them all, or your jaw is going to have one hell of an introduction to my rifle butt. *Comprende?*"

The man stared up at him, one eye narrowing. Navarro gazed down the rifle barrel and repeated the orders in pidgin Spanish. The man slid back his short leather jacket with his right hand, removed a pistol from a shoulder rig and tossed it with the others. When he'd removed another pistol from a cross-draw holster on his right hip, he crouched slowly, bending his knees. Staring up at Navarro, he slipped a long stiletto from the high top of his right boot and tossed it over with the guns. He straightened and, holding his hands straight down at his sides, turned them palms forward.

One at a time, the other two men went through the same maneuver, until there were nearly a dozen pistols and four or five knives in the grass at the base of the ridge. When Navarro ordered them to lie face-down with their hands on their heads, he climbed down from the cliff, his rifle trained on the clearing. He retrieved the coiled rope lying near Alejandro, who stared at him wide-eyed, gaunt cheeks mottled red with exasperation, and trussed up the trio like hogs for a roast, wrists bound to ankles.

Leaving Alejandro and the pistoleros in the clearing, he tramped off to look for their horses. A half hour later, he had the five vaqueros, including the two dead men, tied belly down across their saddles, though the two dead were considerably more sedate than the living. Alejandro wasn't any too pleased, either, and voiced his complaints at the top of his lungs while spitting bits of the pinecone still lodged in his teeth.

Nibbling jerky, Navarro tied all the horses together in a long line behind his claybank. He took a long pull from his canteen, washing down the jerky, then turned to regard his caravan. The dead men were covered with their blankets.

Alejandro brought up the rear, sitting slouched in his saddle, his hair mussed and seed-flecked, his eyes heavy-lidded and dark. His tirade had wound down as the fatigue had set in. Tom was glad. He had to resist the notion to turn the younker belly down across his saddle and throw a blanket over his head.

Navarro mounted the claybank and jerked his caravan down off the ridge and into the playa, moving southeast toward the de Cava hacienda.

■ ■ ■ ■

On a brushy plateau east of the playa, Real de Cava stared through his field glasses at the tall, silver-haired man in the high-crowned black hat leading the horses toward a notch in a jog of olive hills. De Cava followed the procession for nearly a minute, sliding the glasses slowly from right to left, using his gloved hands as visors, shielding the lenses from the sun glare.

Lowering the glasses, Real shook his head, chuckled, and ran a hand across his nose. "If I had a man like that on my role, I wouldn't need you, Cayateno, or half my other gun wolves."

He looked at the blocky-framed Mexican hunkered on one knee beside him. Cayetano Fimbres raised the heavy Sharps buffalo gun to his right shoulder, the octagonal barrel glistening darkly in the midday sun. Real placed his right hand on the barrel, shoved it down.

"No, no."

"Why not?" protested the regulator, frowning beneath the brim of his buckskin sombrero. "Four hundred yards is nothing for this weapon."

"I'll hear what my friend Navarro has to

say back at the ranch. Then, after I've given him a drink for returning the worthless Alejandro, I'll kill him myself." Real glanced at the gunman's younger brother, Pepe, who stood on the other side of Cayetano, holding an old Burnside rifle in both hands, as if eager to use it. "Pepe and I will return to the hacienda. You, my good friend, continue to the Bar-V, as we discussed."

"I wish to go with Cayetano," Pepe protested. When Real's eyes glittered angrily, the boy swallowed and added, dropping his gaze to his rope sandals, "I mean . . . with your permission, *jefe.*"

"You cannot cat around like your brother. You will —"

Cayetano Fimbres had risen to his full six-feet-four, shadowing Real, who glanced up at him warily. Cayetano spoke in a burly monotone, not looking Real in the eye. "The boy comes with me. I am teaching him." Now he slanted a grim glance at Real, the gunman's eyes black as a cave. "So he will not have to take orders from mice like you, Real de Cava . . . unless he is well-paid for the indignity."

Cayetano turned, tapped the boy on the shoulder, and headed down the hill. The boy glanced at Real, a jeering twinkle in his eye, then followed his brother down the hill, trying not to skip.

Real's gaze bored into Cayetano's broad, buck-skin-clad back. *Ungrateful bastard. I never should have given him his first hunting rifle. The peon thinks he's bigger than those he once chopped hay for.* Real spat and scratched his head. Once the Bar-V was taken care of, he'd have Cayetano done for, as well. He'd make it look like an accident. Wouldn't want to put the man's beguiling sister, La Reina, off.

Real followed the two down to where their horses were tied in an ironwood thicket, and watched them mount up and ride away.

"Report back to me as soon as it's done," he shouted, trying to reassert his authority.

Neither Cayetano or Pepe so much as glanced back at him. His chest burning, Real mounted his Thoroughbred and whipped it toward the hacienda.

Riding east behind Cayetano, Pepe said, "I do not wish to insult my brother's abilities, but do you think you can really get into the Bar-V's yard without being seen?"

"Of course," the older Fimbres said simply, not turning around, his thick black hair bouncing on the collar of his elaborately stitched buckskin tunic.

Pepe frowned, studying his brother's back and trying to suppress his apprehension.

"Will we wait till nightfall, Cayetano?"

"At night, the rabbit hunkers in his borough. When the sun is high, his guard is down."

From behind, Pepe saw the dark skin of Cayetano's right jaw rise with a smile.

An hour later, they'd left their horses in a gorge and scrambled like coyotes through rocky swales and over cactus-tufted hills until they crossed Bullet Creek and entered the Bar-V compound. Moving slowly, keeping their eyes and ears open, and having to change course twice when they found their route blocked by Bar-V hands working around the barns and stables, they finally hunkered down behind a crumbling rock wall that had one time enclosed a melon patch. Before them lay the east side of the barracks-like rock house. Voices rose on the patio.

His breath a low wheeze in his throat, Cayetano set his rifle on a rock and slid his cheek up to the smooth-worn walnut stock. Kneeling beside him, Pepe squeezed his own inferior rifle in his hands and tried to slow his breathing.

Ten minutes earlier, Karla Vannorsdell had entered the house with Lee Luther on her heels.

"Grandfather?" she called, walking through the foyer into the house's cool, deep shadows still smelling of the *sope saguado* Pilar had fixed for lunch. She strode through the high-ceilinged sitting room to the old man's office. Finding the room vacant, she headed for the house's other end, her calls echoing off the rock walls.

She was crossing the living room again when she realized Lee Luther was no longer behind her. She turned into the foyer. The boy stood just inside the main door, hat in his hands, shuffling his boots as though the floor were hot.

"Come in, come in," she urged, beckoning.

"Oh . . . no, ma'am . . . I couldn't. . . ."

"Will you get in here?"

She saw movement on the other side of the living room. It was the short, blocky figure of Vannorsdell moving toward her, a half-eaten cookie in one hand, his leather hat in the other. "What's all the yelling about?" the old man gruffed.

"I've been looking for you," Karla said, seeing that Lee Luther was moving slowly toward her on her left. He walked as though afraid he were going to slip and fall. "It's Lee Luther — he thinks he's well enough to ride, and —"

"I am well enough to ride, sir," the boy said as he took just one step into the living room, one step short of the rug.

"He's not well enough at all, Grandfather. Three Feathers said those stitches could pop open anytime, and he could bleed to death."

"But it's just a flesh wound," Lee Luther complained to the rancher, who'd stopped before him and the girl. "The bullet went all the way through, only nicked the bone. I'm tired of playin' checkers, sir. I wanna ride out with the others and look for them cattle the vaqueros got their long loops around."

Chewing his cookie bemusedly, Vannorsdell studied the boy and his granddaughter, standing shoulder to shoulder, looking at him beseechingly. The old man had a sudden nostalgia for a time, long ago, when another boy had romped about the grounds: Karla's father, whom, for reasons obscured by time, Vannorsdell had found himself at odds with about the time the young man had turned Lee Luther's age.

"Son," the rancher said, setting his hat on his head, "let's walk back to the bunkhouse and talk about it." Placing a hand on the boy's shoulder, he turned him around. Side by side, they walked through the foyer to the front door.

Karla wheeled to follow. "I'm going with you. Lee Luther can be very persuasive."

Outside, the three stepped off the porch, crossed the patio, and began angling across the sloping yard toward the bunkhouse. "The way I see it," the rancher said, his right arm draped across Lee Luther's shoulders, "I *could* let you ride out there after those missing beeves. I *do* need them back, and I need all capable hands on the job."

The boy glanced at Karla, a subtle jeer in his eyes.

"But," Vannorsdell added, "I like to treat my men at least as well as I treat my cattle. And when they're sick or wounded, I keep 'em close to the yard until they're well enough to do the work they've been hired for. Saves me time and money in the long run. Now suppose we go back to the bunkhouse, and I challenge you to a game of checkers before I ride out and see how those boys are doin'?"

Before Lee Luther could respond, the old man ran his hand across his right hip and stopped suddenly. "Oh, hell, I forgot my gun." Wheeling and starting back toward the house, he said, "You two go ahead —"

A loud thunder clap cut him off. Facing the house, Vannorsdell jerked his head up with a start. Karla screamed. *"Lee!"*

Confused, Vannorsdell turned sharply left. Karla had dropped to a knee. Her face and blouse were spattered with bright red blood. Lee Luther lay back in her arms, sagging groundward, blinking, his eyes rolling under his eyelids. Blood and brain matter spurted from a gaping hole in the boy's right temple.

"Lee!" Karla screamed.

Vannorsdell wheeled again, facing northeast, the direction from which the shot had come. Gray powdersmoke hovered over the old melon patch. The maw of a big-caliber rifle appeared below the smoke, glinting darkly in the midday sun.

"Karla, get down!" the old man shouted, throwing himself over the girl just as the gun boomed again, echoing like falling boulders around the ranch yard.

As Vannorsdell and Karla hit the ground together, the rancher heard the whine of the heavy slug cutting the air a foot above and behind him. It careened into the ground with a loud thud, spraying dirt and stones.

Voices rose and hands came running. One triggered shots toward the melon patch, his slugs spanging off the rock wall. Beyond, two figures ran into the scrub bordering the yard's north side, heading for the old creekbed and the chalky buttes beyond.

"Get after 'em!" Vannorsdell yelled hoarsely, rising up on an elbow.

Sobs sounded on his right. He turned. Karla lay propped on her elbows near Lee Luther, her left hand squeezing the boy's bloody left shoulder, her head and shoulders quivering as she cried.

The boy lay before her, faceup, arms out, blood pooling thickly under his head.

CHAPTER 19

About a mile from the de Cava headquarters, Navarro acquired an entourage of sorts — two vaqueros armed with rifles appearing out of nowhere and keeping about fifty yards away on both sides of him and his caravan. One of the men glassed him, then whipped his horse eastward toward the headquarters.

A few minutes later, four more vaqueros appeared, riding straight at him. Thirty yards away, they cut off suddenly, two drifting to his right, two to his left, then, keeping a cautious distance, followed him under the brick arch into the de Cava headquarters, past the corrals and outbuildings and through the courtyard's gate.

On the wall over the gate, two guards scowled down at him, fingering their Winchesters. Like the other de Cava riders he'd seen over the past year or so, they looked more like bandits than vaqueros, with their multiple guns and knives and criss-crossed cartridge bandoliers.

Outside the sprawling hacienda, which the falling sun washed with salmon light and purple shadows, Real stood, grinning, arms crossed on his chest. He wore a second skin of dust, as though he'd just ridden into the place himself. Behind him, Lupita was on a low balcony, staring down at him, expressionless. She wore an elaborately stitched black-and-purple dress trimmed with gold lace, her raven hair combed to shining and flowing over her shoulders. Her eyes were as black as her hair, set deep in an ebony face that could have been the model for any Spanish cameo.

Navarro halted the claybank before Real, who stepped forward, throwing his right arm out. "Senor Navarro, how nice it is to see you again, amigo! *Muchas gracias* for bringing my brother home." He ran his eyes from Alejandro to the vaqueros tied belly down across their saddles, adding, "I think." He chuckled with more apprehension and anger than humor.

Navarro tossed the lead rope to Real. "I ran into these boys out on the playa. They were herding the wrong beef."

"Ah, yes." Real shook his head sadly. "It is a tough habit to break."

In Spanish, Alejandro told his brother to cut him free of his horse, in a tone that betrayed both his indignation and pain. He'd been riding with his chin dipped toward his chest for the past few miles.

"Brother, if you were stupid enough to get yourself shot, you can sit there another minute," Real said, smiling again at Navarro.

He'd barely finished the sentence when Lupita and a small, stern-faced Mexican woman in a simple black dress emerged from the hacienda's main door and descended the stone steps. They brushed past Real, heading for Alejandro. Lupita had a pearl-handled knife in her hand. She went to work cutting Alejandro free. Then she and the other woman helped him down from the saddle and, each draping an arm over their shoulders, half carried, half led him toward the house.

Passing between Real and Navarro, Lupita gave Tom an enigmatic glance. Tom pinched his hatbrim.

When the women and Alejandro had ascended the steps and disappeared inside the hacienda, Real cocked his head at the vaqueros who'd followed Navarro into the yard. The men drew their horses up to within ten feet of Tom's claybank, rifles held high and threatening.

"In spite of the fact you returned my brother, Navarro, we are enemies. Tell me why I shouldn't kill you."

Navarro glanced slowly over each shoulder. His chances for surviving a lead swap were nil, but he kept his right hand near his pistol. If he went down, he'd take Real to the dance, as well. "We have no reason to be enemies. My boss didn't kill your father."

"Why should I take the word of Taos Tommy Navarro?"

"My word was always bond with your father. If you inherited his savvy, you'll play it smart and get off this vengeance bronc you been ridin'."

Real lifted his shoulders and opened his hands. "If not?"

Navarro leaned forward on his saddle horn. "If not, I'll guarantee you, there's gonna be trouble like you've never known."

Real's lips closed over his teeth, and his round face colored up. "Are you threatening me, Navarro?"

"I'm telling you the way it is. You been barkin' up the wrong tree. It's time to look elsewhere for your father's killer."

"How do you know Vannorsdell did not kill my father?"

" 'Cause he told me and 'cause he ain't a

killer. Why do I get the feeling you know that?"

A muscle twitched high in Real's right cheek and he seemed to stop breathing for a bit. Tom inched his hand up his thigh to the butt of his Colt. He could hear the men behind him breathing. He stared at Real. Gradually, the man's eyes softened and a slow grin took shape on his face, the curled ends of his mustache rising.

He glanced at the men behind Navarro, sending a silent command. In the corners of both eyes, Tom saw the riders lower their rifles.

Real extended his arm to the house with a flourish. "Stay for a drink? Your horse is tired, as are you, I would think."

Before Tom could answer, Guadalupe Sanchez appeared at the top of the steps, looking trim and fit, his wavy gray hair combed to one side, a curl licking over a temple. He stood there, his face grim, saying nothing.

Real followed Navarro's gaze to the old vaquero. "Ah, *el segundo,* there you are. It is hard to keep track of you now that the women have coaxed you into the house!"

Real chuckled, then quickly sobered. "Perhaps you would be so kind as to show Navarro to a room so that he can wash.

Perhaps, then, you will be just as kind to show him to my father's office. We'll have drinks there — just the two of us. No servants allowed," Real added, jogging up the steps and giving the old segundo's shoulder a mocking pat. He disappeared into the house, the stony clatter of his boots quickly fading.

Navarro swung down from the claybank as Sanchez descended the steps. Moving up close to Tom and taking the claybank's reins, the segundo said in a hushed tone, "You should not have come. Much trouble about."

Without waiting for a response, Sanchez ordered one of the vaqueros to stable Tom's horse. The man, freeing one of Tom's victims from his saddle, scowled at Sanchez, a knife in his hand. Finally, grumbling, he walked over, took the claybank's reins, and led the horse toward the stables.

"My rifle gonna be in that boot when I leave?" Tom asked wryly.

"I cannot guarantee it," Sanchez said, "but in the house it would do you more harm than good."

He jerked his head to indicate the *casa*, then started up the steps. Navarro fell in behind him. As they were walking down an arched hall a minute later, their boots clacking on the tiles, Tom said, "You mentioned trouble."

Sanchez stopped and threw open a heavy door. The room beyond was small and hadn't been dusted in a while, but there was a big four-poster bed to the left, a pine wardrobe, small writing table, and cane-bottom chair to the right. Near the door was a marble-topped washstand with a pitcher, a bowl, and a coal-oil lantern. In the pitcher and the bowl were only dust, dead flies, and cobwebs.

Sanchez peered both ways down the hall, then turned to Navarro, who'd stepped into the room.

"Real has hired Cayetano Fimbres."

"Ain't that nice — a local boy."

"Since the don's death," Sanchez added, "Real has stepped up his night work. A dozen to fifteen men leave at a time. They're gone usually for two, sometimes three, nights."

"Where do they go?"

"I'm not sure, but I have my ideas." Sanchez shook his head. "Not now. I have something more important." He stared gravely up at Navarro. "I found more tracks like those I found near the don's body, and I have an idea who the rider might be."

"Who?"

The sound of light-soled shoes clicked in the hall, growing in volume. Sanchez winced, then grabbed the pitcher and turned to the door.

"No need, *el segundo,*" Lupita said, hefting the filled pitcher in her hands. "I have brought water for Senor Navarro. You may leave."

Sanchez stared at her for a moment, puzzled. As a flush rose in his dark face with its contrasting white mustache, he glanced quickly at Navarro, then turned out of the room, his spurs chinging down the hall.

"You made a nice mess of the boy's arm," Lupita told Navarro, setting the filled pitcher on the wash stand beside the bowl. "I see it's been tended halfway decently, however. No sign of infection."

She set the old pitcher on the floor, splashed water into the bowl, swirled it around, then emptied it into a copper chamber pot. "A doctor is now practicing at the Bar-V?"

"An Indian blacksmith," Navarro said, tossing his hat on a chair and unbuttoning his shirt cuffs.

Her face lit up. "Ah, the *Indio* who busted up the Catalina in Tucson. You had to rise early and bail him out of jail." She poured water into the bowl, then cocked an eyebrow at Tom. "At least, that's why you said you had to leave before even a civilized cup of coffee."

Tom was rolling his right sleeve up above his elbow. "I'm sticking to my story."

As she stepped aside, he moved up to the bowl and splashed water on his face. He lathered his hands from a small cake in a tin tray, worked the suds into his face and arms and across the back of his neck. Lupita sat on the bed and watched him. By the time he was through, the bowl resembled a well-used stock tank.

"I'm sorry about your father," he said, taking the towel she handed to him.

She watched him dry his face, then turned and, crossing her arms, took several steps to the back of the room. "I guess you're here to convince us that Vannorsdell didn't do it."

"You get the cigar."

Lupita turned back to him, her face taut with anger. "Save your words. Of course he did it. Who else would have killed Don Francisco?"

Navarro thought about what Sanchez had told him about possibly knowing who killed the don and wondered why the segundo hadn't shared the information with Lupita. He must have had his reasons. If one of the three siblings had dropped the hammer on the don, Navarro's trip here was for nought. No point in dancing around it, however.

"Someone with the most to gain from his death, right here at Rancho de Cava."

"Who on the rancho would have anything to gain from the don's death? He paid the bills, you fool. He was the only one with any cattle sense. Without him, we'll be ruined in months."

"Real and Alejandro are payin' all those *banditos* out there with something."

"Bandits," Lupita said distastefully. "That is all my brothers are. We are no longer a ranch but a hideout for criminals. And my father is turning in his grave."

Navarro stood before the washstand, rolling down his sleeves and buttoning the cuffs, the expression on his face betraying his confusion. If he'd only had one more minute with Sanchez . . .

"What's the matter, Navarro?" she asked. "Don't you like being caught between two diamondbacks?"

"No more than you will." He tossed the towel on the bed beside her. "I reckon I'll see if Real'll smoke the peace pipe. If not" — he leveled a hard look at her — "there's gonna be a pitched battle between our spreads."

"I have already put in my two cents with Real," she said. "If he won't listen to his older sister, why would he listen to you?"

"To forestall a war?"

"Hah!" she laughed. "It gives him a reason to get up in the morning."

"Maybe he's too cocky for his own damn good and just needs convincing he won't be getting up at all soon. He might have a cavvy of gun hounds on his role, but the Bar-V doesn't hire rabbits, either."

Her dark eyes glittered with admiration. "And they have *you* on their side."

"That's right."

"Maybe you and I should consider another option," Lupita said with a sudden quirk of her upper lip, her left eye still glittering.

Tom had been about to go out, but he stopped and turned back to her. Distant thunder rumbled. "Such as?"

She shrugged a shoulder, looked at her hands toying with the edges of the black cape falling over her ample bosom. "I have friends in Mexico City. You might like it there."

He fashioned a smile. "Don't tempt me."

He turned and left the room.

CHAPTER 20

By the time Navarro found his way to the don's office, Real was already a little tipsy. The rheumy-eyed de Cava sat behind his father's broad leather-topped desk, a cut-glass brandy goblet and two matched Remingtons before him. He had both guns apart and was cleaning the parts with an oiled rag, whistling while he worked.

When Navarro came into the room, Real stood, pointed to a chair on the other side of the desk, then plopped back down in his own chair with too much force. The chair broke, and he nearly went down. He caught himself at the last second, gaining his feet and hurling the chair across the room with a drunken bellow.

"You'd think with all the money he had," he raged, crimson-faced, "he could have bought a new chair!"

Footsteps sounded in the hall. Chewing his cheek to avoid grinning at the firebrand's drunken display, Navarro turned. The grave woman in the simple black dress appeared, a look of alarmed inquiry on her pinched face.

"Go away, Henriqua!" Real pulled a high-backed chair away from a map table, maneuvered it behind the desk. "If I need you, I'll shoot twice into the ceiling." He grinned at Navarro, who'd reached forward to steady the brandy glass, which had teetered when Real had rammed the chair into the desk.

De Cava sat in his chair, shoved an empty glass toward Navarro, and glanced at the decanter. Tom splashed a couple fingers of brandy into the glass, slid the decanter back toward Real, then picked up his glass and sank back in his chair. The curtains over the two arched windows buffeted, and the smell of desert rain filled the room on a chill draft. Thunder rumbled like a giant's hungry stomach.

Navarro studied the new *hacendado,* who studied him in return. Real's round face was flush from drink.

Tom saw no reason to beat around the bush. "So what are we gonna do here, Real? Can I go home and assure Vannorsdell there won't be any more attacks on the Bar-V and no more long loops tossed over his beef?"

Real didn't say anything. Lounging so low

in his chair that his head barely shone above the desktop, and steepling his fingers on his chest, he just stared across the desk at Tom with that funny, drunken grin. "You know Taos —" He stopped. "Do you mind if I call you Taos?"

"Yes."

"You know, Taos, I believe we are cut from the same cloth, no?"

"No."

"I think we are. I think we are both men of high blood. Blood that boils in our veins so that common, everyday things bore the hell out of us."

Tom waited.

"I think I get that from my mother's side. Her people were conquistadors!" Real's lips and mustache swept back from his teeth, saliva beading along his gums. "My father's ancestors were store clerks, and then land-owners, cattle breeders, that sort of thing. Very boring. They could endure day after day of the same. Me, I like adventure!"

"Where's this taking us? It's thundering, and I'd like to get started back to the Bar-V before I need a boat."

Real downed half his glass in a single swallow, then turned and shoved his head up close to the desk. "I am going to set aside the fact that you work for that gringo and offer you a place here with me . . . at Rancho de Cava."

Tom just looked at him.

"Once a gunman, Taos Tommy, always a gunman."

"Not for me."

"*Sí,* for you. Here, riding for me, you can make enough money to retire in two, three years. More money than you would make in twenty years of punching cattle for that gringo bastard."

Navarro cocked an eye. "Doing what exactly?"

"A little of this, a little of that," Real said, lifting a noncommital shoulder and throwing back the last of his brandy.

"Chew it up a little finer and maybe I'll consider it." Tom had no intention of considering any alliance with Real de Cava, but his curiosity was piqued.

Real stared off to one side of the desk, smacking his lips as he thought it over. Sitting behind the broad desk in the cavernous office with its heavy furniture and cultured trimmings, including framed wall maps and imported gas lamps, he looked like a little boy playing grown-up.

Finally, he ran his hand across his mouth, set his glass on the desk, and refilled it from the decanter. When he'd topped off Tom's glass, he sat back in his chair. "You have heard of the Mexican smuggling trains, no?"

Few in southern Arizona and New Mexico hadn't heard of the smuggling trains that regularly came up from Sonora with thousands of dollars' worth of gold or silver. The smugglers would purchase American goods, then slip back across the border without paying the required duty and sell the goods for an enormous profit.

It was an illegal trade, but the Army was too busy wrangling Apaches to stop it, and there were too many well-armed smugglers for the U.S. marshals to handle. Those lawmen that tried simply disappeared or turned up as bleached bones in a canyon or boulder field high in the Dragoons or Huachucas.

Navarro chuckled without humor. "You're running a train?"

"No, no, no, senor. I am *raiding* the trains." Real let that sink in for a time. When Navarro just scowled at him with incredulity, de Cava said, "I need men who are good with their guns."

"You gotta be shittin' me," Navarro scoffed, and laughed again. "You're raiding smuggling trains?"

"*Si.*"

"Why?"

"For the money, Tom." Real pounded his

fists on the arms of his chair. "And because it makes my blood surge in my veins."

"I don't hire my guns," Navarro said.

"From our last raid, we took four thousand dollars in silver. We lost three riders in doing so, but four thousand dollars just the same. I am honest with you. There is risk. But what endeavors do not involve risk, eh, Taos?"

"Stop calling me Taos," Tom said, throwing back the last of his brandy and setting the empty glass on the desk. "Thanks for the drink."

"Taos, you can't go — it's raining."

Real gestured at the two windows behind Navarro. Beyond the veranda, rain came down in a heavy white sheet, the wind blowing it through the window and onto the office floor. As if on cue, lightning flashed, followed several seconds later by a thunder crash Navarro could feel through his boots.

"I can make it," Navarro said.

But when he got outside, he could tell he wouldn't make it. The rain came down in waves. The courtyard was a pond. The trail back to the Bar-V would be a river. After a monsoon rain of this severity, the trail wouldn't be passable until midmorning tomorrow, at the earliest.

"Shit."

"Taos, you better have another drink," Real said, sidling up to him and placing a hand on his shoulder. "Why not?"

Grudgingly, Navarro followed Real back to Don Franscico's office, where they had two more brandies before Real, growing bored and peevish over Navarro's refusal to join his train-raiding pistoleros, bid him an unceremonious good night and staggered toward the door.

"Taos," he said, turning back toward Navarro and holding himself up with one hand on the doorjamb, "I hope you have a comfortable night here at Rancho de Cava." He swayed from side to side and lifted an admonishing finger. "But next time we meet, we will not be friends. *Buenos noches, senor.*"

When Real had staggered off, no doubt to drink and play cards with his men, Navarro poured himself another brandy, then sat, sipping the drink and listening to the rain, cursing the early-summer storm's unfortunate timing.

He was nearly finished with the drink when Lupita came with a tray of sandwiches and invited him into the partially roofed courtyard outside the don's office. They ate by the wan light from a couple of Chinese lanterns and washed down the sandwiches with rich sangria. The rain lightened up but it was still sprinkling and Navarro heard the water gurgling lower down in the terraced court and outside the low adobe wall.

He had finished his sandwich and was working on his second glass of sangria when Lupita said, in a brooding, faraway voice, "It is lonely here."

"Leave." Navarro sipped the wine. He was drunker than he knew he should be in enemy territory. "You said you had friends in Mexico City."

"It takes money to travel."

"Just how broke are you, anyway?" Tom wondered if Real shared his smuggling train plunder with his sister. Maybe she didn't know about it.

"I don't want to talk about money tonight." Lupita stretched like a cat and stood, her wicker chair creaking. She walked slowly over to him, a seductive set to her pretty mouth. Then she brusquely spread his knees and perched her rump on his right thigh.

Before he could get his hands up to ward her off, she kissed him and ran her hands through his hair. The warm, wet, passionate kiss would have stoked the fires in any man. The hot, womanly curves and the full bosom swelling against his chest would have, as well. Drunk, he needed a few minutes to remember he'd asked another woman to marry him, then to push Lupita away and heave himself to his feet.

"Why such a saint?" she snapped, glaring at him as she collapsed back into her own chair and crossed her legs with an angry flair. "I wasn't good enough for you in Tucson? You seemed to enjoy it."

"I enjoyed it, all right. I reckon I'm not as young as I used to be. I'm drunk and tired and need a bed to sleep in."

"You got a woman, Navarro? I won't kiss and tell."

"Thanks for the grub." Navarro swiped his hat off a wrought-iron table and headed for the room he'd washed in earlier.

Looking for the room in the sprawling, cavelike hacienda, he wondered if there was anyone in the house but him and Lupita, until, stumbling down a dark hall, he saw a dim light ahead and heard muffled female voices.

Finding the room, Tom pushed through the heavy door, managed to get the single lamp lit without breaking it, then closed the door and removed his pistol and cartridge belt. He stripped down to his underwear, pulled the dusty covers back, and crawled into bed.

What had he accomplished here?

Besides setting himself up for one hell of a hangover, not a damn thing. His only hope was that Real would get himself killed raiding the Mexican smuggling trains before he could effect anymore attacks on the Bar-V. That was something, anyway.

He leaned over to blow out the lamp on the bedside table and was asleep less than a minute after his head hit the pillow.

Real returned to his father's office for two more bottles of brandy. His men in the bunkhouse had run out of the local firewater but Real's cards were hot, and he was not yet ready to call it a night.

Dripping wet from the rain and cradling both bottles in his right arm, Real closed the office door behind him and moved drunkenly down the corridor, toward the outside door he'd left open and through which wan night light emanated, illuminating his muddy bootprints. He was turning to go out when a girl's muffled laugh rose from the corridor beyond.

Real stopped and, holding a bottle in each hand, strained his ears to listen. After a minute, he heard two voices coming from the same direction as the laugh. He moved down the dark corridor and past the faded paintings and tapestries the don had brought back from trips to Mexico City.

He followed the sounds to a door on the right side of the hall, stopped, and listened through the thick mahogany. A minute later, he threw the door wide and stepped into the big, candlelit room, where Isabelle knelt beside the bed, a medicine bottle in one hand, a tuft of cotton in the other.

On the bed sat the tall, shaggy-headed boy Pepe, soaked to the skin, his muddy cotton slacks pulled down around his ankles. A long cut angled across his brown thigh, red with fresh blood and the lighter red of iodine.

Seeing the door open, the girl jerked her head up with a start and drew air sharply through her teeth. The boy looked up, as well, his back tensing and his eyes widening with alarm. His right hand reached automatically for the old rifle lying beside him on the bed, then froze on the Burnside's gray stock.

"And what do we have here?" Real said through a lascivious grin.

The girl flushed and dropped her eyes demurely.

His gaze glassy with fear, Pepe's mouth worked several times before he said, "Real, it's not what you think. Cayetano and I did what you told us to do. We were chased. I was grazed by the Bar-V riders and simply came to the hacienda, hoping someone would tend the wound."

"Oh, don't shit your pants over it," Real said. "I know all about you and Senorita Flores. Don't think you've been pulling the wool over my eyes."

Pepe stared at him, the color draining from his cheeks.

Real chuckled. "I know you killed the don. It was my idea."

Pepe glanced at Isabelle, who returned the look with a guilty glance.

"I thought your aim would be truer if you did it for love," Real said, staggering into the room. "And my hands would be clean. Tsk-tsk. It is a very grave sin, you know, to kill your own father."

The girl said softly, "Pepe, I —"

"Shut up!" Real snapped. He looked at the boy. "Tell me about what happened at the Bar-V. Did you and Cayetano accomplish your mission?"

Pepe lifted his gaze to Real, still in shock over the girl's manipulations and what they meant about her and Real.

"*Sí,*" the boy said quickly, nodding. "I mean, we think so. We know Cayetano hit someone, and we were pretty sure it was Vannorsdell. But we were far away, and we had to flee quickly, because the Bar-V riders were shooting."

"Where is Cayetano?"

"He went from the stables to the bunkhouse. We just rode in a few minutes ago. They gave us a hard chase, but the rain turned them back." The corners of Pepe's mouth rose proudly. "Cayetano's horse slipped in the mud and fell down a cliff. We had to ride back on my pinto."

Real stood just before the open door, considering what the boy had told him. If Vannorsdell indeed was dead, there would be much to celebrate. He canted his head toward the door behind him. "Pull your trousers up and go on back to the bunkhouse. I'll be along shortly."

Pepe glanced at Isabelle, who still knelt before him, holding the iodine bottle and the cotton tuft. She did not return Pepe's joyful, relieved glance. "Does this mean I will become one of your riders?"

"Don't push your luck this evening, young one," Real growled. "You still have much to prove. And I don't like all this sneaking around my house."

The boy grabbed his soggy hat and rifle and hustled out of the room.

When Pepe was gone, Real took another step forward. The girl looked up at him, her eyes dark with apprehension. She set the bottle and the cotton on the floor and rose slowly, keeping her eyes on Real, standing stiffly before the door. She must have seen some subtle change in his expression, because she ran forward suddenly and wrapped her arms around his waist.

"Oh, Real," she cried, "now we can be together always!"

"But first you must decide," Real said, smiling as though thoroughly enjoying his charade, placing his right hand beneath her chin and gently tilting her head back, "which one of us you love more."

CHAPTER 21

Tom knew neither where he was nor how long he'd been asleep when his eyes snapped open. He'd heard something. A dark figure moved in the darkness.

His heart began hammering when a star-like glimmer of vagrant light flashed off something shiny, and then his left hand snapped up, his fingers closing around a slender wrist.

"*Bastardo!*" came the sound of Lupita's voice.

Tom stopped the knife's descent but not before the tip had penetrated his neck, piercing him like the bite of an angry wasp.

Fighting the hand wielding the knife back away from his face, he reflexively jabbed his right fist straight up with savage force, connecting soundly with the woman's face. Her full lips cracked beneath his knuckles, blood spurting across his cheeks.

Lupita cried out and fell back across the

bed. "Damn you!" she sobbed.

Knife in his own hand, Navarro stumbled out of bed. He peered both ways down the hall. Seeing no one, he closed the door, reprimanding himself for his drunken stupor. Then he lighted the lamp.

The butter yellow light revealed Lupita lying on her back across the foot of the bed wearing only a copper-colored night wrapper. She lolled from side to side, with one knee raised. She sobbed and held the back of her right wrist across her bloody mouth.

Tom could see the naked inside of her raised left thigh, but it didn't do anything for him. His chest burned with fury. That pretty thigh belonged to a cold-blooded killer.

"*Bastardo!*" she snapped, then sniffed. Tears streaked her gaunt cheeks.

"What the hell do you think you're doing?" He was tempted to punch her again.

"Trying to kill you. What do you think, you stupid gringo?" Through a raspy cry, she added, "No one refuses Lupita de Cava!"

"No wonder you're lonely." Navarro tossed the knife into a far corner and stared down at the crying, bloodied woman. The angry light in his eyes softened, and the skin across his cheeks slackened. She was like a lonely, spoiled child, he decided. Grumbling a curse, he turned and poured water into the bowl atop the washstand.

"Who is she, Navarro?" Lupita asked angrily. "Who have you refused me for?"

"None of your business," Tom said. With the bowl in one hand, and a towel in the other, he sat down at the end of the bed and dipped one end of the towel in the water.

"It's that stage station gringa, isn't it?"

Tom looked at her. "How do you know about Louise?"

Lupita's voice was muffled by the hand she held against her nose. "I manage to get to Tucson once a month. I have heard the rumors."

Tom looked at her hard, not liking the fact that she knew about Louise. On the other hand, Louise Talon was fully capable of taking care of herself.

"It's still not any of your business." Navarro squeezed the excess water from the end of the towel, then leaned toward her. "Move your hand away."

"No. You've made me ugly."

"You did it to yourself. Now move your hand away from your face."

She looked at him, slowly removed her hand from her face. Turning toward him, she drew her robe closed and pulled her knees toward her waist. Tom dabbed at her torn lower lip. She winced and jerked away.

"Hold still. It's gotta be cleaned. Could even use some catgut."

"No stitches."

"Hold still, damn it."

She did as he told her, and he dabbed at the split lip. When he got the blood away, he saw that it wasn't as bad as he'd thought, though both lips were already swelling. The top one was only bruised.

She stared at him as he worked, dabbing the blood away and rinsing the towel in the bowl. When he'd wrung the towel out the fourth time, he glanced into her eyes. Her anger seemed to be gone, but the bridge of her nose wrinkled as tears rolled down her cheeks. He brushed at the tears with the towel.

"It's stopped bleeding," he said, squeezing the water from the towel and rising. "Better go back to your room. You can pick up your pig sticker tomorrow . . . after I've gone."

"Let me stay," she said, resting on her side, her left elbow beneath her, her feet curled together. When he turned to her, she added, "I don't want to go back to my room. It's cold after the rain. I won't try anything funny."

He set the bowl on the washstand and regarded her severely. At least, if he had her here where he could keep an eye on her, he wouldn't have to worry about her sneaking back into his room with another knife. "Get under the covers."

Again letting the robe flop open, she crawled up to the head of the bed, peeled the covers back, crawled beneath them, then drew them up to her shoulders. She slid over to the far side and patted the sheets.

"There is room," she said.

Navarro pulled the chair out from the table and sat down. "I'm gonna sit up and have a smoke."

She watched him as he got out his makings and built the cigarette, touched fire to it, and inhaled deeply. By the time he was finished with the quirley, her eyes were closed, and she snored softly, her swollen lips parted. Despite the pain of the split lip, all she'd drunk had finally knocked her out.

"Thank Christ," Navarro said through a sigh.

He got up, blew out the lamp, sat back down in the chair, crossed his arms and ankles, and lulled himself to sleep with thoughts of Louise and their future life together up north.

When he woke, he opened the shutters.

Milky dawn light shone in the window. He turned to the bed. Lupita slept beneath the single quilt, her back to him, her raven hair mussed, knees drawn up to her chest. Turning away, he rolled the kinks out of his neck and shoulders.

His back ached when he bent down to retrieve his clothes and quietly began dressing. When he'd stepped into his boots and wrapped his cartridge belt around his waist, he donned his hat and glanced at Lupita once more.

She lay as still as before, breathing slowly, deeply.

He eased the door open, stepped out, and eased it closed.

A minute later he walked out the front door and strode across the house's main courtyard, inhaling the fresh morning air fragrant with desert rain and the faint smell of lemons. It was so still that he thought he could hear the rain sifting through the orange caliche beneath his boots.

Tramping across the main yard, heading down the grade toward the stables, he kept his hand close to his pistol butt and swung his gaze around warily. He didn't trust Real as far as he could throw the firebrand into a stiff wind.

As he neared the stables, one of the big,

rectangular doors opened. He stopped suddenly as a short, bandy-legged figure with dark skin and a white mustache stepped out, a Spencer carbine in his hands. Navarro's heart sputtered, then resumed its normal rhythm when Sanchez beckoned him forward.

"I was wonderin' where you were," Navarro said as he stepped into the stable's musty shadows.

Sanchez drew the door closed, barred it, and turned to Navarro. "I rode out before the storm to haze a small herd of cattle from a canyon." Sanchez frowned and shook his head with distaste. He kept his voice just above a whisper. "Real's idiots did not think of it. The cattle would have drowned. When I returned to the headquarters, I learned that Real had sent three men to the stables, to wait for you to retrieve your horse."

Tom glanced around, his hand returning to his pistol butt. "To send me off in style?"

"*Sí*. Grand style. I got up early, found them still sleeping off last night's booze — Real had quite a card game going in the bunkhouse — and bashed all three over the head with my rifle butt."

"Ouch."

Sanchez strode back into the shadows and returned a moment later, leading two saddled horses, his own and Navarro's. "They didn't feel a thing. We must leave before Real wakes up from his stupor."

Navarro looked at him. "We?"

Silently, Sanchez peered out the stable doors, looked around the yard, then swung both doors wide. The two men led their horses into the yard and swung up into their saddles. As they reined the mounts toward the main gate, Navarro noticed his rifle wasn't in his saddle scabbard.

"Bastards got a good Winchester," he groused.

"Be glad that is all they got. What happened to your neck?"

Navarro touched the spot where Lupita's knife had pierced his skin. "Cut myself shaving."

The segundo did not turn his head to look at him, but the upswept ends of his mustache rose in a slight, knowing grin. He cantered his horse down the grade toward the rock wall lining the yard's western periphery, barely visible through the dawn shadows.

"I don't know if the guards at the main gate are aware of Real's plans for you." Sanchez drew his carbine and cocked it, snugging the butt up against his hip. "We better be ready."

Riding off the segundo's right stirrup, Navarro flipped the safety thong from his Colt's hammer but left the pistol in the holster. As they neared the wall and the gate, the two Winchester-wielding lookouts standing on the ledge near the wall's lip turned to them. Navarro slid his hand up his thigh toward the Colt, but the guards kept their rifles turned away. With a pulley rope, one of the guards opened the gate while the other said good morning to Sanchez and, in a sneering tone, asked him how he got his old bones out of the mattress sack so early on a wet morning.

"He doesn't have a fat whore to keep him warm," said the other.

Sanchez said nothing, only raised a stiff hand as he and Navarro passed through the gate. When they'd ridden twenty yards along the soggy trail, one of the guards yelled in broken English, "Navarro, I piss on the Bar-V!"

Tom glanced over his shoulder. One of the guards stood on the very top of the wall. With his free hand he directed a stream of piss toward Navarro. Tom waved and turned his head forward, a wry expression on his unshaven cheeks.

"That's quite the crew you have there."

Sitting stiffly in his saddle, facing down

the trail, Sanchez grunted disgustedly.

As they rode along the soft, damp trail, their horses' hooves making sucking sounds as they cantered, Navarro glanced at Sanchez periodically. The old segundo seemed sullen and distracted, frowning over his pinto's ears. Tom noted the inordinate bulge in the man's saddlebags and decided to mention it.

"I am not going back to Rancho de Cava," Sanchez announced, sitting straight-backed in his bouncing saddle and holding his reins high against his chest.

"Where are you going?"

"I don't know, but the rancho is no longer my home with the don dead." He spat off his horse's left wither. "I thought I could help turn it back around. I see now there is no chance." He glanced at Navarro, the growing light revealing a wry twinkle in his old eyes. "I have become a useless old vaquero, weary of living but afraid of dying."

Navarro reached over and pulled back on the bridle bit of Sanchez's big pinto. At the same time, he halted his clay, and the two riders faced each other over their horses' ears.

Navarro said, "What've you found out?"

"I am about to show you." Sanchez reined

his horse left and gigged it forward along the trail. Navarro stared after him, then touched his heels to the claybank's ribs.

CHAPTER 22

Sanchez leading the way, the segundo and Navarro headed west on a seldom-used horse trail. They stopped twice at water puddled in rock tanks along the trace. Navarro pressed Sanchez to tell him where they were going, but both times the segundo merely shook his head and said, "It is best if you see for yourself."

It wasn't long before they were south of the barranca that the Apaches called the Shadows and that Navarro called the tail end of nowhere. The Bar-V riders tried to keep the cattle from drifting down here because it was almost impossible to get them out of the deep arroyos, box canyons, and boulder snags.

Sanchez led the way down a steep game trail into a deep, narrow brush- and boulder-choked defile, just wide enough for the horses to pass. Looking around, Tom saw shod horse prints and apples that weren't more than a few days old. At the bottom, Sanchez dismounted and led his horse into a cave yawning in the canyon's south wall.

Navarro dismounted and followed him.

The cavern was about fifty feet wide, maybe ten feet high. Several picks and shovels leaned against the cave walls. They weren't the old implements found in long-abandoned mines — rusty and splintered and falling apart — but fairly new equipment. There was a big fire ring in the cave's front center, the ashes still mounded and a few freshly chopped branches lying beside it. Broken rocks lay strewn about the floor, streaked with glittering metal.

"What the hell?"

Navarro peered into the cave's shadows. Sanchez had disappeared, leaving his horse ground-tied about twenty paces beyond the entrance. Navarro dropped his own reins. Running his fingers along the left wall when the light grew dim, he carefully planted his feet one in front of the other to avoid tripping over the rocks that had been chiseled out of the walls. The cool air was rife with the musty pungence of bat guano.

A few feet ahead, a match flared, its glow showing the segundo's dark face and low-crowned sombrero and part of the rough rock wall. Sanchez turned to Tom. "Thirty feet back, this cave opens into a room as big as Don Francisco's office at Rancho de Cava."

"Manure and shod horse tracks," Navarro said. "Many men have gathered here frequently and stayed for long periods."

"Real and his pistoleros." Sanchez's match burned out.

"They hide out here to let their trail cool after their raids on the smuggling trains," Navarro mused aloud.

"Let's go back outside."

Leaving the horses in the cavern, Navarro and Sanchez walked back out to the narrow trace in the deep defile, already shaded by the steep, boulder- and brush-strewn walls. A cool breeze whistled through the cleft, rattling the galetta grass.

Facing Navarro, Sanchez said, "I think Real came upon the gold quite by accident, when he and his gun wolves were hiding out here. It is my suspicion that Real had the don murdered because the patron would not have allowed mining for gold on the Bar-V range. Not, at least, without the involvement of Paul Vannorsdell and yourself."

"And Real wanted it all — whatever's here — for himself."

Sanchez stared back at him, his brown eyes in the angular, taut-skinned face both sad and angry. His lips were pursed, and he drew air sharply through his nose.

Navarro said, "How much do Lupita and Alejandro know about all this?"

"I could not say," the segundo said with a sigh, throwing his hands out. "My guess is nothing, and that is why Real framed your boss for the murder. Because his sister and brother would have not gone along with it. And it gave him a good excuse —"

A pistol popped. Sanchez grunted and stumbled forward, his jaw dropping suddenly, eyes snapping wide.

Navarro turned as the segundo fell into him, opened his arms to catch him. He saw over the peak of the segundo's sombrero a Mexican crouched about twenty feet back along the canyon, cocking the hammer of his extended six-shooter, a savage snarl on his patch-bearded face.

"They're down here!" the man yelled.

As he extended the pistol, Navarro brought his own Colt up and fired. At the same time, the pistolero drilled another round into Sanchez's back. The segundo shuddered with the slug's impact into his right shoulder. Tom's shot cored the pistolero's chest, knocking him back as the man fired another round onto the trail, blowing up shale.

Shouts rose on the gorge's rim.

Navarro lowered his gaze to the segundo. Two blood splotches grew on the back of Sanchez's vest, one near the center, the other over the right shoulder blade. Navarro eased the man onto his back, then gently down to the ground. Both rounds had gone all the way through; his shirt was a bloody mess.

"Guadalupe," Tom muttered. "Goddamn it." He removed the sombrero that tipped off as the man's eyes rolled back in his head, and tossed it aside.

Sanchez was dying, but he found enough strength to reach up and grab Navarro's shirt with his bony right fist. "Tom . . ."

"Easy, amigo."

"In my pocket." Sanchez brushed his hand against his right vest pocket. "I wrote out . . . everything."

Tom glanced back along the canyon's sharply pitching trail. On the rim, the shouts grew louder. Stones loosed from the top tumbled onto the trail. Raising his pistol toward the noise, Tom looked down again at Sanchez. With his left hand, he removed the folded paper from the segundo's vest pocket.

"From what I overheard and saw for myself," Sanchez said, his voice weakening, his chest rising and falling sharply. "Real, the girl, the boy . . . the gold . . ."

Tom spotted movement to his right, swung his head toward two more gunmen descending the steep trail single file, rifles in their hands, crouching behind boulders. Navarro whipped his Colt up at the same moment they saw him, and fired twice.

One shot caught the first man in the head, laying him out flat between two split rocks and a cedar. The second man scrambled back up the trail to the rim, shouting epithets in Spanish.

Sanchez raised a hand and extended a finger weakly, indicating the opposite end of the canyon. "That way. *Go!*"

Tom bunched his lips and fired another enraged shot toward the rim, holding the de Cava riders at bay. "Those sonso'bitches. I'll —"

"Kill Real." Sanchez exhaled this last on his last breath. His chest fell still and his chin dipped toward his right shoulder. His hands fell to either side of his slender, slack form and turned palm up.

Navarro jerked his head up toward the trail, saw the boots of another man working his way down. He snapped off two quick shots, watched the man's feet disappear back up toward the rim.

"Sons'obitches!" Tom shouted, his guts on fire. He triggered another enraged shot.

Someone loosed two shots from the rim, the bullets plunking into the trail ten feet in front of Tom. Navarro stood, stuffed the paper into his back jeans pocket, and dragged Sanchez into the cave. More shots sounded from above, the blasts echoing around the gorge, causing dirt to sift from the cave ceiling.

Navarro crouched over the segundo's slack body, placed a hand on the man's belly, looked sadly, angrily down at the wizened face with its half-closed eyes and parted lips beneath the thick, gray mustache.

"*Hasta luego, amigo.* You deserved better."

Real's voice sailed down from the ridge. "Navarro! Come on out of there, amigo. We must talk."

"I'm done talkin'!"

Navarro slipped the segundo's Russian .44 from his holster, wedged it behind his own cartridge belt.

"All right, so you found the mine," Real called. "Let us talk it over, uh? There are solutions to every problem."

"Like having your father killed?"

Real laughed as Navarro walked over to Sanchez's horse, slipped the old Spencer from the boot, then grabbed his own mount's reins, turned the horse around, and led him to the cave's mouth.

Three shots sounded, blowing up gravel ten feet before the cave's entrance. Because of the brush and rocks around the entrance, Real's men wouldn't be able to see the cave from where they were; they were no doubt hoping for a lucky ricochet.

Navarro clucked to the horse, led it out of the cave and onto the path tracing the bottom of the narrow canyon, heading toward the chasm's opposite end, as Sanchez had directed. Another shot barked and spanged off the wall beside the cave. Navarro heard the rock shards spraying the brush.

"Come on, boy, keep movin'," Navarro urged the horse as the walls closed in around them and the horse fidgeted and pulled back on the reins.

Navarro walked quickly. If they caught up to him in the canyon, he could hold them off only as long as his ammo held out — an hour at the most.

The terrain grew rocky, and in one place the canyon narrowed so much that the uneven walls nearly stripped the saddle from the clay's back. Navarro cooed to the horse and applied firm, steady pressure to the reins, easing him through.

He was climbing a shelf and pulling the horse along behind him when gunfire sounded, several echoing cracks growing closer. Real had discovered that Navarro had left the cave.

"Come on, boy. Let's make some time," Navarro urged.

Another gunshot rocked Navarro's eardrums. The horse reared, screaming and jerking the reins from Navarro's hand. Tom turned, ducking under the horse's flailing front hooves. Another shot. The horse's head snapped sideways, spraying blood from the wound below its right ear.

Navarro stumbled back and watched the horse twist around, bounce off the narrow walls, and fall. It rolled back down the trail, splashing the ground with blood. Behind the dead claybank, the de Cava men were running along the trail, zigzagging behind clefts in both sides of the wall. Tom drew his pistol and fired two shots, holding them at bay, then looked at the horse. It had fallen on the saddle boot.

Navarro climbed to his feet and sidled down the slope to see if he could wrestle the long gun from the boot. Two shots stopped him and turned him around, heading him on up the trail, cursing and snapping shots off behind him.

Minutes later, the canyon floor rose sharply. A crenelated wall faced him. The wall was a hundred feet high straight across the canyon. He was boxed in.

Behind, Real's men fired their pistols and rifles and shouted back and forth. Tom heard their pounding boots. He glanced behind him, saw the men approaching about forty yards back along the corridor — flashes of bright serapes and sombreros and gun barrels between the canyon's bulging walls.

Sanchez had said there was a way out. . . .

Navarro looked again. To his right, in the gray-blue shadows of the bulging wall, a black line appeared. Navarro made for the gap as two pistols barked behind him, the slugs careening over his left shoulder and thudding into the rock wall ahead.

Navarro's heart thudded with relief as he saw that the black line was really a gap in the canyon wall. He shouldered through the gap and followed the meandering passageway to another wall, less steep than the other, with corrugations providing hand- and footholds. It must have been the chute for an ancient waterfall that had once tumbled into the canyon. Earthquakes had probably shifted the passageway. Three-quarters of the way to the crest, it canted sharply, tunneling into the limestone and creating a chimney of sorts. The chimney was straight up and down for about twenty feet, only about four feet wide.

Shouted Spanish rose only a few feet behind him. Navarro leapt onto the wall and scrambled up the cleft, loosing rocks and shale behind him. He hoisted himself up by the wall's clefts and bulges, crawling through the right-angling chimney, pushing off both walls with his hands and feet, then stretching his arms over the rim and muscling his legs up and over.

He'd just pulled his head and shoulders away from the hole when several shots sounded from below, the slugs slicing up through the chute and continuing straight up toward the sky. A couple tore rocks away from the lip of the chimney's rim, showering Tom with grit.

Navarro sat back on his haunches, away from the hole. Calmly, he shucked his Colt, flipped open the gate, and pinched out the spent, smoking brass. By the scuffling sounds emanating from the hole, Real's men were climbing the chute. Navarro plucked one cartridge after another from his belt, thumbed them into the Colt's cylinder, then closed the gate.

The scuffling grew louder. He could hear men breathing hard, cursing under their breath.

Navarro spun the Colt's cylinder. He waited. There was no more shooting, just the sounds of climbing.

Presently, the crown of a ratty straw sombrero appeared. Then a swarthy face with a pencil-thin mustache and two coal black eyes slid up from the hole. Spying Navarro, the man dropped his jaw. He didn't have many teeth. His eyes snapped so wide they showed as much white as black.

"Por el segundo." Tom extended the Colt and drilled a neat hole through the man's left cheek.

The man, dead before he could scream, dropped straight down the chimney. The others behind him shouted and cursed.

Navarro peered into the hole. Three men lay tumbled at the bottom in their bright serapes, sombreros falling off their heads.

Another had avoided the falling dead man and was clinging to the left side of the chimney. He looked up at Tom. As his eyes widened, he snapped up his revolver. Tom shot him in the chest, knocking him back against the wall. His hands lost their grip and he fell straight down, careening off the dogleg.

Tom emptied his gun into the hole, then reloaded the Colt and climbed to his feet. He regarded a boulder a foot to the right of the hole, on a slight upgrade. Holstering his Colt, he threw his right shoulder into the boulder, and heaved.

It took him four good heaves, the veins popping out in his forehead, before the boulder even budged. He heaved three more times before he'd rolled the boulder over the hole. Part of the boulder broke the chimney's rim, dropped a good foot, throwing up dust, and settled there.

By the time Real's men got back to their horses and skirted the chasm, Navarro would be long gone. Stretching the knots out of his back, he snugged Sanchez's Russian .44 behind his cartridge belt, looked warily around at the broken country around him — a maze of chalky buttes, greasewood flats, and boulder-strewn arroyos stretching off to olive mesas dimming under a west-falling sun.

A hawk swooped low for a look at all the commotion. It probably thought it had a meal down here.

Navarro took a heading on Bullet Ridge and started tramping north across the long mesa he'd found himself on, then down the mesa's steep wall and into an arroyo, where the de Cava riders would have a hard time tracking him.

He'd walked for three hours, crossing three ancient riverbeds, and the sun had gone down, when he took a smoke break along an old Apache trail. He built a corn shuck cigarette, touched a match to it, and inhaled deeply. The air was cool but he was sweat-soaked, and now that he was no longer moving, the chill crept into his bones.

He was lamenting the fact that he had no horse, and that it was probably another two hours back to the Bar-V headquarters, when something rattled off in the darkness.

A slug whistled past his ear and plunked into a cactus, followed a half second later by the report of a big-caliber rifle.

CHAPTER 23

Navarro dropped the quirley and threw himself to the ground, grabbing his Colt from its holster. He'd be a son of a bitch if they'd found him out here. No way he could be that unlucky.

He pushed himself to his feet and, staying low, scrambled into a patch of buckbrush and low boulders. Scrub crunched and thrashed to the southwest, the direction from which the shot had come.

"I got him. I think I got him!" a man's voice shouted, pitched high with excitement. Running footsteps grew louder.

"Homer, be careful," a woman admonished, from somewhere behind the running man. "Don't just go a-runnin' up like that!"

But the man had already pushed between two spindly ocotillo stands, holding a rifle high across his chest. He stopped and looked around — a medium-tall man in baggy dungarees, hobnailed boots, a shapeless wool coat, and a bullet-crowned hat. He stepped toward the rock Navarro had been sitting on when the shot had sizzled past his head.

Under his breath, the man said, "I thought for sure —"

The air left his lungs in one loud exhalation as Navarro rammed his Colt's butt hard between his shoulder blades. The man stumbled forward, dropping his rifle and hitting the ground on his chest.

Raking air into his lungs and giving exasperated cries and grunts, the man turned on his side and reached for his rifle. Navarro's left foot came down hard on his wrist, grinding it into the caliche as he lowered his Colt to the man's face, and ratcheted back the hammer.

"Homer?" The woman's voice was alarmed. The wooden rattling of a springless wagon sounded like oncoming thunder.

"He's over here, Hattie." Navarro aimed his cocked Colt at Homer Winters's fear-etched face. "Come and pick him up before I stop his clock."

"Mr. Navarro," the miner stammered, staring past the Colt's long barrel into Navarro's hard face. "I didn't know it was you. We seen someone movin' around, heard the footsteps, and thought someone was layin' fer us agin."

Navarro heard the approaching wagon, drawn by two gaunt ponies, roll up behind him. He depressed the Colt's hammer and turned.

Hattie Winters stood in the box, the ribbons in her hands. A thin figure dressed in men's garb and with severely pulled-back hair, she drew back on the reins and cast her gaze from Navarro to Homer and back again. "Sorry, Tom." She frowned down at her husband, who winced from the stinger Navarro had put in the middle of his back. "I told you to make sure who you were shootin' at, ye damn dunderhead."

"If he keeps shootin' at Bar-V riders on their own range, he ain't long for this world."

"I was just —" Homer stammered, pushing himself to his feet.

"Oh, shut up!" Hattie berated him. To Tom, she said, "We were haulin' this deer, which I shot" — she jerked a thumb at the hulking, lank form in the wagon's bed — "back to the dugout when we seen your shadow movin' down that arroyo. I thought we might be in for another bushwackin', so I sent Homer ahead to look into it."

"Well, he did that."

"My worthless brother's back at the dugout, drunker than a peach orchard sow. I'd starve if I couldn't shoot." Hattie was looking around. "What are you doin' out here, Tom? And where's your horse?"

"Long story." Navarro was looking at the beefy, knock-kneed saddle horse tied to the wagon. Just what the doctor ordered to save his feet and to get him back to the headquarters before dawn. "Mind if I borrow yours? I'll send him back first chance I get."

"I reckon that's the least we could do . . . for Homer's bad behavior." Hattie thrust her chin at her thoroughly cowed husband, who was moving stiffly toward the wagon. "Homer, untie ole Jim for Tom here."

"I got him." Navarro slipped the reins from a steel eye on the tail gate where the dead black-tail's feet hung slack, and swung into the saddle. Heeling old Jim into a trot, he called without turning around, "Obliged!"

Behind him, Hattie watched him go. She sighed balefully at his retreating silhouette, touched the vagrant strands of hair fluttering about her sun-seared cheeks. "If only I woulda found me a man like that . . ."

Homer climbed up beside her. "Ye ask me, he ain't so damn smart, traipsin' around out here without a horse."

"I ain't askin' you!" With that, Hattie

turned the horses around and slapped them back toward the dugout.

Navarro could gallop the old horse only for short stretches on flat terrain. But when he gained the wide, graded trail connecting the Bar-V with Benson and Tucson, he gigged him into a gallop. Old Jim showed surprising power as he snorted and lunged through the night.

Galloping, Navarro and old Jim approached the headquarters ten minutes later — the silhouetted corrals and outbuildings stretched out on the rise before them.

Two gun flashes appeared straight ahead, directed skyward. The reports followed a wink later. Old Jim threw his weight forward as he slowed, his muscles rippling with alarm.

"Name yourself!" a man shouted.

Navarro stared at the spot where the flashes had appeared, frowning. It was custom to call out to approaching riders at night, but the shooting was a little extreme. It meant something had put the Bar-V men on the balls of their boots.

When Navarro shouted his name, the sentry repeated it toward the house. Tom heard the squawk of the main gate and gigged the horse forward. A few seconds later he and the horse plunged through the open gate and into the yard, where several men stood facing him between the house and the bunkhouse, both buildings lit up as though for a barn dance. All the men were wearing pistols on their hips, and several carried rifles. The tension was almost palpable.

"Tom, we was beginnin' to think you was a goner," said the big Welshman Bear Winston, who was resting the barrel of a Henry carbine on his yoke-sized shoulder.

"I was beginnin' to think so, too," Navarro said, swinging down from the saddle. "What the hell's goin' on around here?"

He wheeled toward the house as Bill Tobias took his reins. Paul Vannorsdell and Karla were moving down the porch steps, his bulky figure and her slender one silhouetted by the salmon-lighted windows behind them.

"Trouble," Vannorsdell said. He paused, dropped his voice. "They shot Lee Luther."

Navarro didn't move. His heart thudded. "Dead?"

Vannorsdell nodded. Karla's fists were balled at her sides, and her eyes were bright with tears.

"Came right into the yard — Cayetano Fimbres and some shavetail," the rancher said. "They were aimin' for me and they hit the kid. I sent riders after them, but the rain turned them back. The men were certain it was Fimbres."

Karla was staring at Navarro. Her voice was thick. "We have him inside."

Feeling weary, Navarro moved toward the house, only vaguely aware of his burning, blistered feet. Lee Luther was dead. He walked passed Karla and Vannorsdell, who followed him across the courtyard and up the porch steps. Inside, Tom removed his dusty hat. In the parlor, a fire had been laid in the field rock fireplace.

A simple pine coffin had been set up against the far wall, on saw horses. The rug before it was gritty with sand from the boots of the men who'd come to pay their respects. Pilar stood in the kitchen doorway, her face drawn with sadness, her hands folded across her stomach.

Lee Luther looked much smaller than Tom remembered. The boy wore a crisp plaid shirt and dark blue dungarees — his Sunday duds. He had a blue-striped neckerchief knotted around his neck and another, bloodstained one around his head, covering the bullet's entrance and exit wounds. The head lay at an awkward angle, chin tipped down and toward his right shoulder, and his lips were pursed as though from pain. The boy's eyelids lay lightly, so that Tom could see some light reflecting off the eyes beneath the light brown lashes.

Sometimes the dead appeared only to be sleeping. That wasn't how Lee Luther looked. He looked dead, the life drained out of him along with the brains the bullet had shredded.

Staring down at the boy, Tom dug his fingers into the side of the coffin until his knuckles turned white. His lips stretched back from his teeth in a grimace.

Behind him, Vannorsdell said, "I was going to send more men out today, but I figured I'd better wait till you got back — if you were *coming* back. Didn't want to catch you in a cross fire."

Navarro turned, stared at the man unseeingly. All bets were off. It was war now. Real had made certain of that. Vannorsdell could call in marshals, but there weren't enough marshals and rangers in the territory to take down Real's riders.

It was up to the Bar-V. Navarro knew it, and so did Vannorsdell.

Peering into Tom's dark face, the rancher said, "What happened over there?"

Tom reached into his back pocket, handed the folded paper to Vannorsdell. "Sanchez

wrote this out. It explains everything."
Knowing that Lupita would translate the segundo's Spanish, he began walking stiffly toward the door.

"He still over there?" Vannorsdell asked.

"He's dead."

The men gathered outside the courtyard watched Tom walk down the steps, expectant looks on their drawn faces. They squeezed the rifles in their hands or smoked fervently, angrily. Tom moved toward them and stopped.

"Be ready to ride at first light."

"Why not tonight?" protested Ky Tryon, his arm in a sling, a quirley dangling from his lips.

"They could be laying for us along the trail tonight." Tom shuttled his flinty glare from man to man. "We'll ride tomorrow."

They stared at him hard, shuffled their feet and squeezed their guns. By ones and twos, they gradually turned and, lowering their rifles to their sides, moved off toward the bunkhouse.

"They'll be ready, Tom," Bear Winston said, coming up behind Navarro, then moving along with the others.

Navarro sighed and headed toward his cabin back in the chaparral. In spite of his mental and physical weariness, he had trouble getting to sleep. His blood pounded with fury, and images of Lee Luther and Guadalupe Sanchez kept careening before his eyes. He'd slept a total of only three hours before his own inner clock woke him.

He skipped coffee and his usual breakfast, wrapped his cartridge belt around his waist, grabbed his second Winchester, Sanchez's .44, and three extra boxes of .44 shells. Then he headed outside. False dawn limned the eastern sky, behind jagged-peaked mountains. A lone coyote was still yammering, and a night breeze rustled the tops of the aspens behind the cabin.

It was not yet dawn, but when Navarro walked into the main yard, he saw that the other Bar-V hands were already up, moving back and forth behind the bunkhouse's lighted windows. The bunkhouse door was open, and the riders were heading out, donning hats and cartridge belts, quirleys smoldering between their teeth, some still thumbing cartridges through their rifles' loading gates. A couple held freshly oiled saddles on their shoulders.

There were a few strange faces — the extra shooters Vannorsdell had sent to Tucson for. Bringing in unfamiliar, untested riders went against Navarro's grain, but facing de Cava's hired killers, they'd need every gunhand they could find.

Tom fell in beside Bear Winston and was heading to the stable when he saw Vannorsdell moving toward them, the lit windows of the house silhouetting his bulky, hatted figure clad in a dark duster. He carried two rifles, one in either hand. A freshly fired stogie drooped from his lips.

"Where're you going?" Navarro asked.

The stumpy rancher stopped and removed the cigar from his mouth. "Where the hell you think?"

"Things are gonna get a mite hairy out there."

"You don't think I been through wars before?" Vannorsdell sucked air through his nose, puffing up his chest. "Or you think I'm too old?"

Navarro lifted a shoulder. Seeing a slender, hatted figure with long tawny hair coming up behind the old man, he said, "What about her?"

"What about me?" Karla said. She had a pistol strapped around her waist and held bulging saddlebags over her left shoulder. "I'm coming."

Vannorsdell turned to her sharply, as though he hadn't known she was back there. The old man opened his mouth to speak to her, but Karla cut him off. "Don't worry. I

317

don't intend on joining the fracas. I'll stay behind you, well out of harm's way, and help the wounded."

"The hell you will!" the rancher and Navarro barked at the same time.

"I should say you won't, young lady!" The woman's voice, familiar to Tom, carried down from the porch. Navarro looked behind Karla. Louise Talon strode quickly out from the front yard, a cape about her shoulders, her red hair piled in a loose bun atop her head. "We'll stay here and help when they get back . . . if any get back," Louise added, sending a half-scolding, half-encouraging look at Navarro.

Tom's frown deepened. Under any other circumstances, he would have been thrilled to see her. "What are you doin' here?"

"Your rider stopped at the stage station on his way to Tucson and filled me in. I came to offer my doctoring services." She draped an arm over Karla's shoulders. "I hope they're not needed."

Karla shuttled her gaze between Tom and her grandfather. "Guess I'm outgunned." She let the saddlebags slide off her shoulder and hit the ground with a thud. She crossed her arms on her chest. "You boys come back in one piece."

Tom gave them both a stretched glance.

Then he and Vannorsdell turned and headed for the stable, from which the other men were leading their saddled horses, including one for Tom and one for Vannorsdell.

Navarro slid his rifle into his saddle boot. "I doubt Real gets out of bed much before noon, but I want to get over there before those drunks he's got riding for him get all their wits about 'em."

"Shit, they'll be expecting us," said the rancher, grunting as he pulled himself into the leather.

"Yeah, I reckon," Navarro growled, gigging his sorrel toward the head of the waiting pack. He glanced again toward the house. Karla and Louise stood there, staring toward him gravely.

"Let's ride!" Navarro yelled to the men behind him and galloped his horse through the open front gate.

Behind him, arm in arm, Louise and Karla watched them go, the ground shuddering beneath their feet.

CHAPTER 24

"How we gonna do this, Tom?" Vannorsdell asked, reaching down and shucking his Winchester from his saddle boot.

He was staring toward the de Cava hacienda from beneath the brim of his shabby leather hat. Between the Bar-V riders and the hacienda, Real's men sat their horses stirrup to stirrup, a cool, killing calm in their eyes. The climbing morning sun canted their shadows across the sage. In the middle of the group, nearly straight ahead of Navarro, sat Real de Cava, his brown felt sombrero thonged taut beneath his chin. To Real's right, Cayetano Fimbres slouched in his saddle under what appeared to be about thirty pounds of brass in his crossed cartridge belts. To Real's left was a lanky kid in white pajamas and a tattered straw hat; he held an old-model rifle across his scrawny chest. Cayetano's brother. The don's killer. Navarro didn't cotton to killing kids, but he was willing to make an exception for this deadly little brush wolf.

Navarro shucked his own Winchester and levered it one-handed. He had a brief image of Guadalupe Sanchez thrown toward him with a bullet in his back, then another of Lee Luther lying pale, small, and dead in his coffin.

Snapping his Winchester to his shoulder, Tom drew a quick bead on Cayetano's forehead. The killer, cocky and red-eyed from drink, was slow to react. Spying Navarro's rifle aimed at him, he jerked up straight in his saddle. But he'd only just started raising his big-caliber Sharps when Navarro's rifle barked. The killer's head jerked back, as if he'd been punched in the chin. His eyes blinked a few times, as if he was trying to clear his vision; then his fingers opened and his rifle dropped from his hands.

"Like that," Navarro said, watching the killer sag back over his horse's rear. The mount suddenly lunged sideways and craned a look at the man sliding off its left hip.

The peon kid shouted, *"Cayetano!"*

His voice was nearly drowned out as the Bar-V riders, following Tom's lead, extended their own rifles at their counterparts sitting thirty yards away, and began firing. Almost simultaneously, the stunned de Cava riders commenced their own fusillade. Holding his jittery mount's reins in his left fist, Navarro extended his rifle at Real but held the shot. De Cava had ducked from lead fired by Vannorsdell, and his horse was rearing.

Tom turned to his left as two shots cut the air on either side of him, one so close it trimmed several whiskers he hadn't had time to shave that morning. As Tom swung his Winchester over the saddle horn, he lost his grip on his reins. The sorrel swung hard right, screaming and bucking. Tom dropped his rifle to grab for the horn.

He missed it, and the horse's motion swung him hard right. The horse leapt out from beneath him; slung like a rock from a slingshot, he flew out sharply, then straight down, hitting the ground on his hip. His left boot hung up in the stirrup. He gave the boot a yank as the horse lurched him forward so hard his teeth cracked together and his head snapped back with blinding force. Suddenly, he was careening and fishtailing over the rocky, brushy ground.

The screaming sorrel dragged him a good twenty yards before his boot slipped free. Navarro continued sliding on his butt for another fifteen feet, then smashed through a tough clump of silver sage, and stopped with a jolt against an ironwood shrub, his head pounding, the world spinning, the gunfire sounding a good mile away.

He shook his head to clear it, turned over, took quick stock of his condition, then pushed up on his hands and knees. He looked around, blinking, trying to get the world to stop spinning. His ringing ears started picking up the gunfire, the angry shouts, and the screams of the horses.

His eyes focused, and he saw the wafting powder smoke and the fallen horses and men and those men still living crouched behind rocks or shrubs or their dead mounts, slinging lead with their rifles or pistols. Ahead about twenty paces and to Tom's right, Vannorsdell crouched behind a small rock buried in sage. His hat was off and his gray-brown hair hung in his dusty face. He was bleeding from a couple wounds. Extending his old Walker Colt, he cut loose on one of the de Cava men still shooting from his prancing horse.

The man clutched his chest with a groan. He turned his own pistol on Vannorsdell, but the old rancher shot the man off his horse before he could return fire.

Navarro reached for his Colt Navy; he was relieved to feel it still in its holster. He slipped it out, gained his feet, and ran crouching back the way the horse had dragged him. Glancing right and left, he figured the bulk of his men were still alive, while more than two-thirds of de Cava's men were down in bloody humps, one lying half under his own steeldust stallion.

A brown face appeared from the right side of a rock not far from the low brick wall marking the border of the main yard. The man snaked his rifle out, extended it toward Tom. Navarro snapped off a lucky shot without aiming, drilling the man through the right temple and sending him sprawling back in the dust.

As shots continued around him, a slug nicked Navarro's right side, sending a fiery chill deep into his loins. He turned toward the source of the shot. Real was hunkered down behind his dead horse, two smoking pistols extended over the saddle. As Real fired another shot, Navarro dropped to his right knee and fired two quick rounds.

De Cava spun back away from his horse as Tom's second shot cored his right shoulder. Real climbed to his hands and feet; both pistols still in his hands, he crawled toward the brick wall. Squinting through the eye-stinging powder smoke, Tom triggered two shots, blowing up dirt about a foot right of Real's retreating figure. Again, he cocked the Colt and aimed, but before he could fire, a bullet slammed into a rock just ahead of him, spraying him with sharp rock and lead shards.

Squinting through the blood dribbling through a small wound over his left eye, he glanced left. The shooter ran crouching northward. As he dove behind a dead horse, he screamed and slumped onto his back. Tom turned sharply to see Ky Tryon throw up his left arm in a wave, his Henry rifle in his right hand.

"We got 'em on the run, Tom!"

Navarro squeezed off his last shot, then holstered the empty Navy and pulled Sanchez's Russian .44 out from behind his cartridge belt. He glanced right, where Vannorsdell sat with his back to his rock, reloading the heavy Colt with fresh caps and balls, his left hand bloody.

The shooting had died down. One of the downed pistoleros was shrieking in Spanish somewhere off to the south.

Navarro looked toward the brick wall in time to see Real crawl over it and fall to the ground on the other side.

"I'm going after Real!" Tom yelled to Vannorsdell.

"Go ahead, Tommy. I'll cover you!" The

rancher snapped his loading lever down beneath the Walker's barrel, turned forward, and extending the gun over the rock.

As Vannorsdell's ancient Colt roared, Navarro sprinted toward the wall, leaping over several dead bodies and horses and triggering two shots at one of the three or four surviving de Cava men. His left leg was sore from the dragging, so he eased himself over the wall. Ahead, Real de Cava was moving toward the hacienda, skipping and awkwardly dragging one foot. His hat was gone and his leather jacket was torn and bloody.

Navarro walked toward him. "Real!"

The man wheeled, almost fell, and raised both pistols in his hands. Navarro fired the big Russian. Real flinched and stumbled backward, firing both pistols into the ground, then dropping the one in his right hand. Tom fired two more shots, but he wasn't used to the high-shooting weapon, and both slugs tore up dust several yards beyond Real.

"Don't kill me, Taos!" Real turned and stumbled up the grade toward the house now bathed in the lemon light of the rising sun. "You're fighting for the wrong brand. I could make you rich!"

Looking around in case any of the *pistoleros* had retreated into the yard, and feeling the blood from the rock and lead shards dribbling down his face, Navarro headed after Real. Movement near the house caught his attention, and he turned to see a girl with long black hair and wearing a violet dress and black shoes run toward him through the gate of the main courtyard.

"Real!" she cried.

Startled, de Cava spun toward her and fired his Remington. The girl screamed, did a grotesque pirouette, hair flying, flinging her arms out from her sides. Blood stained the dress over the girl's chest as she he lay on her back in the dust, arms thrown out from her shoulders, hair splayed beneath her head.

Giving the dead girl only a moment's scrutiny, as if she were only a bird fallen from the sky, Real turned into the main courtyard, passed under several long-dead pecan trees, and stumbled up a wide set of stone steps toward open double doors at the top.

He turned as Navarro gained the foot of the steps. He fell with a curse, turned on his right hip. His face was sweat-streaked and pale, his eyes bright with terror. "You can have my sister. She wants you, Taos."

"You're a blight on the de Cava name, Real. Killed your own father for gold. I'm

327

gonna put you down like the sick cur you are."

"I didn't shoot *mi padre*! It was Pepe!" Laughing hideously, Real extended his pistol and fired.

A wink later, Navarro fired the Russian, the .44 slug tearing across the top left shoulder of de Cava's short leather jacket. Navarro climbed three steps. Six steps away from Real, he extended the Russian and aimed at the firebrand's forehead.

Real squeezed his eyes closed and winced, tears dribbling down his cheeks. "Don't kill me, Taos. *Por favor!*"

Navarro pulled the trigger. The hammer clapped on an empty cartridge. He fired again. Nothing.

Real smiled, chuckled. "I have one more, Taos." He stared at Navarro, his expression suddenly sober. "You, like *mi padre,* are old and washed up." He thumbed the pistol's hammer back. "Say good-bye to life."

Navarro muttered a curse and stared at the wide maw of the Remington leveled at his head. No Wyoming horse ranch with Louise. Just as well. She deserved better than an aging gunman who'd no doubt have a price on his head until the day he died.

"Sure you don't want me to turn around," he snarled, "so you can drill me in the back like Sanchez?" Tom drew a breath. "Sure you don't want to get a kid to do it?"

Real leered at him. "Go to hell, old fool."

The gun barked, the shot echoing off the low adobe walls lining the steps. Navarro blinked, stared at the gun from which no smoke appeared. It sagged in Real's hand, fell and clattered down three steps and lay still.

Navarro looked at Real. He lay slumped on his left shoulder, cheek against a step upon which dark red blood pooled. On the landing above him stood his sister, a small silver-plated pocket pistol extended in her left hand. Smoke curled from the barrel.

Lupita stared coldly down at her dead brother. "Coward." She slowly lowered the pistol, let it drop from her hand.

Lupita looked at Navarro. "I should have killed him when Alejandro told me about the gold mine."

"Was Alejandro in on it with him?" Navarro asked.

"No." It was Alejandro himself, stepping out through the double doors, his arm in a sling. He didn't have a gun in his hand or on his hip. "I knew about the gold and Real wanting to squeeze out Vannorsdell so he could have it all for himself, but I didn't know he had our father killed till I heard him talking to the girl in her room one night."

The younger de Cava stared grimly down at his brother. "I wanted to kill him then myself but I couldn't bring myself to pull the trigger."

"There wasn't any gold."

The voice had come from behind Navarro. He turned around. Vannorsdell stood a few feet back in the courtyard, dusty and bloody from several bullet burns, his left trouser knee torn. He was wearing his hat, and he still had the big Colt in his hand, hanging low at his side. Bear Winston and Ky Tryon flanked him. Navarro realized that the shooting had ceased, that he hadn't heard any reports for several minutes now.

"I prospected that cave years ago, when I first came to this country," the rancher said. "I had a couple Army assayers take a look. There's one vein that pinches out about ten feet inside the mountain." He shook his head. "The gold Real and his killers got out of that cave is about all there is. All there ever *will* be."

Lupita sighed and tottered back against the wall, her face bleaching. She dropped her chin to her chest and sobbed at the irony and horror of it all. The de Cava's spidery, silver-haired maid, her face even more grave than usual, walked through the doors holding a shawl about her shoulders as if chilled to the bone. She moved carefully down the steps and strode stiffly toward her daughter lying dead outside the courtyard gate.

Alejandro stepped forward and faced Navarro and Vannorsdell, his back straight and soldierly. "My sister and I will leave here, turn over the de Cava grant to you."

"I don't want it." Vannorsdell ran the back of his wrist across his mouth, smearing blood and dirt. He glanced at the house. "This is de Cava land. Always has been, always should be. If we can be friends like me and your old man, I'll give you all the help you need getting back on your feet."

Alejandro stared back at him, wary caution in his gaze. Lupita held her head down, sobbing.

Navarro turned. Feeling as old and tired as he'd ever felt, he started back across the yard toward the battlefield over which powdersmoke still wafted and the smell of blood emanated.

Frank Sharpe met him, grabbed his arm. "De Cava's men are all dead or run off, Tom."

"How bad they hit us?"

"Five dead, seven wounded."

Navarro stared grimly at the dirt before his boots. "Get a wagon and some shovels."

He brushed at the blood on his face and limped through the main gate.

EPILOGUE

Two months later, in the Vannorsdell dining room at the crack of dawn, Tom sipped his coffee and said over the rim of the mug, "Ready to head north, Mrs. Navarro?"

"Ready and raring." To Paul Vannorsdell, Louise said through the side of her mouth, "Let's see. Since we're leaving in July, we'll get up there just in time for winter, won't we?"

"A little snow never hurt anyone," Navarro said, throwing back the last sip of his coffee. "Besides, we'll want to get those pregnant mares all cozied up in their new pastures before they drop their foals in the spring."

"If you'll excuse me" — Karla slid her chair out from the breakfast table and turned to Tom — "I'll be off on my morning ride. Don't think I can take the sight of you riding away . . . for the last time."

Tears came to her eyes. Dressed in her

333

riding clothes and a beaded denim jacket, she moved around the table to Navarro, threw her arms around his neck, and kissed him hard on the cheek. The girl straightened, turned, and hugged Louise. "You promise to take good care of him?"

Louise glanced at Tom. "I'll do my level best."

" 'Cause he can't take care of himself. He thinks he can, but he really can't. You know how many times he's been wounded in the few years since I've known him?"

Tom snorted. Half of those times had been due to Karla's own antics, not the least of which was getting herself kidnapped by slave traders and hauled to Old Mexico.

"I'll take care of him, Karla," Louise said. "And as soon as we get settled into our new ranch house, I'll send you a letter."

Tears streaming down her cheeks, Karla forced a smile. Without another glance at Tom, she grabbed her hat and left the room.

When the outside door slammed, Vannorsdell said, "That girl's gonna miss you, Tommy." He sighed and stared down at his stone coffee mug. "And I am, too. That's a fact."

"I'm grateful for what you've done for me, Paul. Not too many men would have given this old gunfighter a new start, but you did, and for that, I owe you my life." Tom wiped his mouth with his napkin and stood. "And thanks for those mustangs. They're prime. Sired by the Appy and that Morgan, they'll produce some of the finest cow ponies in all of Wyoming."

"Hell, you paid for 'em," the rancher said as he, too, gained his feet. "I just threw in a couple scrubs for saving my ranch. And that you did, Tom. Let there be no mistake. Without you, this ranch would now belong to Real de Cava, and my bones would be strewn around Bullet Creek Canyon."

"How's everything going with Lupita and Alejandro?" Louise asked the rancher as they walked out onto the porch.

"Good so far. I've lent them six of my top hands to get their herds back together and to work on their wells and such. Lupita's doing the hiring and firing and keeping the books. I think Rancho de Cava will be back on its feet again by spring."

"Maybe the don's kids aren't turning out so bad, after all," Tom said, descending the steps.

"At least two of them," the rancher replied as they made their way into the ranch yard and headed for the corral, where Tom's twenty-five mustang mares milled with the two stallions, their coats glistening as the sun climbed.

The five drovers Tom had hired to drive the cavvy north waited outside the corral, smoking and talking and looking over the run-ready, eager-eyed remuda. Mordecai Hawkins and Billie Brennan had gone ahead in the chuck wagon.

"Chivvy 'em out, boys!" Tom yelled.

One of the men swung the gate wide, and Tom, Louise, and Vannorsdell stepped back to watch the cavvy thunder through the gate, the cowboys whistling and waving their reatas. The ground vibrated beneath Navarro's boots. Dust rose, tinted pink by the sun.

Navarro wrapped an arm around Louise's waist. "That's a fine-lookin' bunch. A damn nice start."

"A brand-new beginning," Louise said, her eyes bright beneath the brim of her man's cream hat. "For both of us."

"Just stay clear of Colorado, Tommy," Vannorsdell warned. "Whatever you do."

"No need to even straddle the line. We're gonna head straight north through Utah."

Tom shook Vannorsdell's hand, then helped Louise into the saddle. He bid the rancher a final good-bye, then mounted his pinto. He and Louise trotted their horses through the gate. Tom reined up suddenly.

"You go on," Tom said, staring after the

dust of the cavvy being hazed on down the road. "I'll be right behind you."

Louise gave him a questioning glance, but before she could say anything, Tom had reined his horse off the trail and up the low hill covered with desert scrub and stippled with chiseled stones and wooden crosses. He rode up to the freshest grave and looked down at the stone he'd carved himself.

Lee Luther
1863–1879

"You didn't have time to grow old, boy. Maybe you're better off. Wherever you are, I know you're makin' big tracks." Tom blinked back tears. "Man tracks."

Navarro reined the pinto around, galloped down the hill, and headed west, into the dust of his north-heading herd.

The employees of Thorndike Press hope you have enjoyed this Large Print book. All our Thorndike, Wheeler, and Kennebec Large Print titles are designed for easy reading, and all our books are made to last. Other Thorndike Press Large Print books are available at your library, through selected bookstores, or directly from us.

For information about titles, please call:
(800) 223-1244

or visit our Web site at:
http://gale.cengage.com/thorndike

To share your comments, please write:
Publisher
Thorndike Press
10 Water St., Suite 310
Waterville, ME 04901